THE WRONG MAN TO TANGLE WITH

The small Texan caused Blitzer to think he was on the point of collapsing with fear. Feeling the grips on his neck and wrist relaxing slightly, he knew he had achieved his purpose. Crouching a little on his slightly bent knees, Fog rotated his torso to add impetus as he thrust back with his left elbow.

Caught totally unprepared, a startled and pain-filled gasp burst from Blitzer. His erstwhile compliant captive wrenched free, and the force of the elbow's jab to the solar plexus sent him backwards to collide with the screen door.

Startled by the change that had come over Fog, Willie led the way as the brothers rushed forward. Both had boxed in their eastern college, and neither envisaged any difficulty in dealing with a person they regarded as nothing more than a small country bumpkin.

Which was a dangerous mistake when confronted by the grandson of Dusty Fog!

Alvin Fog,
Texas Ranger

J. T. EDSON

A DELL BOOK

Published by
Dell Publishing
a division of
Bantam Doubleday Dell Publishing Group, Inc.
666 Fifth Avenue
New York, New York 10103

This book was originally published in Great Britain under the title *You're a Texas Ranger, Alvin Fog* by Corgi Books, a division of Transworld Publishers, Ltd.

ISBN: 0-440-21034-8

Printed in the United States of America

Published simultaneously in Canada

November 1991

10 9 8 7 6 5 4 3 2 1

OPM

For Myrtle Molloy, who—unlike her husband, Bob, and myself, who are growing old and decrepit—still looks as young and beautiful as ever.

INTRODUCTION

"So you're the young feller from England who's been writing about the 'Hardin, Fog, and Blaze clan' all these years?"[1]

"Yes, sir," I replied, wondering what would come next.

"You're doing a right satisfactory chore," the man to whom I had just been introduced declared in his Texas drawl. "And forget the 'sir,' you-all aren't *that* young. Call me 'Cap.' Then haul off and tell me what I can do for you."

I must admit that I had been experiencing a slight sense of apprehension ever since I was told who was to be the dinner guest at the home of my friends, Ellen and Chuck Kurtzman, that warm July evening in 1975.

---

1. Just how many years this has been was brought home to me recently. I was standing at the bar of my "spiritual" home, the White Lion Hotel in Melton Mowbray, one evening when one of the Women's Royal Army Corps' dog trainers from the Royal Army Veterinary Corps' Depot came up and asked, "Are you J. T. Edson?" When I modestly admitted I was, she went on, "My dad was reading your books when I was in kindergarten." J.T.E.

Having attended the Twenty-second Annual Convention of Western Writers of America at Carson City, Nevada, I had accepted Elley and Chuck's kind invitation to return to Fort Worth, Texas—the Twenty-First Annual Convention having been held there—and spend a few days with them. Although Elley had hinted there was a surprise in store for me, I *never* would have guessed what it was to be.

What is more, to this day I still do not know how she brought it about.[2]

I had, of course, been in written communication with various members of what I will continue to refer to as the "Hardin, Fog, and Blaze clan" for several years, but this was my first meeting with one of them. My requests to do so on my two previous visits to the United States—attending the Twentieth Annual Convention of W.W.A. at Olympia, Washington, having been the first—had been politely, but definitely, refused. Yet Elley had not only arranged the meeting, but it was with the current patriarch of the clan, Alvin Dustine (Cap) Fog himself.

Despite being over seventy, Cap looked a good twenty years younger. Small, and still with an excellent physique, although he no longer trimmed down at the waist as much as he had on photographs I had seen that were taken in the 1920s, it was his face that impressed me most. One would not call him handsome, but his tanned features had a strength of will mingled with a sense of humor that told of an exceptionally potent personality. It caused one to forget his lack of height, for he had the undefinable aura of a person possessing an inborn ability to command. He was, in fact, everything I had always assumed his paternal grandfather, Captain Dustine Edward Marsden (Dusty) Fog, C.S.A.—for whom I have the honor to be official biographer—to be.

---

2. As "Cap" Fog's clothes clearly came from there, I suspect that the management of Luskey's Western Stores, Inc., of Fort Worth may have helped organize the meeting, but neither Ellen Kurtzman nor David Luskey will confirm my supposition. J.T.E.

"I keep getting asked by readers why Tommy Okasi,[3] who was a trained samurai,[4] came to be in the United States in the 1830s," I hinted. "And I hope I'll be able to give them the answer."

"Well now," Cap said, his voice dry although his gray eyes sparkled with amusement. "I reckon that's *one* hope you're going to be shy on when you-all head back to home. Trouble being, with what caused him to light out and the folks involved being so important—all of whom have kin alive and holding down pretty influential positions in Japan to this day—we don't figure it's advisable to let the truth get out even at this late date. So those readers are just going to have to stay curious."

"Whatever you say, Cap," I assented.

"*Bueno,*" this Texan of Texans drawled, and I sensed that my acquiescence without argument had satisfied him. "Say, did you-all ever run across an *amigo* of mine, Mr. J. G. Reeder?"

"I only wish I had," I confessed, having read all of this great detective's biographies, which had been written by Edgar Wallace.[5] "But I didn't know you'd met."

"It was back in twenty-eight," Cap said reminiscently, and I formed the opinion that the meeting held a number of pleasant

3. For the benefit of new readers, Tommy Okasi is not the man in question's real name. It is an Americanized corruption of the one he gave when rescued from a derelict vessel in the China Seas by a ship under the command of the father of General Jackson Baines (Ole Devil) Hardin, C.S.A. Details of the general's and Tommy's early careers are given in the author's Ole Devil Hardin series. J.T.E.

4. For the benefit of new readers. A samurai was a member of the Japanese lower nobility's elite warrior class and who usually acted as a retainer for the *Daimyos,* the hereditary feudal barons. A masterless samurai who became a mercenary was known as a *ronin.* During the mid-nineteenth century, shortly after Tommy Okasi's departure, an increasing contact with the Western World was bringing an ever growing realization that the retention of a hereditary and privileged warrior class was not compatible with the formation of a modern and industrialized society. Therefore, various edicts issued by the Emperor between 1873 and 1876 abolished the special rights of the samurai and, although some of their traditions and concepts were retained, they ceased to exist. J.T.E.

5. Told in: *Room 13, The Mind of Mr. J. G. Reeder, Red Aces, Mr. J. G. Reeder Returns* and *Terror Keep,* by Edgar Wallace. J.T.E.

memories for him. "Yes, sir, good old James Garfield was one he-bull on his home range, same as all his kind."

" 'James Garfield'?" I repeated, remembering that I had read another name in Mr. Wallace's biographies. "I thought his name was John Grant?"

To say I was interested is putting it mildly!

At first, Cap was reluctant to go into greater detail. However, he finally offered—with the proviso that I obtain a clearance, before starting to write, from the executors of Mr. J. G. Reeder's biographer—to present me with all his notes on the affair for publication.[6]

Changing the subject, I asked how he had acquired the sobriquet "Cap." I was informed that it had come into being when he, the youngest man ever to attain the rank of captain in the Texas Rangers, took over command of Company "Z." I remarked that I had never come across a reference to such a company in any of the histories of the Texas Rangers I have read. Cap explained that, because of the unconventional fashion in which he and his men carried out their duties, their existence had been kept secret.

I immediately pointed out how many would be interested to learn about Company "Z" and Cap's participation in its activities, but he stated that this was not yet permissible. All he could promise was that, should the time become propitious, he would notify me. After that, although he has continued to supply me with information upon which further books were based,[7] he did not refer to the matter and I was starting to believe he had forgotten. However, a few days ago a package arrived addressed

---

6. I subsequently did as Cap Fog suggested. In addition to giving me permission to publish what became *"Cap" Fog, Texas Ranger, Meet Mr. J. G. Reeder,* Ms. Penelope Wallace presented me with the notes her father had made concerning the affair. She also introduced me to Mr. James Garfield Reeder at the preopening reception of the Edgar Wallace Pub on Essex Street, London W.C.2 and he added his own details. J.T.E.

7. These include *Set A-Foot, Beguinage, Beguinage Is Dead!, The Remittance Kid, The Whip and the War Lance, The Gentle Giant,* plus Belle "the Rebel Spy" Boyd, Martha "Calamity Jane" Canary, and Betty Hardin episodes of *J.T.'s Ladies.* J.T.E.

in his familiar handwriting. Much to my delight, I found it contained the necessary authorization and several casebooks.

So here at last is some of the story of Cap Fog, Company "Z."

J.T. Edson,
Active Member, Western Writers of America
Melton Mowbray,
Leicestershire, England

Case One

ALVIN FOG'S MISTAKE

"This'll be him now, I reckon," Major Benson Tragg remarked, coming to his feet as there was a knock on the door of the room he was renting at the luxurious Cattlemen's Hotel in Austin. "Push it open, Jubal, it's not locked."

Alvin Dustine Fog had been trained since childhood to be a peace officer by two acknowledged authorities in all matters pertaining to such duties.[1] These included the handling of firearms, which was still as necessary on occasion in the early 1920s as it had been when Texas was growing—out of hide and horn—from the poverty left in the wake of the War Between the States.[2] At twenty, he had already served for two years in the Rio Hondo County Sheriff's Office as one of his father's deputies and had

1. Although Jackson Marsden Fog has not received the acclaim accorded to his father, Dustine Edward Marsden—details of whose career are given in the author's Civil War and Floating Outfit series—or his son, Alvin Dustine, the records of his exploits as the sheriff of Rio Hondo County prove he was equally competent as either a peace officer or a gun fighter. J.T.E.
2. How this was brought about is told in *Goodnight's Dream; From Hide and Horn; Set Texas Back on Her Feet* and *The Hide and Tallow Men.* J.T.E.

had a commendable number of successful cases to his credit. For all that, he felt more than a trifle uneasy in his mind as the door began to open. He wondered how the latest visitor would react on being appointed as his partner and to the discovery that, although he had just been sworn in as a Texas Ranger, he was to be granted the rank of sergeant immediately after his period of probation was over. He was all too aware that, on the surface at any rate, he appeared anything but a likely candidate for acceptance into the Lone Star State's best known and most respected law-enforcement agency, much less warranting such an early promotion.

Not more than five foot six in height, Alvin had a bronzed face that was moderately handsome and yet made him appear somewhat younger than his actual age. A wide-brimmed, low-crowned black J. B. Stetson hat hung by its *barbiquejo* chinstrap on his shoulders to exhibit curly, short—and newly trimmed—black hair.[3] He had on a waist-length brown leather jacket that gave little indication of there being a Colt Government Model 1911 automatic pistol in a spring retention holster against his left ribs, or the two spare magazines filled with rimless .45 bullets in a pocket inside its right side. Tight rolled and knotted, a multihued silk bandana trailed its long ends over his open-necked dark-green shirt. A brown waist belt, with a fancy buckle and floral pattern carving, held up new Levi's pants. Their legs, cuffs turned back a good three inches deep, hung outside Justin boots carrying Kelly "Petmaker" spurs on the heels.

If Alvin looked like a cowhand who had donned his best clothing to celebrate paying a visit to the state's capital city, Major Benson Tragg conveyed the impression of being a prosper-

---

3. The author suspects that the trend in movies made since the mid-sixties to portray cowhands as long haired and filthy had risen less from the producers' desire for "realism" than because that was the only kind of performers available. In our extensive reference library, we cannot find a dozen photographs of cowboys—as opposed to mountain-men, army scouts, or prospectors—who have long hair and bushy beards. In fact, our reading on the subject has led us to assume that the term "long hair" was one of derision and opprobium in the cattle country then as it is today. J.T.E.

ous rancher. There was little about him to suggest he belonged to a family that had long been associated with the law enforcement of Texas.[4] A good six foot tall, he had the lean and wiry build of one who still followed a strenuous occupation. He had on a light-weight brown suit of excellent cut—although the tailor had not been able to make the jacket so that it entirely hid the bulge of the short-barreled Colt Storekeeper Model Peacemaker holstered butt forward on the left side of his waist belt—a white shirt and sober blue necktie, but his footwear was as suitable as that of his young visitor for riding a horse and working cattle.

From all appearances—so alike were they in height, build, and general demeanor—the man who entered could have been cast in the same mold as Tragg. His attire also suggested he was connected with the cattle business, but closer to Alvin's level. White haired—he was carrying an ancient grayish-green Stetson in his left hand—his leathery brown features gave little hint as to his age—except that he was well on in years—or the feelings behind its impassive mask. Yet they were far from surly or disapproving. In fact, there were wrinkles at the corners of the keen blue eyes and the lean slash of a mouth suggested a dry sense of humor. He was wearing a somewhat baggy brown coat, a gray shirt buttoned to the neck, but without a necktie. Like the hat, his Levi's pants and Justin boots looked old enough to have been part of the original batches put on the market by their respective manufacturers.

Despite being keen sighted and trained for such detection, Alvin could not see any trace of the newcomer being armed. He found this rather surprising. As was the rule with most law-enforcement agencies, a Texas Ranger was expected to have a weapon on his person at all times; including when he was off duty. Nor did it appear likely that a man with Branch's considerable experience as a peace officer would have forgotten such a basic precaution.

4. And, as is demonstrated in the author's Rockabye County series covering the work of a present day Texas sheriff's office, still are. Some details of two earlier members of the Tragg family who served as peace officers in the Old West are given in *Set A-Foot* and *Beguinage Is Dead!* J.T.E.

A dog followed the man into the room and there was something about it that diverted Alvin's attention from trying to discover where he was carrying his weapon. Standing a full twenty-
six inches at the shoulder and weighing at least one hundred
pounds, it had a dark bluish-gray coloration with a black head,
saddle and the speckling by numerous irregularly shaped small
spots that was responsible for its breed's name of "bluetick"
coonhound. However, its size suggested that it was more likely
to be used for hunting big game such as cougar, black or grizzly
bear, rather than raccoon.[5]

Being a keen hunter and follower of coonhounds, the young
Texan found the dog's appearance and attitude as intriguing as
its owner's apparent lack of armament. Straight up, of racy type,
it was well muscled without being chunky or clumsily built. Its
coat was medium coarse and, lying close to the body, had the
glossy smoothness that told of excellent health and fitness. Anything but goose-necked, its head was carried well up and the
longish ears were set low. Square from the top to the end of
the nose and in perfect proportion with the rest of the skull, the
muzzle had flews well covering the lower jaw. They combined
with clean, keen eyes to give a pleading hound expression that
was neither wild nor cowed. Attached slightly below the back
line, well rooted, tapered, and of moderate length, its tail was
carried high in a forward curving crescent. Yet, despite all the
evidence of its unexceptionable physical condition, it moved in
such a lethargic fashion that it might have been tired almost
beyond endurance.

"This is Alvin Dustine Fog, Jubal," Tragg introduced. "The
young feller I was telling you-all about. Alvin, meet Sergeant
Jubal Branch."

"Right pleased to make your acquaintance," the newcomer
declared, his Texas drawl implying his background was lower on
the social scale than that of the other men present. Strolling
forward, his leisurely seeming gait giving a deceptive speed, he
extended his right hand and went on, "Knowed your

5. A description of hunting big game with a pack of hounds and of some of
the other breeds that are used is given in *Hound Dog Man*. J.T.E.

grandpappy, Colonel Dusty,[6] and your daddy. Jackson and me did a hitch together in the army and rode side by side more'n once when I was a deputy under Sheriff Billy-Bob Brackett down to Jack County."

"I've heard them both speak of you-all, Jubal," Alvin admitted, shaking hands. As he was doing so, the bluetick ambled up. Sniffing at his left leg in passing, it gave a single languid wag of its tail before crossing to flop down in the corner of the room, and apparently falling asleep. Having watched it, Alvin swung his gaze back to its owner. "Have you-all come far?"

"Drove over from Widow Haskey's rooming house on Thirty-eighth street is all," the sergeant replied, drawing an accurate conclusion over what had caused the question. His voice took on a slightly defensive note as he continued, "Mind you, ole Lightning 'n' me *walked* all the way up here, 'stead of riding that fancy 'el-ee-vator.' "

"Lightning?" Alvin repeated, unable to prevent himself from throwing another glance at the sleeping bluetick.

"Sounded like a right good name to call him—once," Branch stated, his bearing suggesting a kind of defiant exculpation for what he knew to have been an all-too-obvious error of judgment on his part. "Anyways, when a feller gets to my age, he don't want no fool hound dog's goes dashing and rushing about wild-like."

"One thing's for sure," Alvin conceded, suspecting that the bluetick's demeanor was deceptive and that he was repeating comments on the matter that had been frequently made. "Nobody's ever going to start accusing *him* of doing that."

During the conversation, the elderly sergeant had continued the examination of his future partner, which he had commenced on entering, and was now drawing conclusions. The youngster did not have his daddy's height and heft. Rather he favored his

6. As was the case with master cattlemen Charles Goodnight, Captain Dustine Edward Marsden (Dusty) Fog, C.S.A., never attained the rank of colonel. It was a term of respect given in his later years, gained by his courage, integrity, and ability as a fighting man and leader. See Chapter Four "The Death Bringer's Orders" of *Sidewinder.* J.T.E.

paternal grandfather, except he had his grandmother's black hair.[7] There was the same kind of spread to his shoulders and trimming down at the waist Cap'n Dusty had had, hinting at his small frame being packed with muscle power that a bigger man would not have scorned to possess. His face gave little away and his gray eyes looked capable of boring through a man. From all accounts, he had done pretty well as a deputy down in Rio Hondo County and was reckoned to be a regular snake with a handgun. Branch knew Jackson Fog too well to think he would have been retained in the sheriff's office unless he was worthy of the badge, kin or not. Of course, there were differences in being a deputy and serving in the Texas Rangers. Somehow, Branch felt sure he would be willing to listen and learn when any of those differences came up.

Taking everything into consideration, the sergeant was confident that he and the young man would be able to work together harmoniously. Nor was he in the least put out by the knowledge that, once Major Tragg was satisfied, the other was to be promoted to his own rank when they joined the new company that the governor of Texas was having formed.

Conscious that he was being subjected to a thorough scrutiny, Alvin had been doing the same to the observer while wondering whether he was being found acceptable. He hoped that he was. Not only had Branch many years' practical experience of law enforcement, much of it had been acquired in the Texas Rangers. Their statewide jurisdiction gave a greater scope and variety of duties than came the way of a deputy sheriff, whose authority was restricted to the county in which he held his office. That would be particularly the case when Company "Z" came into being and commenced its specialized, unconventional task. Having the elderly sergeant's guidance and access to the wisdom he had accrued would be more than merely a source of valuable information, or the means of carrying out an assignment correctly. It could spell the difference between life and death.

7. Lady Winifred Amelia (Freddie Woods) Besgrove-Woodstole. How she and Dusty Fog met is told in *The Making of a Lawman* and *The Trouble Busters.* J.T.E.

"The major here allows you-all 'n' me's going to be working along of each other," Branch remarked, in such a neutral tone it was impossible to deduce how he regarded the arrangement. "Don't know about you-all, but I'm right pleased. A smart young feller like you'll certain sure be able to show a wored-out 'n' old-fashioned goat like me how all these newfangled scientifical wonders's going to make life easier for us John-Laws work."

"Why now, you couldn't have come to a better man to ask," Alvin asserted, his voice and attitude redolent of mock false modesty mingled with pride. "Back home to Polveroso City, we've not only traded in our *Dragoon* Colts for some of these fancy new metal cartridge guns, we've even got us a *telephone* in the sheriff's office."

"Trust your pappy Jackson for *that*," Branch drawled, his eyes twinkling. "Allus was a mighty 'per-gressive' sort of feller 'n' willing to try anything new."

"Why sure," Alvin agreed, sensing he was making the correct impression. "Trouble being, nobody else in Rio Hondo County has a telephone and, even should they have, ours isn't wired up. We don't have electricity yet."

"Well, you-all can't have *everything*," Branch consoled. "Which's what I told your daddy Jackson the night him 'n' me went a-visit—to raid Minnie Ogilvie's chicken ranch—"

"We don't either of us want to know *that*!" Tragg interrupted firmly, satisfied that the sergeant was in agreement with the decision to enlist the young man and would be willing to act as his mentor through the probation period. Ignoring Alvin's sotto voce but audible comment, "I wouldn't mind," he went on, "Why don't you pair go some place and do something useful, or just waste your time and the good taxpaying citizens of the fair state of Texas's money. I don't care much which, just so long as you leave me to get on with my work."

"Whatever you-all say, Major," Branch drawled, oozing well-simulated unctuous respect. "What say we head out to the National Guard's ranges 'n' shoot us a few, amigo? Way my eyes're going back on me, I'll need me spectacles to see the targets. But I reckon you'll be able to hit enough for both of us. It's surely a

comfort to know I've got me a young 'n' lusty partner to 'per-
tect' me should it be needed."

"I'll do my level best to justify your faith in me, sir," Alvin
promised, as soberly as if he was taking a solemn oath, then
nodded to the dog. "Do you-all reckon he can make it down to
the parking lot on his own, or should I carry him?"

"He can make it for sure," Branch declared, if a touch doubt-
fully, and gave a low whistle that brought the bluetick to its feet
with what, in a human being, would have been an air of dejected
resignation. "Just so long's we don't walk too fast."

As if to be in keeping with the elderly sergeant's emphasis on his
age and general state of decrepitude, his car was a hard-used
1920 Ford Model T center door, four-seater sedan, the exterior
of which looked badly in need of a clean. There was a low-
horned, double-girthed Texas range saddle on the backseat.
When Branch opened the passenger door, the bluetick climbed
aboard, and acting as if the effort had been almost beyond its
capacity, curled up alongside the rig with an air of proprietor-
ship.

"We could always ride over in *my* jalopy," Alvin suggested,
nodding to the sleek silver-gray 1920 Cunningham V-8 sports
car, which had been a present from his family to celebrate his
pending enrollment as a member of the Texas Rangers. "My
saddle's in the rumble seat, but there'd still be room for that fool
hound dog as well."

"I'd sooner stay as we are, happen that's all right with *you*,"
Branch refused, and despite the polite way they were uttered,
there was a slight suggestion of challenge in the words. "It'd
mean disturbing him, which'd be a sinful shame. Anyways, ole
Lightning 'n' me, we're just plain country folks and aren't used
to riding in nothing that fancy nor fast-looking."

"Have it *your* way," Alvin assented, starting to swing into the
front passenger seat. "After all, you *outrank* me."

"I hadn't give it a thought," Branch lied, but sounding as if he
was speaking the unvarnished truth. He knew that he had just
received an assurance with regard to their status quo, which
settled his thoughts on the subject. "Allus did take real well to a

young feller's who's respectful to his 'olders' and knows his place."

"That's me from here to there and back the long way," Alvin declared, sealing the unspoken agreement. Glancing over his shoulder at the Winchester Model 1873 rifle in the boot attached to the left skirt of the saddle, he went on, "Hey, though, shall I fetch my carbine along?"

"Was figuring on using sidearms," Branch replied. " 'Less you-all'd sooner show me how it's done with a saddle-gun."

"Like I said," Alvin drawled, not averse to finding out where the sergeant was carrying the obligatory handgun. "You're the boss."

Having noticed that the Ford's wheels were equipped with demountable rims, the young Texan was not surprised to discover—when his companion settled in the driver's seat—that it also had an electric starter, although both were still optional extras on such vehicles. What was more, as the engine purred into life, he realized it was a far more powerful unit than the one with which the car had left the factory. He considered the improvements further proof of his suspicion that the sergeant was far more progressive than appeared on the surface.

"What do you-all reckon about this Company 'Z' we'll be joining?" Branch inquired, driving the sedan westward across the city with a laconic aplomb.

"Seems to me like it's an outfit that's badly needed," Alvin replied, remembering all he had been told by Major Tragg and the governor of Texas when they had met the previous evening. "We've both seen too many times when a son-of-a-bitch who's guiltier than all hell gets away scot-free because his shyster lawyer comes up with some ruling that's supposed just to protect the innocent. I'm all for *anything* that'll stop it happening."

"There's some as won't see it that way," Branch warned, giving no indication of whether or not he approved of his companion's sentiments. "They'll allow it's not right."

"Hell!" Alvin protested. "It's not that we're being let take away the rules to protect the innocent. We'll just be making sure the guilty sons-of-bitches don't use them to escape. It's only shyster lawyers, criminals, soft-shells and liberadicals[8] who'll be against Company 'Z.' Honest, law-abiding folks will back us all the way."

"Trouble being, them said honest, law-abiding folks are too busy working and earning their livings to go spouting off about what they reckon in the newspapers or on the radio," Branch pointed out. "Which same, seems like the soft-shells and liberadicals can allus find time to do. Way some of them take on about the way things're going to be now the 'people' have took over in Russia, there won't be no laws, police, nor criminals over there 'n' I believe 'em. Mind you, though, I'm just a half-smart ole country boy's believes in Father Christmas 'n' the Tooth Fairy."

"I'll have to remember to buy you a Christmas stocking to hang on your bed," Alvin said with a grin, then became more serious. "Anyways, once Company 'Z' gets going, we have to make sure that *nobody* gets to hear about how we work."

"I'll say 'amen' to that," Branch replied and changed the subject. "Have you-all ever been on the National Guard's new hand-gun range?"

"No," Alvin admitted. "Is it different from the others I've shot on?"

"Well, now," the sergeant drawled. "I'd say that all 'deepends' on what they was like. One thing I will say, though, it's sure not the easiest son-of-a-bitch *I've* seen."

A movement in the bushes caught Alvin's eye as he walked with Branch along the path at the bottom of a wood-covered valley to which they had been directed by the controller of the National Guard's shooting range. Seeing what caused it, the young Texan realized he had been deliberately misled. They were not going to the mysterious pistol range, but were already on it.

Stopping instantly on spread-apart feet, Alvin bent his knees slightly while tilting his torso forward a little. Working in smooth coordination with the other movements, his left hand

8. For the benefit of new readers: soft-shells and liberadicals are left wing intellectuals, or liberals of radical persuasion. J.T.E.

rose to grasp and draw open the near side of his jacket and the right crossed with equal alacrity to swivel the Colt automatic from the spring retention clips of the shoulder holster. Turning outward at waist level and aimed by instinctive alignment, the weapon barked just seven tenths of a second after he had appreciated the situation. For all that, the .45 bullet struck the center of the man-sized and shaped target, which had swung into view from behind a tree some twenty feet from the trail. Against a human being, the hit would have proved fatal.

Anticipating what was to happen, Branch had been watching with interest. He liked everything he had seen, and despite having expected a display of skill, was impressed. Caught unawares, the youngster had not become flustered. Yet, swiftly as he had reacted, his right forefinger only entered the triggerguard and the thumb refrained from pushing down the manual safety catch until after the muzzle of the Colt was pointing outward.[9] That was the mark of the truly expert *pistolero,* and a major criterion by which the sergeant judged such matters.

"You sneaky cuss!" Alvin exclaimed, looking at his companion as the target turned to disappear from whence it had come.

"Land's sakes!" Branch gasped innocently. "Didn't I *tell* you-all's we was on the pistol range? That's the worst of getting old. You turn sort of 'fer-getical.' That fool gun of your'n jammed?"

"No," Alvin replied, after glancing in surprise to the weapon he was holding and at which the sergeant was staring disdainfully. "What made you think it might have?"

"I've heard tell all them new-fangled 'auty-matics' jam every time anybody's *loco* enough to shoot one off," Branch explained. "*Could* be I wasn't told it right."

"Way I heard it, revolvers throw flames out of the sides of their cylinders," Alvin stated, having encountered a similar prejudice against automatic pistols on other occasions. "That's why I don't use one. What now?"

"Might as well keep walking," Branch suggested.

"Shall I holster my iron?" Alvin inquired.

9. For the benefit of new readers: a description of how dangerous a failure to take such a precaution could be is given in *The Fast Gun.* J.T.E.

"I'd say that's up to you-all," Branch answered in an offhand fashion. "I don't *know*, mind, but there *could* be some more of them sneaky targets along the way."

Starting to walk, with the sergeant following in a way that allowed him to keep the fairly dense woodland on each side of the trail under observation, Alvin decided whoever laid out the unconventional—yet very practical—range was a man with experience where using handguns was concerned. It presented a demanding test of alertness and skill. With one exception, the targets were situated between fifteen and thirty feet from the trail. All were brought into view with only sufficient commotion to make it possible for the ears to play their part in the detection as well as the eyes.

Advancing steadily along the winding three-quarters of a mile length of the range, which was controlled by a man in a high tower on the rim of the valley signaling to the operators of the targets when he wanted them to appear, Alvin contrived not only to locate but to hit each in turn—even the third, which was a good fifty yards away. Nor did the fact that he had retained the Colt in his hand, instead of replacing and drawing it after each shot, lessen the admiration he was arousing in Branch.

All in all, the sergeant concluded he was witnessing a masterly display. He had asked the range master to signal for the third target, which was normally used only when the man on the trail was carrying a rifle, more as a joke than part of the test. Yet, bringing the pistol to shoulder height at arm's length and supporting it with both hands while using the sights, Alvin had made a hit. Then, when the fifth target emerged slightly behind and to the left, the weapon was transferred swiftly to that hand instead of being delayed while turning his whole body, and he fired with no loss of accuracy.

Although the sixth, seventh, and eighth targets appeared close together and in rapid succession, Alvin was able to deal with them all because he had developed reloading the pistol into a fine art. Having returned the Colt to his right hand after the fifth target, he had extracted a full magazine with the left as he started walking. Firing the sixth shot, he pressed the stud on the left side of the pistol with his right thumb. As the empty maga-

zine slid from its housing in the butt, he deftly replaced it with
the reserve and was able to continue shooting. Having dispatched the eighth bullet to puncture its intended mark, he could
not resist commenting to his companion that such a feat would
have been impossible for a man who was old-fashioned enough
to make use of a slow-to-reload revolver.

Despite his continued success and feeling sure he was leaving
his future partner with no doubts regarding his competence at
handling a gun, Alvin was aware that he had not achieved his
secondary purpose. As yet, Branch had made no attempt to participate, and by doing so, display where he was carrying his
sidearm. Deducing from a sign announcing, "Unload Weapon
Before Passing This Point"—which was nailed to a tree on the
bend they were approaching—that they were reaching the end of
the range, he was unable to restrain his curiosity any longer.

"I'm empty, Jubal. Happen there's another target, you'll have
to take it."

"Danged if I wasn't feared as you'd say something like *that*!"
the sergeant protested plaintively, having counted the number of
shots expended since his companion last changed magazines and
being aware that there were still two bullets in the pistol. Arch-
ing his spine with a wince and reaching around with his right
hand as if to rub it, he continued, "And me with 'screwmatics' in
my back fit to—"

Rising from among a clump of bushes some thirty feet beyond
Branch's side of the trail, a target caused him to stop speaking
and turn, bringing the hand into view quickly. It was grasping
the ivory butt of a Colt Civilian Model Frontier revolver.[10]
Adopting a gunman's crouch with remarkable ease for one who
claimed to be suffering from rheumatism, he pressed his right
elbow tightly against his side and brought his left hand in a
circular motion that drew back then released the hammer.

Unlike when Alvin had been firing his more modern "smoke-

10. The Colt Frontier is the name given to a Peacemaker chambered for the
Winchester .44-40 bullet—caliber .44 of an inch and with a forty-grain
powder charge—permitting the same ammunition to be used in the revolver and the Model 1873 rifle. J.T.E.

less" ammunition, the gasses produced by detonating the revolver's forty grains of black powder gushed from the four and three-quarter inch barrel in a white cloud. There was little breeze on the trail to disperse it and it was added to that which was generated from the four shots fanned by the sergeant's rapidly moving left hand in the wake of the first bullet. Despite the target being partially concealed by the smoke, he contrived to put three of the bullets into its "chest."

"Well now," Alvin drawled, after the smoke wafted away. "Is that a trick you learned in France when you-all and my daddy were over there fighting the Germans?"

"Shucks, no," Branch replied, having mentioned during the drive to the range that he had served in the same regiment as Jackson Fog during the World War. "I learned fanning from my old grandpappy. Over there, I used me a lucky ole B.A.R."[11]

"I was meaning putting down a smoke screen that way," Alvin corrected with a grin. "I'll give you it's a sneaky trick, though. Happen you-all miss despite spraying so much lead around, the other feller couldn't see to shoot back at you."

"Smart-alecky young cuss," Branch sniffed, returning the revolver to the holster, which rode horizontally instead of vertically on the back of his wide waistbelt. "Anyways, like you say, it's a smart trick. Trouble being's how they don't give out no smoke, you-all couldn't do it with that blasted 'auty-matical' pistol gun you're loco enough to be carrying."

The screeching of tires brought Alvin Fog to the front window of the accommodation he was renting while in Austin. Although the term "motel" had not yet come into use, the Greenville Inn could have qualified for such a title. In addition to the main hotel building, it offered several small detached cabins surrounding the parking lot.

Rocking on its springs from the violence with which it had been turned from the street, an open, four-seater, black 1923 Buick Sport Tourer was crossing the parking lot faster than was prudent. Before it swerved and skidded to a halt in front of the

11. See Part Two "Jubal Branch's Lucky B.A.R." of this volume. J.T.E.

next but one cabin to his own, Alvin had been able to study its
occupants. Guided by comments from an obviously disgruntled
neighbor, he deduced they were the Holstein brothers, Willie
and Karl, and their cousin, Hubert Blitzer. Certainly the physical resemblance of the two young men on the front seat suggested they were closely related. Tall, slim, with good-looking
features, they were bareheaded and their dark hair was slicked
down by oil. Like the shorter and more heavily built passenger in
the rear—who had on a white fedora hat and whose sun-red-
dened face was sullen—they were dressed in lightweight, costly
alpaca suits, white shirts, and multihued ties. Climbing from the
vehicle, they were clearly in high spirits. Laughing, exchanging
comments he could not hear, and slapping each other on the
back, they disappeared into the cabin.

There had been something besides the reckless fashion in
which the man behind the steering wheel—his neatly trimmed
mustache suggested he could be the elder brother, Willie—had
been driving to attract Alvin's attention. A brown leather strap
passed across the chest of his shirt as if he was wearing his waist
belt unusually high for some reason. The young peace officer
doubted whether this was the case. In fact, unless he missed his
guess, it formed part of a shoulder holster that was not so well
designed for concealment purposes as his own. He was also
aware that, if the assumption was correct, it opened the way to
other and more disturbing speculations.

After completing the "Walk and Shoot" course, Alvin and
Branch had returned to the range master's office. There, while
cleaning and reloading their weapons, they had been joined by
three members of the Austin City police department. After being
introduced, one of them had commented upon a wave of holdups
that was plaguing the municipal law-enforcement agency. Although eight had taken place so far, very little was known about
the perpetrators other than that two were tall and slim, the third
shorter and stocky. They invariably wore masks and coveralls
that effectively concealed whatever clothing and features were
beneath. However, witnesses in two of the robberies had claimed
the tallest of the trio produced his Luger automatic pistol from
what appeared to be a shoulder holster.

While there was not a great deal in it, Willie Holstein had a discernible height advantage over his brother!

The trio also could fit the description of the robbers!

Against that, according to the embittered neighbor, all three were the pampered sons of well-to-do families and should have no need to repeatedly commit crimes that had brought only small amounts of money and a few items of not too great value as loot.

On the other hand, neither did there appear to be any valid reason for Willie to be carrying a gun in a shoulder holster. At least, not in one that announced its presence in such a fashion. The party's clothes precluded the possibility that they had been out hunting and were equally unsuitable for even target shooting on a range.

Having drawn his conclusions, Alvin found himself on the horns of a dilemma. He had not yet been sworn in as a Texas Ranger, which would simplify matters. Even if he had not already resigned his commission as a deputy sheriff in Rockabye County, his appointment would have given him no legal jurisdiction in Austin. So, whatever action he decided to take, he must carry it out in the capacity of a private person and could only make a citizen's arrest if his suspicions were confirmed.

One solution presented itself.

Before they had parted at the Cattlemen's Hotel, where Branch had delivered Alvin on leaving the National Guard's range to collect his Cunningham, they had arranged to meet that evening and take dinner together. The sergeant was due to arrive shortly, but Alvin did not know exactly when he would put in an appearance. Nor could he guess how Branch would react when he came. There was so little to go on and it seemed pushing the bounds of coincidence to extreme limits that three criminals they had only heard about a few hours earlier should be staying in the same place as Alvin. What was more, there was a chance that they would leave before Branch arrived. Or they might conceal all the evidence that could incriminate them.

Taking everything into consideration, Alvin felt sure the elderly sergeant would prefer him to act on his own initiative under the circumstances rather than wait for guidance. Even if he did no more than try to look into the trio's cabin, or eavesdrop on whatever conversation might be taking place, it would be better than waiting passively until Branch joined him.

Reaching his decision, Alvin went into his bedroom. He had changed into a white sports shirt and flannels earlier, removing the spurs, but retaining the boots. Drawing on his shoulder holster, which had a webbing loop that passed behind his back and around the right shoulder, he slid the strap at the rear of the rig through his waist belt and secured it by joining a press-stud. Thrusting home a loaded magazine, he drew and released the cocking slide to feed the uppermost round into the Colt's chamber. Having set the manual safety instinctively, he placed the weapon in the spring clips. Unlike in Willie's case, once he had donned his navy blue blazer, there was nothing visible to show he had such a device on his person.

Leaving by the back door, Alvin made his way to the rear of the trio's accommodation. He paused, listened, and looked into the bedrooms. They were empty and nothing suspicious was to be seen in either. So, guessing that the layout would be similar to the quarters he was renting—with the sitting-cum-dining-room and kitchen at the front—he decided to try his luck in that direction and via the side door.

There was one problem, Alvin realized. The cabins on either side had occupants who might draw the wrong conclusions and betray him if they saw what he was doing. A moment's thought supplied the solution. While three young women lived on the opposite side to his cabin, he had seen them leave earlier, and as their car was not outside, he felt sure they had not yet returned. So he would be able to carry out his reconnaissance with less chance of being observed in the gap adjacent to their quarters. What was more, the sitting room was on that side and he expected his quarry would be in it rather than the kitchen.

Arriving at his objective, Alvin found as he had hoped that—although the outer mesh screen was closed—the door stood open. Peering around stealthily, he saw only the brothers in the room. Having removed their jackets, collars, and ties, they were sitting at the table drinking beer. However, Willie was not wearing a shoulder holster. Yet their conversation was suggestive, if not incriminating.

"When do we hit another one?" Karl was asking.

"Soon," Willie answered.

"I should hope so," the younger brother declared, gesturing toward a cigarette case that lay open on the table. "Those are expensive."

"But worth it, brother mine, *well* worth it!" the elder stated. "When those girls have taken a few drags, they're game for *anything.*"

"You can say that again!" Karl enthused. "Millie's the cat's meeow, and boy, can she neck!"

"*Neck!*" Willie scoffed. "She does a whole lot more than *that.*"

Engrossed in the conversation and drawing conclusions about the type of cigarettes in the case, Alvin failed to notice that he was under observation himself.

Coming from the rear corner of the girls' cabin, Hubert Blitzer paused as he saw the small figure clearly listening at the side door of his quarters. A scowl came to his surly features. Then, hoping his cousins were not saying anything indiscreet, he began to advance on tiptoe. Closing into reaching distance without being detected, he grabbed and twisted the eavesdropper's right wrist around in a hammerlock.

"All right, you nosy son-of-a-bitch!" Blitzer growled, throwing his left arm around and across his victim's throat to stifle any outcry. "If you're so interested in what's being said, go in and you'll be able to hear better."

While speaking, the burly young man reached with his left foot to draw open the screen door. Retaining his hold, he pushed his captive in ahead of him.

"What the hell?" Willie exclaimed, coming to his feet. His action was duplicated by his sibling.

"I caught this little bastard 'on the Erie' outside," Blitzer replied.

"Why would he be?" Willie demanded, knowing the term "on the Erie" meant to eavesdrop.

"You heard the man, squirt!" Blitzer snarled, sounding as tough and menacing as he could manage while loosening the pressure his left arm was applying. "Why should you be doing a columnist on him?"

"Well, now," Alvin drawled, standing passive and giving his voice the timbre of a less well-educated person. "Could be's how I *know* the way you good old boys's buying your muggle 'n' want in."

"You *know*—?" Karl commenced, alarmed by the prospect of an outsider having discovered the means by which the money to purchase the marijuana cigarettes in the case had been acquired.

"Bag your head!" Willie yelled, his Midwestern accent growing more pronounced in his consternation as he brought his brother's incautious words to a halt. "So you think you know—"

"No, *hombre*," Alvin corrected, but remaining motionless in his captor's grasp. "I *know* I know."

"To hell with what you know!" Blitzer spat out, drawing his left arm back and starting to force the trapped limb higher with his right hand. "It's not going—!"

The actions, based upon their recipient's behavior to that point, proved to be a mistake!

Although Alvin had been aware of Blitzer's quiet approach, he had allowed himself to be grabbed when it had become apparent—from the shadow on the wall, which the other had overlooked—that he was not going to be assaulted in any other way. He had guessed, correctly, that he would be taken into the cabin for questioning, and as this served his purpose, he had seen how it would be advantageous not to prevent it happening. In the event of his suspicions proving unfounded, he would be able to claim truthfully that he was compelled to go in and had not entered uninvited.

Feeling the hold being tightened, Alvin concluded that the time for staying passive was over. If he continued to behave submissively, he might suffer an incapacitating injury. So he accepted that he must now take the offensive.

Slumping a little, the small Texan caused Blitzer to think he was on the point of collapsing through fear. Feeling the grips on his neck and wrist relaxing slightly, he knew he had achieved his purpose. From standing apparently in a state of terror, he was transformed instantly into sudden and very effective motion. Crouching a little on his slightly bent knees, he rotated his torso to add impetus as he thrust back with his left elbow.

Caught totally unprepared, a startled and pain-filled gasp burst from Blitzer. Not only did his right hand leave the wrist, he was unable to retain the position of his left arm. His erstwhile compliant captive wrenched free and the force of the elbow's jab to the solar plexus sent him backward to collide with the screen door. It burst open and he toppled through, but managed to remain on his feet.

Startled by the change that had come over Alvin, Willie recovered first and led the way as the brothers rushed forward. Both had boxed in their Eastern college and neither envisaged any difficulty in dealing with a person they regarded as nothing more than a small country bumpkin.

Which was a dangerous mistake when confronted by the grandson of Dusty Fog!

Alvin had learned self-defense from a relative of the man who had taught the Rio Hondo gun wizard a devastatingly effective form of unarmed combat that in the 1920s was still but little known in the Western Hemisphere.[12] Putting his training to use, he had no hesitation over going to meet the brothers. Leaping into the air, he kicked the ball of his right foot against Willie's chest to send its recipient spinning helplessly into a corner of the room.

Nor did Karl fare any better. As the small Texan alighted from the assault on his brother, Karl shot out a classic left jab at the face. It failed to connect. Ducking below the blow, Alvin struck back in a different—yet highly efficient—fashion. Instead of clenching his right fist, he kept the fingers extended together and folded the thumb across the palm. The fingers thrust just below Karl's breastbone, and experiencing a similar sensation to

12. It was not until the author received the notes upon which this volume is based that he learned a nephew of Tommy Okasi, who was also trained as a samurai warrior, had come to the United States and taught Alvin Fog ju jitsu and karate. J.T.E.

a time when he had been jabbed in the stomach with the end of a baseball bat, he went into reverse, displaying his discomfort.

Snarling with rage, Blitzer plunged into the cabin. Hoping to spring a similar surprise to the one inflicted upon himself, he reached, meaning to grab the small Texan by the shoulders. Alerted to the possibility by hearing him returning, Alvin needed only a brief backward glance to assess the situation. Turning, he caught the outstretched left hand, and stepping aside, swung around to propel his attacker onward. Blundering into and falling across the table, which collapsed under him, he was precipitated to the floor.

Completing his turn with the Colt in his right hand, Alvin directed its muzzle to where Willie was getting ready to attack again. Having brought the elder brother's movements to a halt, the weapon swung and quelled his sibling's desire toward further aggressive action.

"That's better," Alvin stated. "You're all under arrest."

Coming at the end of the words, there was a crash and the front door burst open. Even as the small Texan was about to swing the automatic that way, he found to his relief that the precaution was not necessary. Stepping warily, a star-in-the-circle Texas Ranger's badge pinned prominently on his shirt, Jubal Branch entered. He had the Colt Frontier revolver in his right hand and Lightning was at his left side. However, the bluetick's earlier appearance of sloth was absent, being replaced by a demeanor that suggested the alertness and menace of a wild predatory creature.

"Howdy, you-all," the sergeant greeted, with an air of laconic yet purposeful authority. "What's coming off here?"

"These are the three who've been pulling all those holdups around town," Alvin supplied, the words having been directed to him.

"It—it's a goddamned lie!" Willie shouted.

"I'll say it be," Branch spat out, running his gaze over the trio and then turning it to Alvin. "How in hell could you-all have made such a goddamned fool mistake?"

* * *

To say the young Texan was taken aback by the sergeant's furious words was an understatement. He had expected that he
would receive support even if he was wrong in his suspicions.
Instead, Branch's whole bearing suggested contempt for him and
his actions.

"Them three!" the sergeant continued, before Alvin could
speak. "Look at 'em, goddamn it! Those stickups were pulled by
men. These're nothing but a bunch of *college boys.* Worse any of
'em dast do'd be go on a panty raid for their 'fraternical initera-
tion' and not then, happen they thought the gals'd fight back."

"Hey!" Karl yelped indignantly, writhing with growing annoyance at the disdainful way in which the elderly peace officer
was looking at and speaking about them.

"And whoever pulled the stickups wouldn't've got whupped
by a short-growed button like you-all," Branch went on remorse-
lessly, paying no attention to the younger brother. "Why, nobody with one goddamned lick of half good sense'd reckon any
one of 'em could do sic 'em 'cepting live offen their folks's
money."

While pleased by the declarations, which clearly presumed
their innocence, Willie and Blitzer were finding the sergeant's
reflections upon their manhood increasingly distasteful. The effect was even greater upon Karl. Always treated as very much
the subordinate by the other two, he was uncomfortably aware
that much of what was being said came close to being applicable.
None of them had managed to hold down a job since being
"requested" to leave college after an incident too many. Nor,
apart from the robberies they had been committing, had they
ever succeeded in anything they had attempted. The comment
about them being dependent upon the bounty of their parents
was also true. None of which appealed to Karl's arrogant, snob-
bish nature, particularly when he was being reminded of it—
taunted about it, would be a better term—by a person he considered to be typical of the semi-illiterate, incompetent law-enforcement officers he and his companions had been outwitting with
such ease.

"What about—!" Alvin commenced, meaning to mention the marijuana cigarettes that were now scattered across the floor.

"What about you-all keeping your goddamned flapping mouth shut?" Branch suggested. "The last son-of-a-bitching thing I need is for you to try convincing me these three half-baked college-boy pin-brains'd have the guts, or sense, to do more'n go to the backhouse without help—'n' not that, happen it was after dark!"

"Is that so!" Karl howled, jumping forward as he was unable to control himself any longer. "Well, you're the one who's making the mistake. We did the—"

"Shut up!" Willie yelled, starting after and meaning to restrain his sibling by force if necessary.

Before the elder brother had taken his second step, despite having remained lying at its master's side when Karl advanced, Lightning rose in a swift motion. Standing on stiff legs and with tail rigid, a low growl full of menace rumbled from the bluetick and caused Willie to halt.

"Sure," Branch supplemented, without taking his mocking gaze from Karl. "Shut up, for shame. Trying to make a poor ole cuss like me think you-all'd be *men* enough, or *smart* enough even, to have done them."

"We *did* do them!" the young man howled, so beside himself with rage that he did not care what the consequences of his behavior might be. "You'll find the coveralls we wear, the guns, and the loot we haven't got rid of yet in the next cabin."

"Will we, now?" Branch drawled. "Well, happen that's so, I reckon I'll apologize most humble and admit you did them stick-ups after all."

"Whooee!" Alvin exclaimed, watching the three young men being escorted from the parking lot by the policemen the sergeant had summoned. "I thought I'd made a mistake there."

Half an hour had elapsed since Karl had made his damning admission. A check on the girls' cabin had produced the items Blitzer had taken there just before finding Alvin eavesdropping outside the trio's quarters. They had included the Luger mentioned by the witnesses and the poorly designed shoulder holster that had attracted Alvin's attention when Willie had been injudicious enough to wear it instead of taking it off during the journey from their most recent robbery.

Throughout the waiting period, the young Texan had been worried by the way in which the sergeant had acted since arriving. While he had provoked a confession from Karl, he had not given any indication of whether his opinion of Alvin's judgment and behavior had changed for the better. In fact, beyond mentioning that he had seen Blitzer forcing Alvin to enter the cabin and "done snuck over to find out why," he had conveyed the impression that he considered the affair was over.

"Depends upon what you-all mean," Branch commented. "I conclude you allowed you'd got reason to figure they were the ones."

"Not a whole heap, but some," Alvin confessed and explained the circumstances.

"Like you say," Branch drawled. "Not a whole heap, but enough to take a whirl on. 'Cept that stacking up against odds of three to one's not the smartest thing to do. I'm not overtaken with that old 'one riot, one Ranger' notion,[13] less'n there's no other way. But I'd say you did right by going in, 'stead of waiting and maybe letting 'em get away, and you handled 'em real good."

"All right, I give up!" Alvin asserted, deciding that acting on his own initiative was not the error. "What was my mistake?"

"Figuring how I was riled at *you* in there," the sergeant answered with a frosty grin. "When all I was doing was trying to get one of them fancy-pants city slickers all pawin' and bellerin' mad 'cause a poor, wored-out, un-eddicated, ole country hick like me was disrespecting 'em something fierce."

"So *that* was it!" Alvin said, unable to conceal his relief. "I was thinking you'd reckoned it was a mistake to say you'd have me for a partner."

---

13. According to the legend, arriving alone in a town that had requested assistance to quell a riot, a Texas Ranger was asked how many more of his companions were coming. "None," the Ranger replied. "There's only one riot, isn't there?" J.T.E.

"Nope," Branch admitted and indicated the dog, which, having reverted to its usual languorous behavior, was sprawled on its side at his feet. "I *knowed* you-all'd work out fine, way ole Lightning here took to you soon's you and him met up."

"You knew from *that*?" Alvin inquired, remembering the bluetick's far from vigorous response when passing him in Major Tragg's room at the Cattlemen's Hotel.

"Why sure," Branch confirmed. "He took on real 'enthusiasti-cal'—for him."

Case Two

JUBAL BRANCH'S LUCKY B.A.R.

It was shortly after noon on September 29th, 1918. What was to become known as World War I was, although few realized it, entering its final stages. However, despite the fighting that was taking place elsewhere, all appeared peaceful enough along the wood-lined stretch of road in the west of the area in France to which its residents—with typical Gallic local pride and stubbornness—still insisted upon referring to as the Province of Champagne rather than, as had become law in 1790, the Department of Meuse.

The pacific appearance was *very* deceptive!

In fact, men were on the point of taking the lives of other human beings!

Hearing the sound of an aircraft approaching, Sergeant Otto Eisenfaust of the *Graf Barfuss (4. Westphalia)* No. 15 Infantry Regiment was prevented from seeing it by the fairly dense foliage of the woodland where he and his ten men were waiting in concealment. Watching the dozen khaki-clad figures who—having emerged from the trees at the opposite side and crossed the road —were advancing in an extended line through the hip-high grass that formed an almost one-hundred-yard-wide border toward his position, he hoped that they would consider the plane as friendly. Convinced that they had no suspicion of the presence of himself and his men, the last thing he wanted was for them to be disturbed by the arrival of a flying machine they would regard as being hostile.

The hope did not materialize!

Flieger-Lieutenant Manfred von Crimmitschau was flying his garishly painted Albatross Va scout aircraft[1] in search of whatever targets of opportunity might present themselves along the wood-lined road from Montmédy to Verdun. Due to bad liaison, he had not been notified that any of his country's infantrymen were patrolling in the vicinity. Nor, being a newly promoted officer of the elite German Imperial Air Service's *Jasta* 8, would he have changed his intentions if he had discovered they were there. Such was his feeling of superiority over the humble foot soldiers that it would not have bothered him if he had known they were on the point of launching the ambush they were laying. He regarded their intended quarry as offering him some legitimate and comparatively safe prey as he came over the trees and obtained a view that had previously been concealed by a bend in the road.

Oblivious of the plan he was about to disrupt, von Crimmitschau smiled pityingly as he studied his proposed victims. He assumed from what he had been told about the area over which he was flying that they must be Americans, but he was neither interested in, nor disturbed by, the discovery. As far as he was concerned, they were merely enemy to be killed. He was confident that the Springfield Model 1903 rifles in the hands of the doughboys would pose no more of a threat to him in his swiftly moving aircraft than the Short Magazine Lee Enfield of the British "Tommy Atkins" or the Lebel M1886/93 used by France's poilus. They would be just as helpless against the twin Spandau machine guns—each being synchronized to fire five hundred

1. As yet, the term "fighter" had not come into general usage. Despite an ever increasing employment for aerial combat, airplanes designed specifically for such duties were still referred to as "scouts," which had been their original function during the earlier days of World War I. J.T.E.

rounds per minute without the bullets striking the whirling propeller—with which his Albatross was armed. Having that comforting thought in mind, he started to deliver what was already becoming known as a "strafing" attack.[2]

Possessing a far greater length of service and combat experience than the pilot, as well as being in a better position to make a visual examination, the sergeant had drawn a similar conclusion with regard to the nationality of the approaching enemy. Although they wore round-topped steel helmets and khaki uniforms much like those of the British army, there were obvious differences to be detected by trained eyes. The webbing ammunition belts around their waists had two sets of five pouches in line, instead of two being positioned above three. Nor could the Springfield rifle be mistaken for the British S.M.L.E. In addition to a bayonet, each enlisted man had a trench knife with a knuckle-duster hilt in a sheath tucked down the right leg of the leather leggings, which many members of the American Expeditionary Force wore instead of the difficult-to-affix long cloth puttees issued to "Tommy Atkins" if not to his officers. Even the man with the insignia of a first lieutenant was supplementing the Winchester Model of 1912 "trench gun" in his hands and the Colt Government Model automatic pistol in the low-hanging leather holster at the right side of his belt with the same kind of knife. It was, in fact, those weapons—and one other even more so—that established beyond any doubt to which army they belonged.

The sight of that particular weapon, noticed through his field glasses while scanning the woodland at the other side of the road, had aroused Eisenfaust's interest to such an extent that he had been delighted to discover the enemy patrol was coming in his direction.

Things had been going badly for the Germans recently and the sergeant had felt that, provided he handled the situation properly, he might be able to supply an aid to swing the tide back in

2. "Strafing": to attack troops, emplacements, and other enemy positions with machine-gun fire, and later, bombs or rockets, delivered by low-flying aircraft. From the German word "strafen," to punish. J.T.E.

his country's favor. Rumor had claimed that during the past few weeks, the doughboys had been employing some kind of new and very portable machine gun. It was apparently far lighter and less cumbersome than even the drum-fed Lewis guns with which troops of the other enemy nations were equipped,[3] permitting it to be carried easily, and it was said to have been used very effectively to help break up his army's mass infantry attacks.

Usually skeptical where reports of "wonder weapons" were concerned, Eisenfaust had heard it described by senior noncommissioned officers upon whose veracity he was certain he could rely. Remembering the descriptions he had been given, brief though they had been, he believed one of the new firearms was in the hands of the patrol, and he could visualize how useful it might prove if he could capture it. Once it reached them, he did not doubt that the arms' manufacturers of his homeland could duplicate or even improve on the design and soon put something more effective at the army's disposal in large numbers. Once this happened, the recent setbacks—he was too race-proud to consider them defeats—would be turned into the kind of victories that had characterized the earlier years of the war.

Eager as the sergeant might be to ascertain whether his supposition was correct, his military instincts had demanded that he avoid any rash action. Such a weapon would render the position of his men extremely precarious if all he had been told about it was true and if the soldier who was carrying it should be given an opportunity to bring its firepower into use. So, explaining how

3. Developed by Colonel Isaac Newton Lewis, U.S.A., from a design invented by Samuel McClean, the "Lewis" was one of the earliest and most successful "light" machine guns. Although by 1918 a stripped-down version had been produced for use in aircraft, it had been discovered that—lacking the slipstream to produce the effect—the "ground" model required a cooling system to prevent jams being caused by the mechanism overheating. This gave a weight, inclusive of the bipod mounting and drum magazine filled to its forty-seven-round capacity, of up to thirty-seven pounds. Believing that the Lewis gun could not handle the chamber pressures and velocity of the .30-06 cartridge in general service, the United States Army refused to accept it and it was put into use by Great Britain but not by the American Expeditionary Force. J.T.E.

he intended to deal with the situation, he had ordered his squad
to refrain from shooting, or doing anything else that would make
their presence known, until he gave the command. The losses
suffered in the earlier fighting, and increasing pressures, had ne-
cessitated their being brought onto active service shortly after
recruitment. So it was his intention to wait until the doughboys
were near enough to ensure that his inexperienced and far from
fully trained young soldiers would be unlikely to miss.

Measuring with skilled eyes the distance separating his squad
from the approaching enemy, Eisenfaust listened to the aircraft
roaring nearer. From all appearances, the doughboys did not
consider it to be any threat to them. This led him to assume it
might pose a threat for his squad. Wanting to avoid any chance
of its pilot spotting them and alerting their quarry, he decided
that he might give the order to open fire somewhat earlier than
he had intended. Having done so, he would immediately launch
a bayonet charge to get them to such close quarters that the
aircraft would not be able to turn its machine guns upon them.
Drawing consolation from his assumption that the doughboys
did not appear to be any more experienced than his men, he
opened his mouth to give the command.

Also estimating how close to an effective distance he was coming, von Crimmitschau was smiling even more mockingly as he
watched the lack of reaction from his proposed victims and concluded that they had not identified his Albatross as a hostile
aircraft. Telling himself that they would soon be taught their
error, he grasped the spade-grip of the control column more
firmly and placed his right thumb upon the firing button that
was attached to it.

There were two factors that were to spoil the aims and intentions
of both the young flieger-lieutenant and the middle-aged sergeant. One was created by a mutal ignorance, and the other
through underestimating the quality of the men with whom they
were dealing.

Although the term doughboy should properly have been given
to infantrymen, the twelve soldiers were members of the United
States' 18th Cavalry; currently dismounted and predominantly

comprised of Texans. In fact, each of the dozen had been born
and raised in the Lone Star State. While, along with others of
their countrymen who were serving with the American Expeditionary Force, they might be less experienced and well schooled
in the disciplines and techniques of modern warfare that had
been acquired by the British "Tommies" and French poilus—
who had suffered the sheer hell of it for close to four years—it
was not this particular patrol's first contact with fighting. Even
before arriving in France, every one of them had had the need to
take up arms in defense of his life, family, and property. Their
previous antagonists had been Mexican revolutionaries. No matter how the liberals of a later generation might seek to glamorize
or justify their behavior, these were no more than cold-bloodedly
murderous thieves who had—under the pretense of righting social injustices—crossed the Rio Grande into Texas searching for
plunder.

Having learned their fighting business against such a wily and
ruthless enemy, whose ability at lurking in concealment and the
laying of ambushes could not be matched by a Prussian-trained
professional soldier, no matter how many years' experience in
formal warfare he might possess, the Texans were far from being
the easy victims Eisenfaust and von Crimmitschau were anticipating. In fact, the tall, wide-shouldered and ruggedly good-
looking officer and the eleven enlisted men under his command
were fully aware of the dangers they were facing.

Wishing to ascertain the state of the morale and willingness to
sue for peace among the rank and file of the German army,
regardless of what the High Command and governments of the
Central Powers[4] might be contemplating, orders had been given
to have prisoners taken for interrogation. Leading a patrol on
such a mission, First Lieutenant Jackson Marsden Fog[5] had seen

---

4. "Central Powers": Germany, Austria-Hungary, Bulgaria, and Turkey,
the countries opposing the Allied Nations—Great Britain, France,
Belgium, the United States—in World War I. J.T.E.

5. Although in general the male members of the Fog family were shortish in
stature, those with Jackson Marsden's build occasionally cropped up. His
grandfather, Alvin Baines (Hondo) Fog, was another example of this diver-
gence. J.T.E.

the glint of the sun on the field glasses with which Eisenfaust was scanning the woodland through which he and his men were passing. The discovery had been made in time for him to prevent his party from being detected until it suited his purpose for them to be. Studying the terrain, he had formulated a scheme by which a trap could be baited and he had set about putting it into operation.

Although he was not a professional soldier, Jackson Fog had seen the dangers of the line of action he had proposed to take. They were such that he would not have attempted such a hazardous undertaking without being convinced it was justifiable and likely to produce the required results. Certainly he would never have set about it if he had not been sure it could be accomplished without endangering his men's lives recklessly. He had complete confidence in the courage and fight savvy of every member of the patrol, particularly as it would be backed by the capability his second in command had attained in handling the weapon which—although he did not realize it—had aroused the German sergeant's interest. In return, he had earned their trust and respect sufficiently for them, on hearing how he proposed to handle the situation, to have no hesitation over accepting that it offered the best chance of successfully carrying out their assignment.

Skilled in such matters, by the time they had arrived at the road and created the impression of being blissfully unaware that any danger threatened, Jackson Fog and his men had already pinpointed the positions of every one of their "concealed" enemies. Furthermore, the continued lack of response to their appearance and advance appeared to be verification of his summations about the nature of their enemies. Having noticed the youth of the German privates compared with the age of the sergeant, he had been given an added indication by watching them fixing bayonets on what he had recognized as 7.9mm Kar. 98 carbines.[6] Although originally intended as an arm for engi-

6. In military parlance, a carbine was an arm designed for use by cavalry and other mounted troops. The Kar. 98 was actually a slightly shortened rifle. J.T.E.

neers, pioneers, and artillerymen, the exigencies of the current situation were causing them to be issued to the recently recruited and hurriedly trained replacement foot soldiers who were being rushed to the front line in an attempt to stem the Allies' advance. Taking these points into consideration, he had surmised correctly what Eisenfaust was meaning to do and based his own tactics accordingly.

The arrival of the Albatross had brought an urgent need for the Texans to revise the plan they were in the process of implementing.

Contrary to von Crimmitschau's suppositions, neither Jackson Fog nor any of his men had believed the aircraft was friendly. Although they had been aware that it was hostile, they were too battle-wise to have let this become apparent. Having witnessed the effects of strafing, they had all appreciated the folly of making an attempt at evasion too early and had known the best way to save themselves when subjected to it, particularly while traversing such terrain.

Displaying an even more astute judgment of distance than that of the pilot, Jackson Fog timed his response to the threat perfectly. More so, in fact, than he realized. Just as von Crimmitschau was on the point of pressing the firing button, and with the German sergeant giving the order for the infantrymen to start shooting, he snapped out the one word for which the members of his patrol had had the courage and confidence to wait.

"Down!"

Instantly, like puppets operated by a single string, every Texan dived forward with great rapidity into the high and wind-stirred grass through which they were walking. This offered them the concealment which had formed a major part in their officer's decision to put his plan into operation, although when making his plan he had not considered the possibility of a strafing aircraft.

The disappearance of what he had considered to be unsuspecting and certain victims caught von Crimmitschau completely unawares. Even with such a maneuverable aircraft as the Albatross Va, he could not change his point of aim swiftly enough to

prevent the hail of bullets from the twin Spandaus flying harmlessly above rather than through the bodies of the Texans.

Nor did Eisenfaust and his men fare any better!

Brought about by the aircraft launching its attack, the evasive
action came so unexpectedly that the sergeant was unable to
hold back the order to fire. Having been waiting in a state of
nervous tension for the command, the inexperienced soldiers had
had sufficient discipline drilled into them to make them obey
immediately when it came. More seasoned troops might have
been able to restrain themselves long enough to correct their aim
on seeing what the doughboys were doing, but not them. Every
one squeezed his Kar.'s trigger, or jerked spasmodically at it in
most cases, but their bullets met with no greater success than
those that had begun to pour from the Albatross's machine guns.

To make matters worse, from the sergeant's point of view, the
young soldiers had not forgotten the rest of his instructions. Nor
had his grimly profane warnings about their fate if they should
fail to carry out without hesitation all he had told them passed
from their recollection. So, having discharged their weapons,
they sprang from their hiding places to deliver the bayonet
charge that he had stated would follow the volley. Although he
had seen exactly what would happen, they were less perceptive
and rushed forward without heeding his bellowed warning. Seeing they were too excited to pay attention, he ran after them,
spluttering curses at their and the airman's stupidity.

As he continued to follow the soldiers, Eisenfaust wondered if
he had been mistaken and the shooting was more effective than
he had imagined. There was no sign of the enemy as his men
emerged from the trees and began to enter the grass. A glance
told him that the Albatross was rising and the man in the cockpit looking back. He hoped that the pilot would have the good
sense to keep going and leave any further fighting which might
prove necessary to men who were so much more capable of doing it properly. His thoughts on the subject were distracted in no
uncertain fashion.

"Yeeah, Texas Light!"

Following the shout, which rang out in front of the Germans
so closely that they had clearly understood what it meant and

had even been waiting for it,[7] the Texans rose with the same alacrity they had exhibited when disappearing. Each of them returned into view with his weapon ready for instant use. Which was more than could be said for their would-be assailants.

Of the Germans, only Eisenfaust was in a position to start shooting immediately. This was because he had not discharged his Luger automatic pistol when ordering his men to fire upon the doughboys, and none of them had taken the precaution of operating the Kars.' bolts to eject empty cartridge cases and feed live rounds into the chambers. The sergeant had refrained from shooting because he had been too far away to hope to make a hit. Nor was he yet at a distance where he could use it with much greater accuracy, particularly while he was running. With that thought in mind, he skidded to a halt and twisted until standing sideways. Then he began to bring the Luger up to shoulder level at arm's length as he had been taught was the way to use it.

Having deduced that the sergeant would be the most danger-ous of their attackers, Jackson Fog was looking for him while rising, and seeing what he was doing, was holding a weapon ideally suited to coping with him. Before he could finish raising the Luger, much less take aim and fire, two sprays of nine buck-shot ball apiece issued in very rapid succession from the twenty-inch-long barrel—which had a radiating cooling sleeve and was equipped to take a bayonet—of the five-capacity tubular maga-zine, pump-action shotgun. Intended for use in trench warfare, as its official designation suggested, it was a most efficient close-quarters' weapon. Not only could it be discharged rapidly when in skilled hands, the spreading out of its multiple ball loads gave it a greater effective range than a revolver or an automatic pistol. Struck in the body by six of the .32-caliber buckshot, Eisenfaust was knocked from his feet without being able to use his own weapon.

Leaving their officer to deal with the German sergeant, the

7. For the benefit of new readers: the signal shouted by Lieutenant Jackson Fog was the battle cry given when his father and other members of the Texas Light Cavalry were attacking the Yankees in the War Between the States. See the various volumes of the author's Civil War series. J.T.E.

other Texans continued to obey their orders and set about trying
to take prisoners. They had found no cause to doubt his estimation of their opponents' quality as fighting men, so none of them
offered to duplicate his actions by opening fire with their respective weapons. Instead, while five dropped their Springfields—two
drawing their trench knives and three going in with bare hands
—the remaining pair who had rifles demonstrated that they had
received superior training to that of their attackers in such fighting even though they had not offered to fix their bayonets.

Kars. were deflected or wrenched from their users' grasps before their bayonets could drive home. Then their butts, those of
the Texans' Springfields, or the knuckle-duster hilts of the trench
knives, began to fell the startled and alarmed young Germans
before any defensive action could be taken.

On seeing the field-gray-clad figures emerging from the woodland, von Crimmitschau had been content to let them do whatever mopping up might remain after what he believed to have
been a highly successful strafing. Then a furious exclamation
burst from him as he saw the Texans erupting from the grass and
realized he had failed to achieve any noticeable results. Cursing
savagely, he began to bring his Albatross around. By the time he
had done so, he discovered that they were well on the way to
defeating his countrymen.

"Much good *that* will do you, doughboys!" the young pilot
snarled, watching the infantrymen being felled without any difficulty, guiding the aircraft on its second strafing attack and determined it would be more successful than its predecessor.

Once again, von Crimmitschau was committing the error of
underestimating the enemy. He paid not the slightest attention to
the doughboy who had aroused Eisenfaust's interest and desire
to bring off the ambush, apart from noticing that he was standing a few feet clear and was taking no part in the fighting. It was
to prove a costly omission and one from which the young flieger-
lieutenant would be unable to profit in the future.

Sergeant Jubal Branch's assertion that such a newfangled device
as the Browning Automatic Rifle could only be a liability rather
than an asset, regardless of how many other excellent firearms its

designer had produced, had soon proven to have been made from habit and not out of any deep-seated conviction upon the subject. It had not gone unnoticed by his comrades-in-arms that he had displayed no reluctance over accepting the rifle when he was offered one of the six which had been allocated to the 18th Cavalry. Nor had the respect which he had developed for it escaped their attention.

Produced out of the mind of arguably the greatest and undeniably the most prolific designer of firearms the world has ever known, John Moses Browning,[8] the B.A.R.—as the weapon was already becoming known by the men to whom it was issued—came close to offering the concept of "walking fire" so desired by military minds as an answer to the trench warfare of World War I.[9] While heavier by some nine pounds than the Springfield rifle, at seventeen pounds, six ounces with its fully loaded twenty-round box magazine it weighed far less than the Vickers "medium" or the Lewis "light" machine gun. It could be carried by an individual soldier and fired single shot, or with instant conversion fully automatic, which emptied the magazine in two and a half seconds—at four hundred and eighty rounds per minute—from the shoulder or the hip. Furthermore, it was also of such a simple construction that its seventy pieces could be disassembled and reassembled by a trained man in no longer than fifty-five seconds. Nor was its mechanism so complex that the requisite skill required to use it demanded exceptional manual dexterity.

Despite having been aware that Branch was lying about his age, which was above the stated maximum, the officer in charge of the enlistment center in Polveroso City, Texas, had accepted him when he arrived to volunteer. Even before acquiring the

8. In the course of his lifetime, John Moses Browning (1855–1926) designed some sixty-four types of firearms, ranging from single-shot rifles via the Colt Government Model automatic pistol, pump action and semi-automatic shotguns, to 37-mm. aircraft cannon, the majority of which had different principles of operation. He makes a guest appearance in the author's *Calamity Spells Trouble*. J.T.E.

9. "Walking fire": the concept of a line of men advancing with hand-held weapons capable of maintaining a fully automatic sustained fire so that it would literally sweep the enemy out of the way. J.T.E.

B.A.R., he had had combat duty. Having seen and admired the Texans' fighting abilities during the punitive expedition he had led into Mexico during 1916, the commander of the A.E.F., General John J. (Black Jack) Pershing, had soon made use of them on reaching France; and the 18th Cavalry, complaining over being deprived of their horses, had been one of the first American regiments to see active service against the Germans.

Gaining considerable proficiency in handling the B.A.R., Branch's protests about being "compelled" to carry its weight and its "newfangledness" notwithstanding, he had proved its value as a combat weapon. What was more, the men who served with him had declared its possession had imbued him with considerable luck. On three occasions, being armed with it had been all that stood between him and death. Each had been in circumstances when a fortunate chance rather than conscious effort on his part had saved him. The first had come about when, approaching a wood, the sight of a bird that had been flying toward a tree suddenly veering away in alarm had alerted him to danger, and a burst of fire from the B.A.R. had tumbled an unsuspected sniper from concealment among the branches. The second lucky escape had come when the German gunner of a captured French Char Renault FT 17 light tank had started shooting prematurely while approaching the Texans' patrol, and missed. Before he could correct his aim, sufficient of the B.A.R.'s twenty bullets— expelled at a speed no manually operated rifle could attain—had entered via the turret's observation slits to kill the whole crew. The latest rescue had occurred when a machine gun opened fire on them while they were wading across a muddy river. Despite being soaked when its user and his companions dropped for safety beneath the water, the B.A.R. had functioned perfectly as soon as he emerged above the surface, and once more, its high rate of fire had proved the deciding factor.

This, then, was the man and the weapon that von Crimmit-schau was disregarding. Nor did he see any cause for concern when, while the others were breaking off their attacks on the foot soldiers and diving for concealment, the doughboy merely sank to one knee and began to take aim at him. Convinced he had little to fear from a rifle while traveling at the Albatross's maximum speed of 187 kilometers (116 miles) per hour, he devoted his full attention to the rest of the enemy and gave not a single thought as to how he was also placing the lives of his countrymen in jeopardy by delivering the attack.

This time, von Crimmitschau told himself exultantly, nothing could go wrong. The doughboys' attempts at duplicating their previously successful evasive tactics would be of no avail. Not only had the struggle flattened sufficient of the grass for him to have a clear indication of where to aim, but he could see some of the khaki-clad soldiers trying in desperate haste to find what little concealment remained. Once again his right thumb went to the firing button and he was confident that there was nothing to cause him to miss.

While the B.A.R. was equipped with a rear "leaf" sight graduated for ranges up to sixteen hundred yards and that could be adjusted for windage, allowing considerable accuracy up to at least half that distance, Branch did not offer to erect and use it. Instead, he aimed via the V-notch battlesight, which was fitted for use when the more sophisticated device was lying flat in its protective housing. Taking sight and swinging the weapon as if employing a shotgun against a swiftly passing Canada goose, he tightened his right forefinger. He had already moved the change lever on the left side of the frame from the position of safety marked S to cover the letter A ahead of it.[10] So, on the first bullet being discharged, others followed in rapid succession and without the need for further manipulations of the trigger.

Despite the first three bullets passing in front of the Albatross, its forward momentum and the lateral motion given to the B.A.R. caused those that followed to converge with it. Some struck the engine and the forward part of the fuselage without inflicting any serious damage. Then one entered the cockpit and grazed the pilot's shoulder in passing. Surprise rather than pain caused him to jerk back in his seat, tug the steering column toward him and thumb the firing button involuntarily. The aircraft's nose rose sharply under the impulsion of his actions, and

10. The change lever was pushed forward to the letter F to fire single shots. J.T.E.

again, the bullets emitting from the two Spandaus passed harmlessly over their intended victims.

With his thoughts disrupted by the unexpected, if not too serious, injury he had sustained, von Crimmitschau was unable to regain control of the Albatross. Banking steeply, it turned, and rushing toward the woodland from which the infantrymen had emerged, crashed into the trees.

Having saved his companions by preventing the intended strafing attack, Branch found himself to be in danger. Not from the aircraft, but by a threat much closer at hand.

Struggling to prevent himself from being disarmed by the Texan who had grabbed his Kar., one of the Germans had had a very narrow escape. Seeing the Albatross returning, his assailant had let go and dropped hurriedly to the ground. Unprepared for being released, the soldier stumbled forward. By doing so, he passed clear of the machine gun's bullets which—although they were flying over the men who had been felled, or had deliberately taken cover—would have struck him if he had not moved. Instead of being grateful for his salvation, he rushed toward the kneeling sergeant who had contributed to his deliverance.

Catching sight of the German approaching as the magazine's last round was expended, Branch responded with the kind of speed that invariably replaced his normally leisurely movements when danger threatened. Thrusting himself from the kneeling position, he deftly interposed the B.A.R. between himself and the Kar.'s bayonet. Having deflected the jab that was being directed at him, he disengaged and swung a blow with his weapon. The side of the butt struck the rim of the German's "coal scuttle" steel helmet, snapping his head sideways and causing him to be half strangled as the chinstrap was jerked savagely against his throat. Knocked in a half circle, with the Kar. being sent flying from his grasp, he sprawled to the ground half stunned, rendered incapable of further attempts at aggression.

Coming to his feet as soon as the aircraft had gone overhead, Jackson Fog looked around and found the situation was being brought under control. The enlisted men were rising, and without needing instructions, were preparing to cope with any hostility on the part of the German foot soldiers. All of these, however, were either too dazed to resist or saw the futility of even making the attempt to do so. Whichever the cause, all were surrendering.

"Are you all right, Jubal?" the lieutenant inquired, strolling to where his sergeant stood glowering downward.

"Well enough," Branch answered.

"It's right lucky for us you had that old B.A.R. along," Jackson Fog asserted, glancing to where flames rose from among the trees to mark the point at which the Albatross had crashed.

"Why, sure," the sergeant answered, but he sounded aggrieved, and holding out the weapon, displayed the groove carved into the wood of the butt as a result of the impact with the rim of the German's helmet. "Just take a look at what that son-of-a-bitch's done to this lucky ole B.A.R. of mine."

World War I came to an end on November 11th, 1918. Shortly after, along with other members of the Allied armies, the Texans who had participated on the patrol to capture prisoners were returned to their homeland.

On arriving in the United States and being discharged, while Jackson Fog went to become the sheriff of Rio Hondo County, Jubal Branch traded his military uniform and weapons for the plain clothes and armament of a Texas Ranger. However, as has been recorded elsewhere,[11] he never forgot his lucky B.A.R. Nor, although he occasionally thought of trying, did he ever find an opportunity to discover what had happened to it after it had left his possession.

Although there were many who hoped for everlasting peace, fortunately there were also sufficient cynics—or realists—who doubted whether this would be the case. So, along with various other firearms that were no longer required by the men to whom they had been issued, the "lucky" B.A.R. was not destroyed. Instead it was allocated for storage to the armory of the National Guard at Wichita, Kansas. It might have remained there until the urgent need, which arose out of Socialist and Liberal politicians having prevented the British Armed Forces from retaining

11. See Case One "Alvin Fog's Mistake" of this volume. J.T.E.

sufficient men and reserve equipment between the wars, caused many of its kind to be disinterred and sent to replace the losses of material at Dunkirk.

However, this was not to be!

Early in 1923, having been "conscientious objectors" during World War I, Cranston Scargill and the band of anarchists he had gathered decided that they should follow the example of their comrades in Russia and strike a blow for the "oppressed peasantry" of the United States. With that in mind, they raided the National Guard's armory at Wichita. Surprised by the guards, they fled with what little loot they had been able to acquire. It was comprised of half a dozen Colt revolvers, an assortment of ammunition, and snatched up in passing by Scargill, Jubal Branch's "lucky" B.A.R. Hotly pursued by a police car as they were fleeing, it had fallen upon the latter to prevent them from being captured.

To avoid any repercussions that might otherwise have arisen over his "conscientious objections," Scargill had enlisted as a medical orderly in the army. His contribution to the war effort had been small, as he had made sure he was not sent out of the United States and did as little of any kind of work as possible. However, despite his noncombatant role and his expressed abhorrence of killing, he had contrived to acquire some knowledge of how to handle various infantry weapons. So he knew how to charge the B.A.R.'s magazine and prepare it for shooting. Smashing their vehicle's rear window with its butt, he had opened fire. He was far from being an expert marksman, but apparently the "luck" of the weapon still held. More by chance than intention, he had the mechanism set for automatic fire and some of the twenty bullets he sprayed behind him smashed the engine of the police car, to bring the pursuit to a halt.

On the strength of his having saved them, Scargill was able to assume the mantle of leadership over the gang. A petty criminal before he had decided the adoption of anarchistic principles might offer an easier way of obtaining money, he had proposed that they should use the weapons they had "liberated" and emulate Robin Hood. So they had embarked upon a succession of robberies. However, instead of donating the proceeds to the poor, they had kept all they gathered on the pretext that it would be required to finance the forthcoming "revolution."

As was usually the case with their kind, the gang were completely ruthless in the commission of their crimes. They also took as few chances as possible. Their victims were never the big "capitalist" institutions, such as banks or the railroads, but were owners of small stores, cafés, gas stations, or other one-family businesses. Traveling across the Midwest, they never pulled more than one raid in a county and avoided larger towns, which would have a well-equipped police force. This, taken with their habit of killing without hesitation on the slightest provocation, allowed them to continue their depredations unchecked.

Lacking any great skill in the use of their weapons, the gang grew increasingly reliant upon the firepower of the B.A.R. Obtaining ammunition for it and their other arms posed no problems. Living in a democracy, which did not have laws restricting the ownership of firearms, they were able to purchase a supply on the few occasions when thefts failed to procure it. Enough service rifles and handguns had been sold to civilians since the end of the war for ammunition to be readily available, the B.A.R. being chambered to take the standard .30-06 bullets used in the Springfields and Enfields that had been sold as surplus to requirements when peace came. So, by the summer of 1924, they had attained considerable notoriety. None of them had been identified, or were known to the authorities. Instead, newspapers and radio newscasters referred to them with more dramatic quality than accuracy as the "Machine-Gun Gang."

In spite of adhering to their policy of changing locations after each robbery, which allowed them to retain their anonymity, the gang began to appreciate that they were making the United States too hot to hold them. Yet disbanding and going their separate ways did not appeal to them. None trusted the others sufficiently to chance an accidental, or deliberate, betrayal once they were apart. There was also another problem preventing the dissolution of the gang. The acquisition of moderate wealth had led them to acquire a taste for good living that none of them wished to forgo. However, maintaining such improved standards in food, clothing, and accommodation, excused on the grounds that their appearance of affluence helped to avoid suspicion falling on them, caused the funds supposedly for financing the "revolution" to be expended instead on their various expenses.

Discussing the situation after a narrow escape following a holdup in Oklahoma, the gang decided that Mexico could offer them a greater, and hopefully safer opportunity to continue with their "great work." So they set out for the international border. As usual, they traveled in three groups of two men. By taking one of the "airliners," which were operating in ever-growing numbers, Scargill and his companion, Benjamin (Bengie) Woodwedge, reached the rendezvous in San Antonio, seat of Bexar County, Texas, a few days ahead of the others. When the rest arrived, they found their self-appointed leader filled with enthusiasm over the prospect of pulling off a final and much more lucrative robbery than any they had so far attempted. It was, he assured them as he sat patting the scarred butt of the "lucky" B.A.R., a cinch. Everything had been cased and nothing could go wrong.

The wheels of fate were turning to produce the kind of coincidence no author of a work of fiction would dare introduce into his plot.

Opening the passenger door of Sergeant Jubal Branch's swiftly moving 1920 Ford Model T four-seater sedan, Alvin Dustine Fog eased himself carefully onto the running board and contrived to close it again. Moving forward, the spare tire having been removed, he hooked his left arm through the lowered forward window and the raised upper section of the two-piece windshield. Holding himself in place, he turned his attention to the first of a line of seven Olympic "man" pattern targets. Six were positioned at intervals of about twenty yards, the seventh being nearly twice that distance, and some thirty feet from the edge of the narrow dirt road along which the vehicle was traveling.

Although the small Texan had a Colt Government Model automatic pistol tucked into the front of his Levi's pants' waistband, its butt pointing forward to be accessible to either hand, he drew its mate from the spring shoulder holster under the left flap of his brown leather jacket. As he approached the first target, he raised the weapon, and extending it to arm's length at shoulder height, began to take aim with all the skill he could muster. He had already passed along the same stretch of road twice, but the uneven surface was causing the vehicle's motions to be unpredictable. So he knew he must remain constantly alert if he was to counter their effects and improve upon his previous scores of four and five hits on the six targets while going by. The seventh had to be dealt with in a different manner and he had already scored the maximum number of hits on each occasion.

It was almost three o'clock on the afternoon of the third day following the arrest of Hubert Blitzer and the Holstein brothers. The previous evening, the other ten Texas Rangers who had been selected as members of Company "Z" had congregated in Austin, arriving separately and meeting in the privacy of Major Benson Tragg's home. While they had been amiable enough when Alvin was introduced to them, he had sensed they had some reservations about his inclusion in their number and was aware of what was creating their misgivings. Not only was he a newcomer to their organization, he was junior by four years to the youngest of them.

As Company "Z" still existed only in name, and its members had had no duties to carry out, Branch had suggested they spend the following day in target practice. Wanting to avoid arousing speculation by having them seen together, Major Tragg had stated this must be done at a place where there would be no witnesses. So, having borrowed the equipment they would require from the National Guard's ranges, Branch had taken them to a little-used side road in the rolling, open country about ten miles to the west of Austin.

From the start, it had been apparent to Alvin that his partner's main reason for proposing the target practice was to give him an opportunity to exhibit his prowess in handling firearms. Although he had no liking for the feeling that he was being put on display, he realized it was essential for him to win the confidence of the men with whom he would be working, and he was determined to present a creditable performance.

After Alvin had shown himself to be competent with his Win-

chester Model 1894 carbine and a Model 1912 pump-action riot
gun manufactured by the same company, he had demonstrated
his ability at drawing and shooting a Colt Government Model
automatic. Despite believing he had impressed his audience, he
had found he was being subjected to another test and in competi-
tion with a man who was clearly an expert at it. Fortunately, it
was a variation of one that he had engaged upon often enough in
Rio Hondo County to have acquired a creditable proficiency.

Being progressive in all matters pertaining to law enforcement,
Sheriff Jackson Fog had appreciated that even in the Texas range
country pursuit of criminals was becoming increasingly mecha-
nized. So, as other forward-thinking peace officers throughout
the United States had been doing, he and his deputies had devoted much thought to the matter of shooting from a vehicle
while it was in motion. They had soon discarded the idea of
leaning out of the passenger window, along with firing over the
bottom portion of the windshield, having reached the conclusion
that standing on the running board offered a greater scope and
potential for accuracy.

Like all the members of the Rio Hondo County Sheriff's Office, Alvin had expended time and effort on developing the tech-
nique. Nor, under the prevailing conditions, did he regret having
done so. While making three runs past the line of targets, Sergeant Colin Breda had scored five, four, and six hits upon the
first half a dozen and only missed once on the seventh. If the
small Texan could "go clean" on his third run, he would have
beaten his opponent by one hit.

Bracing himself as securely as possible against the side of the
car, Alvin made ready to put his training into use. Centering the
blade of the foresight in the V-shaped notch of the rearsight,
he directed it at the middle of the target's chest and squeezed the
trigger. The automatic cracked and the cocking slide was thrust
backward to eject the spent cartridge case. Before it had been
driven forward again, feeding the next round from the magazine
into the chamber, he had gone by. For all that, he knew he had
made a hit. Nor did he have any greater difficulty in delivering
the next four bullets to their intended marks.

"One more hit and I've done it!" the small Texan thought, and considering the seventh target was the easiest in spite of the way in which he must shoot at it, he was confident he would achieve his purpose.

Even as Alvin was taking aim and tightening his forefinger on the trigger, the car struck a bump it had missed on the previous runs. While he was able to prevent himself from completing the pressure and discharging the weapon, which was jolted out of alignment, he could not control an instinctive reaction to tighten his arm's grip on the side of the vehicle for a moment. When he had done so, fighting down a desire to rush, he twisted his torso and pointed the Colt to his rear. Sighting was not easy as the target was falling behind him, but he forced himself to make sure of his aim before firing. As the bullet was leaving the muzzle, he felt the Ford's pace slowing and knew the delay was creating an unanticipated difficulty. There was a need for haste, but he realized that—particularly with Sergeant Benny Goldberg, second in length of service to Branch, occupying the rear seat—he must not permit himself to become flustered because of it.

One glance ahead as he was turning to the front warned Alvin that, as he had feared, he was much closer to the seventh target than on either of his earlier approaches. The proximity was increasing rather than diminishing his problem. He had to jump from the vehicle while it was still in motion and run toward the target, shooting as he went, to complete the sequence. On each prior occasion, he had been able to employ the first three or four steps to establish his equilibrium before opening fire. Being so near would prevent him from gaining this advantage. Nor could he leap from the running board immediately. Under normal conditions, he would have been carrying his automatics with one round in the chamber and seven in the magazine. However, as his opponent was using a pair of revolvers, he had only been allowed to load each with six bullets and would have to exchange them before he could continue.

In addition to being conscious of Goldberg—who looked more like a chubby, jovial storekeeper than a tough and competent peace officer—subjecting him to a very close scrutiny, Alvin was equally aware that the other members of the company were paying just as much attention to his actions from where they were standing a short distance away. So he had no desire to make any mistakes in front of such a discriminating and knowledgeable audience. With that thought in mind, he tossed the empty Colt onto the Ford's front passenger seat and drew its mate from his waistband. The action was cocked and the manual safety catch applied, but he neither pressed the latter down into the firing position nor put his forefinger inside the trigger guard once the muzzle was directed away from him, as he would have done on completing a normal draw. He refrained without the need for conscious thought, but was sure the precaution had not been overlooked by the nearest of the spectators.

Having exchanged his empty automatic for a loaded weapon, the small Texan sprang from his perch to land on the verge of the road. He came down running, but still refrained from altering the position of the manual safety catch. As he was taking his second step, with the Colt lifting into alignment and his thumb reaching for the catch's spur, his advancing foot descended on a tuft of grass that tilted over beneath it. Feeling his forward impetus causing him to lose his balance, reactions conditioned by a lifetime of horse-riding took control. He realized that he could not prevent himself from going down and sought not only to break his fall, but to prevent it from ruining his attempt to shoot at the target.

Alighting in the prone position without suffering any injury or discomfort, Alvin did not offer to rise. Instead, he commenced another aspect of training at which he had attained competence. Almost as soon as he landed, he thrust the Colt ahead, and thumbing down the safety catch while taking aim, squeezed the trigger. Although the target jerked as the bullet passed through its chest, he had no intention of continuing to fire from that position. Rolling swiftly onto his right side, he cut loose the second shot from there. Still in motion, the third bullet sped away while he was on his back and the fourth was discharged when he lay on his left side. Then, transferring the weapon to his other hand, he completed the roll on his stomach and sent the remaining pair of bullets to join their predecessors in a group no more than three inches in diameter. Letting out a sigh of relief, he stood up and glanced to where the Ford had stopped, then swung his gaze to where the other Rangers were advancing.

"How's about *that* for gun handling, Benny?" Branch inquired, hoping the perturbation he had felt when he saw his young partner stumble had not been noticed by his passenger, and although nothing showed on his leathery face, was delighted at the way the small Texan had utilized the mishap to such good advantage.

"He's better'n fair with weapons," Goldberg conceded. "Which, seeing as who his daddy and granddaddy are, isn't a whole heap surprising."

"Being 'ambidextrical' same as Colonel Dusty helps some, I'd reckon," Branch remarked, but he could tell the other sergeant was more impressed than had been suggested by the laconic comment. "And he sure got out of that fall real well."

"I'm not gainsaying he's a regular snake with a handgun, or he's not a smart young feller who's had good training as a peace officer," Goldberg pointed out. "But has he ever had to *use* his gun?"

"Not that I know of," Branch admitted, being aware of what the question implied.

"Thing being," the stocky sergeant said soberly, "can he pull the trigger on a *man* should he have to?"

"That's something none of us knows until the first time comes," Branch answered, just as solemnly although nothing in his demeanor showed he had had the same thoughts on the subject. "Anyways, let's go and see how well he's scored."

Before the suggestion could be put into effect, a Buick came into view traveling at a good speed. Identifying it as belonging to their new commanding officer, the Rangers decided to postpone checking the small Texan's score until they had learned what was bringing him out with such obvious haste to join them. However, catching Alvin's eye, Colin Breda gave a wry grin and shrugged his shoulders in a way that implied he had already counted the holes in the seventh target, and adding them to those in the other six, was resigned to conceding a very close defeat.

"Howdy, you-all," Tragg greeted, stepping from the vehicle as his subordinates gathered around the driver's door, and despite their attempts to conceal it, sensing their interest in the reason for his arrival. "I've brought some good news and some bad news. The good news is we've got that ranch down along the Colorado River as our headquarters.

"Bueno," Branch enthused, appointing himself spokesman for his companions, as his big bluetick coonhound—summoned by a whistle from where it had been lying apparently asleep and paying not the slightest attention to the shooting—loped up to collapse at his feet as if exhausted by such unaccustomed exertion. "How soon can we figure on setting up down there, Major?"

"Not as soon as I'd like," Tragg confessed, making no attempt to conceal his annoyance over the delay. "Which's where the bad news comes in. There's been a call for help from the Rangers arrived at the state attorney general's office, and as we're the closest to hand, we've been told to go tend to it."

"That's *bad* news?" Breda inquired, his voice having a timbre in its Texas drawl that was suggestive of origins in the Highlands of Scotland. [12]

"It's not the special kind of chore Company 'Z's' been formed to handle," the major replied. "And happen I'm guessing right about what we'll be asked to do, there's a better than fair chance we'll just be wasting our time by going."

"Yes, sir, Sergeant Fog," Jubal Branch asserted in tones of contentment, lounging at his ease on a saddle blanket and with his back supported by a pillow on the left side running board of his Ford. He had his Winchester Model 1873 rifle resting across his lap and Lightning was sprawled with the appearance of being asleep by his feet. "There's one right good thing about being a Texas Ranger. You-all can for sure get straddled with some mighty soothing chores."

"You-all won't get any argument from me on that, Sergeant Branch," Alvin Fog declared, being seated so he was propped up just as comfortably against the front wheel of the vehicle and

---

12. As is recorded in *.44 Calibre Man* and *A Horse Called Mogollon*, Tam, Sergeant Colin Breda's paternal grandfather, also had been a peace officer in Texas. J.T.E.

nursing his Winchester Model 1894 carbine. "Was we deputies working as deputies out of the Bexar County sheriff's office, or serving with the San Antonio police department, we wouldn't be out here in the back country taking things easy in all this good, fresh Texas air."

"Like I allus say," Branch drawled. "There's most times something good comes out of bad happen you-all leads an upright 'n' blameless life."

"Hallelujah, brother!" the small Texan intoned, like a member of the congregation exhorting a "hot-gospel" preacher. Then, becoming serious, he continued, "Do you-all reckon there's anything to this story they've picked up about the 'Machine Gun Gang' planning to raid the car taking the payroll to that big construction company in town?"

"Why shouldn't there be?"

"If they've hit anywhere in Texas, we've never had word about it while I was working out of daddy's office. Which, happen they had, the cold-blooded sons-of-bitches, I'd reckon we'd've been sure to have heard."

"It for sure wouldn't've been kept secret," Branch admitted laconically, yet soberly. "Folks tend to talk up a storm and yell for the law to do something, happen they've had a machine gun spraying off at 'em, which that bunch of bastards do 'promise-callous' just about every time they pull a stickup."

"So they've never hit in Texas up to now," Alvin repeated.

"I ain't gainsaying *that*," the older sergeant answered. "Could be they've done got everybody so riled up north of the Oklahoma line they figure it's come time they gave us good old Texas boys a whirl and picked on San Antone 'cause it's handy for the border should they find us longhorns down here a mite tougher to chew on than the folks they've been hoorawing back to home."

"Which brings this meeting to another point of order," Alvin stated, without inquiring whether his partner had the necessary qualifications to use the words, "San Antone."[13] Instead, he be-

13. Local tradition stipulates that only those citizens who have been residing for at least five years in San Antonio, Texas, are entitled to employ the colloquial name "San Antone." J.T.E.

gan to raise the same points Cranston Scargill had used to persuade the rest of the "Machine Gun Gang" to change their mo-
dus operandi. "They've never tackled anything this big before,
going by all I've read about them, or made a hit in a town the
size of San Antonio."

"Could be they conclude it's time for them to make a change,
or they've gotten tired of the chicken feed their other stickups've
brought in," Branch suggested, just as unconsciously yet accurately duplicating the anarchist's arguments. "What I heard, the
feller's passed the word about and told a story convincing
enough to make the local John-Laws allow there's something in
it."

"I reckon the sheriff could be right with what he said about
them being a bunch of anarchists instead of real criminals, although I'd say most folks would allow they're real enough for
them," Alvin remarked, wondering how his companion had
learned so much. Despite having requested aid from the Texas
Rangers, the heads of the county and municipal law-enforcement
agencies had not been forthcoming about their source of information. "That could explain why they've not been identified before now. Regular owlhoots would have used some of their
kind's hangouts and been named by a stool pigeon by this time,
but anarchists might not even know where places like that can be
found, much less go in them. They've only taken money, arms,
ammunition, or new stuff that couldn't be identified and traced
back to the owners, so far in their holdups. So they could sell it
at a legitimate pawnshop and wouldn't need to know or use a
fence."

"That's just about the way I see it," Branch affirmed. "Anyways, what we've been told to do, there's not a whole heap *we*
can make of it. Unless the local John-Laws get their ropes tan-
gled so's those bastards slip through the noose 'n' run this way,
that is"—There was a brief pause while he gestured languidly
toward the rear of the car, where much to the big bluetick's
obvious disapproval on boarding at San Antonio, a radio had
replaced the saddle that usually occupied the backseat, then he
went on—"And happen, which *I* for one wouldn't want to

count on any too much, they can get word to us about it on that blasted newfangled 'wirey-less' contraption."

In spite of being eager to acquire the acclaim that would accrue from bringing about the apprehension of the notorious "Machine Gun Gang," the sheriff of Bexar County had nevertheless considered it would be tactful to ask for the assistance of the Texas Rangers. However, bearing in mind the thought of the credit he hoped to attain as the commander of the local law-enforcement agencies involved, he had also been determined to prevent Major Tragg's company from playing too conspicuous a part in the capture. Although he had deduced what lay behind the invitation he had received even before setting out from Austin, the major had not quibbled when informed of how little would be required of his men. As he had pointed out when some of them protested over the minor role they were compelled to play, it was important to try to maintain cordial relations with the local peace officers, as this could be a means of ensuring a spirit of cooperation and make their own work easier.

So Alvin and Branch were waiting on the southern side of a blind curve on a dirt road leading through the wood-covered hills to the border, and something over three miles from San Antonio. Along with the other Rangers, working in two-man teams, they had been dispatched to points on the ways out of the city so as to block the escape of such members of the "Machine Gun Gang" who might escape from the trap that was to be sprung by the deputies and police officers when the holdup was attempted.

Like Alvin's father, Major Tragg was always interested in any developments that could improve the operational efficiency of the men under his command. So, knowing enough about the sheriff of Bexar County's aspirations to have suspected that the request for aid would probably offer Company "Z" no more than a marginal participation, he had decided to ensure the affair should be made to serve some useful purpose. Since the end of the war, he had been hearing from colleagues in London, England, and various major cities throughout the United States about the way in which their respective law-enforcement agencies were making use of the radio.[14] As yet, two- and three-way communication[15] was not possible because of the bulky equipment required for transmission. However, receiving sets installed in vehicles were proving effective when it was a matter of dispensing information hurriedly to large numbers of widely scattered men who could not be reached by telephone.

Wanting to experiment with the potential offered by such a means of communication, the major had obtained sufficient sets to equip each of the teams he was sending to act as what would become known as "road blocks." While they were taking up their allocated positions, he had established himself at the local radio station. Having acquired the use of a different wavelength to which their sets were tuned, he was in touch by telephone with the sheriff at the location of the holdup and hoped to be able to keep them informed about whatever might develop. As a precaution against being overheard by somebody other than members of his company, he had devised code names and words to cover various eventualities. He had not believed the gang would be monitoring the calls, but he knew such eavesdropping might occur in the future should the use of radio by peace officers become the standard practice, as he believed would be the case.

"So you-all reckon the local badges will take them all without needing us?" Alvin wanted to know.

"There's a fair chance of it," Branch replied. "Sheriff Heath might be more politician than peace officer, but he's got just enough good sense to listen to somebody who knows what he's talking about, and the way things've been set up for him, a mouse couldn't get out of what's waiting for 'em, much less a gang six-strong and full-growed. No, sir, we're going to be sat here all quiet and peaceable until the major sends somebody out

14. In London, although the sets could only receive, the Metropolitan Police had had the first of their vehicles equipped with radios in 1922. J.T.E.
15. "Two-way" communication is only between the dispatcher's transmitter and a vehicle, but with "three-way" communication messages can be passed between the dispatcher and a vehicle, or between one vehicle and any other with similar equipment. J.T.E.

to fetch us back 'cause that danged 'wirey-less' can't do it for him."

"Well, I'll be damned, Cran!" Bengie Woodwedge hissed in tones of admiration, staring from among the trees at the top of the rim that he and his companion had reached on the southern side of the bend in the road, which had previously been concealed from their view. Two men were sitting by the side of an apparently hard-used Ford Model T four-seater sedan, and a big hunting dog was sprawled sleeping in front of the larger. Although they were a good two hundred yards away, clad in cowhand-style clothing and there was no sign of either wearing a badge of office, the Winchesters across their laps implied they could be peace officers. "You were right when you said we should come and look before driving around here. They have got somebody waiting for us."

"Those two are going to wish they weren't," Cranston Scargill replied, glancing at the B.A.R. he was carrying and starting to kneel down. "Not that they'll be alive long enough to do any wishing."

While the arrangements for trapping the "Machine Gun Gang" were sufficiently thorough to have achieved their purpose, having been thought out by the experienced deputy sheriff whose long-standing friendship with Jubal Branch had caused him to pass on information that his superior would have preferred to remain confidential, events had transpired to render them unnecessary.

Scargill's assumption that he was the leader of the gang had never sat well with any of the other members. Like most of their kind, they were self-centered, avaricious, and even when it was being exercised for their own good by one of their number, resentful of any kind of authority. Nor had his repeated assertions that he alone stood between them and failure or capture when committing the robberies, and his demands for a proportionately greater share of the spoils on that account, done anything to increase their liking for him.

One member of the gang in particular had concluded that the state of affairs produced by Scargill was becoming intolerable.

Having been more thrifty than the others, Jeremy Bessel had contrived to build up a sizable bank balance while they were squandering their respective shares of the loot. With the attainment of affluence, he had found his zeal for "anarchism" was waning, and suspecting that the hazards involved would be far greater than on previous occasions, he had not relished the thought of attempting the proposed robbery in San Antonio. Nor was he any more enamored by the prospect of going into Mexico to continue their depredations. He was aware that, being employed by a less democratic form of government than their contemporaries in his homeland, the law-enforcement agencies of that country tended to inflict summary punishment up to and including executions against malefactors who fell into their hands. So he had no desire to be a party to either of Scargill's latest schemes.

Being all too cognizant of the vindictive natures of his associates, Bessel had considered it was inadvisable for him to disclose his objections and intentions. They would never let him quit the gang of their own accord. Nor did he wish to break away unless he could be sure they would be unable to betray him out of spite before they left the country, or at some later date when he had established himself in a safe and lucrative occupation. He had no doubt that the peace officers involved, knowing against whom they were in contention, would be disinclined to take chances and were likely to start shooting at the slightest suggestion of resistance, which would almost certainly be given. Knowing this he had seen a way out of his dilemma if they came into contact with the gang. He had also appreciated that any information he should lay must be supplied in such a way as to prevent himself from being present when the knowledge was used. So the letter he had sent to the sheriff of Bexar County told when and where the robbery was to be committed, but avoided supplying any clue as to where they could be located before it took place. With that done, he awaited the appropriate moment at which to take his departure. When the time came, he was confident that he had made the way clear to set off for the new life he planned for himself. He felt sure he need not be afraid of repercussions at the hands of his former companions.

Possessing a mistrustful nature, however, Scargill had been suspicious when Bessel announced he was suffering from severe diarrhea on the morning of the robbery and would not be able to accompany the rest of the gang. Scargill had pretended to accept the excuse and had even gone to the extent of warning Bessel that there would have to be a reduction in the absentee's share of the loot, as he was not participating. Bessel's concurrence to this without argument or complaint had increased Scargill's misgivings. So, instead of following the plan he had outlined earlier in the week, he and the other four men had waited in their two cars where a watch could be kept on the ways out of the hotel that had served as their headquarters since their arrival in San Antonio.

Seeing Bessel emerging through the rear entrance carrying a suitcase, Scargill had not needed to ponder over what he might have done and what harm he was up to. Sharing the belief that they had been betrayed, the rest of the gang had informed their self-appointed leader—as soon as the second pair had learned of the development—that they would not continue with the intended robbery. The declaration was unnecessary, as he had already decided against going through with it. So, having agreed, he had joined in the brief debate about how much information the deserter had given to the authorities and what was their best course of action. Having devoted some thought as to how he would carry out a similar desertion if the need arose—although he did not mention *that* aspect to his companions—he had stated that Bessel would have avoided divulging any details that, by leading the peace officers to them before he had left their company, could also bring about his own capture or death while they were resisting arrest. It was obvious he was hoping for the latter result.

There had been no argument when Scargill suggested that the most prudent course was to take an immediate departure from San Antonio. Nor had his proposal that they split into two parties and made for the small border town of Chuckville by different routes produced any objections. He had stated that, even if Bessel had supplied their descriptions to the authorities, the cars would not have been included in the information as that might have led to a premature discovery of the gang's whereabouts. So, as the peace officers would be watching for five men in a group, they would have a better chance of passing unnoticed by traveling separately, and once across the Rio Grande, they would be safe from pursuit.

Taking Woodwedge and Toby Minehead with him, as he considered them to be the bravest and most easily controlled members of the gang, Scargill had set out along what he knew from an earlier study of a map to be the less frequented of the routes that would eventually bring the two parties together at the rendezvous.

While Scargill had never been in such a position before, he possessed a low cunning that caused him to do the right things instinctively. He might have professed a deep contempt for the forces of law and order at other times, but he was aware that in the past the gang had only been in contention with the peace officers of the small towns they had raided. Nor had evading pursuit proved too difficult in the past. A set of wire cutters with which to sever the few telephone wires that existed had been sufficient to ensure that no word of their activities could be sent ahead until it was too late to endanger them.

San Antonio was a fair-sized city. Not only did it have too many telephone wires leading from it for the gang to be able to cut them all, but there was a radio station that could not be silenced and would spread the news of what was happening even more quickly and over a far wider area. What was more, there was a much larger police department than had been available in any other town that had suffered from the gang's depredations. In addition, considering the notoriety their robberies—in which at least nine people had been killed—had attained, the aid of the county sheriff's office and even the Texas Rangers was almost certain to have been procured. So, having deduced that men might have been placed on the roads out of town to cut off their escape, he had insisted upon halting and making a reconnaissance when they found themselves approaching a corner and could not see what was on the other side.

Although his companions had protested over the delay, Scargill had insisted upon taking the precaution. As soon as he

had seen the two men sitting by the car, he had not needed
Woodwedge's comment to suggest what their status might be.
Although they had neither uniforms nor badges, the weapons on
their knees implied they were either peace officers of some kind
or private citizens who had been temporarily deputized by the
local sheriff to carry out what was hoped to be an unnecessary
task. Scargill did not care which it might be. Nor did he envisage
any difficulty in removing them.

Supporting the weight of the B.A.R. with his left elbow on his
bent right knee, the self-appointed leader of the "Machine Gun
Gang" found the unaccustomed posture far from comfortable.
Nor, as all his previous killings had taken place at much closer
quarters and he had never taken the trouble to practice, had he
fired over such a long distance. However, he was confident that,
as on every other occasion, the weapon's capability for automatic
fire would compensate for any lack of skill. After a moment's
thought, he decided to shoot the older man first—as looking the
more dangerous of them—then swing the barrel so that the remainder of the bullets encompassed the younger, and although
he doubted there was any need, the sleeping dog.

With the sights aligned as well as the inexperienced user could
manage, the trigger was squeezed and the B.A.R. fired.

But only once!

Alarm ripped into Scargill when only a single shot left the
weapon and he realized something must be radically wrong. He
knew the change lever was set for automatic fire. Regardless of
how potentially dangerous the practice might be, it was *always*
left in that position. Yet, for some reason he could not understand, no further bullets emerged from the muzzle. However, the
one that had been expelled appeared to have made a hit.

The jamming of the B.A.R. had been caused by a combination
of ignorance and neglect!

When the weapon had come into his possession, Scargill had
known only sufficient to be able to load and fire it. A chance
meeting with an acquaintance of his army days had enabled him
to learn the basic maintenance, such as stripping and cleaning,
the informant having been rewarded by a bullet through the
back of the head at the conclusion of the lessons. While the

instructions Scargill had received had been enough to allow him to carry out ordinary servicing, there was much he had been too impatient to learn. Nor had he given the mechanism all the attention it required to ensure it continued to work properly. In fact, it was a tribute to the inventive genius of John Moses Browning rather than his own care that everything had functioned as intended for so long.

The B.A.R. was operated by some of the gas from each detonated cartridge being vented through a small hole in the underside of the barrel, a few inches from the muzzle, into an expansion chamber. Once there, it forced back the piston, which in turn caused the action to eject the spent case, and by having compressed the recoil spring, allowed the top round to be fed from the magazine into the chamber; whereby, when the change lever was on its "automatic" setting, the firing cycle would continue as long as the trigger was held back and rounds remained undischarged. To save the working parts from undue strain as the piston was being driven back, it was necessary for the bolt, bolt lock, and link mechanism to start their rearward movement comparatively slowly and avoid having them attain the speed of the slide itself until after the high breech pressure was over. This condition was achieved by means of a regulator attached to the end of the gas cylinder. It had three different settings known as "ports," the one which was selected controlling the amount of gas, so only sufficient was used to ensure the correct functioning.

Under normal conditions, the weapon was set to operate on the smallest port. Having been told that the other two were for emergency use only, Scargill had never experimented or found the need to make any adjustment. Nor, due to his lack of knowledge, had he realized that the smaller vent was becoming fouled to such an extent that insufficient gas was entering the cylinder. The cumulative result was that at last the mechanism had not recoiled far enough to permit the complete ejection of the spent cartridge case. He was not given an opportunity to locate, much less deal with the stoppage.

Scargill's belief that he had made a hit was caused by his having seen the Stetson jerked from the head of the man at whom he was aiming. Despite his consternation over the B.A.R.

having jammed, he soon discerned that he had been in error with regard to the effect of the shot.

While he had lost his headdress, Jubal Branch was uninjured. In spite of having been taken by suprise, neither he nor Alvin Fog was frozen into terrified immobility. Rather, the narrow escape that the elderly sergeant had had spurred them to react with alacrity. Two Winchesters were already rising as their owners were leaping up, the butts settling against right shoulders with the precision that told of considerable training. A glance up the slope from whence the bullet had come gave the small Texan and his partner all they required. Neither of them realized the weapon that had been fired was now jammed, so they behaved as they believed the situation demanded.

With the sights aligned swiftly, the rifle and the carbine barked at almost the same instant. Nor was the shorter barrel of the latter any disadvantage under the circumstances. Powered by only thirty grains as opposed to the forty in the cartridges of the Model 1873 rifle used by Branch, they were of the vastly more potent "smokeless" powder. So the Model 1894 carbine possessed a greater range and velocity, allowing Alvin's .30-caliber bullet to reach their objective first. There was not much in it. Branch's .44 ball passed beneath the barrel of the B.A.R. and into Scargill's chest closely on its predecessor's heels as, in a state of panic, he was trying to rise. Either of them would have been fatal.

Seeing his companion jerked almost erect by the impact of the lead, spin around, throw aside the B.A.R. involuntarily, then sprawl facedown, Woodwedge made no attempt to draw the revolver tucked into his waistband in order to try to take revenge. Nor did he give the slightest thought to ascertaining the extent of the other's injuries. Instead, he twirled on his heels and dashed back in the direction from which they had come as fast as his legs would carry him. When no bullets came his way, he felt relieved and was confident that he could join Minehead, who was waiting at the wheel of their car, and make his escape before either of the peace officers could ascend the slope to endanger him.

There was a snag to Woodwedge's plan, but he had failed to notice it!

Like its master and Alvin, the big bluetick had responded instantly upon receiving the warning that there was at least one hostile presence in the vicinity. As the bullet passed through Branch's Stetson and struck the side of the Ford, the dog leapt to its feet in a manner that justified the name "Lightning" more adequately than its usual apparently slothful behavior. Guided by the sound of the shot, it started to dart forward. Being at its back, the wind had prevented it from becoming aware of the anarchists' arrival on the rim and it still gave no indication of where to go. So the dog made for the point from which the crack of the detonating powder had originated.[16] While sprinting up the slope, however, its keen ears detected the noise being made by Woodwedge's headlong flight through the woodland. On reaching the top, it gave chase with no more than a glance in passing at the motionless figure that was sprawled there.

Although most of its breed were noted for being "open voiced" and giving tongue freely when pursuing a quarry, a factor that made them so highly prized as hunters of nocturnal prey such as raccoons, Lightning was running mute as it rapidly closed upon the fleeing man. So great was Woodwedge's eagerness to reach the safety of the vehicle he had left when accompanying Scargill on the reconnaissance,[17] he paid no attention to

16. During the campaign against Communist terrorists in Malaya, the Royal Army Veterinary Corps used ambush-breaking dogs in a similar fashion. Selected for size and aggressiveness, the dogs were trained to attack when a shot was fired in their direction, and by doing so, create a diversion that would allow the handler and his patrol to locate, then deal with the assailants. J.T.E.

17. Benjamin Woodwedge would have been disappointed if he had reached his destination. Hearing further shooting after the B.A.R.'s solitary discharge, Toby Minehead deduced that Cranston Scargill had failed to deal with whoever was beyond the bend. So he had turned their vehicle without waiting for confirmation of his supposition, or to see whether his companions would join him. Setting off in the direction from which he had come, he was intercepted by two police cars dispatched out of San Antonio, and surrendered without a fight. J.T.E.

the far from noisy but rapidly approaching patter of feet to his rear. So he was unaware of his peril until the last moment.

By then, it was too late!

On coming close enough, the bluetick let out a roaring snarl and left the ground in a bound. Its powerful jaws closed upon the man's right arm and its one hundred pounds of hard-muscled body crashed into him from behind. Thrown off balance by the impact, he pitched forward and might have considered himself fortunate that his head struck the trunk of a nearby tree with sufficient force to render him unconscious. Finding he did not struggle when he slumped to the ground, Lightning behaved as trained. Releasing the arm and jumping clear, the dog moved so quickly it would have avoided any kick that might have been directed at it. Having done so, it sat down and watched, ready to attack again if necessary.

"Jubal, Alvin!" Major Benson Tragg's voice crackled from the radio in the Ford, the urgency of the information he was about to impart causing him to forget to employ the code names he had allocated to the two Rangers. On the point of setting out after Lightning, they paused as he continued, "Two of the gang gunned down the feller who informed on them, then ran into some police. The one that survived the shooting says three more of the gang could be headed your way."

"God-blast all newfangled devices!" the older of the sergeants exclaimed, directing a venomous glare at the radio. "We for son-of-a-bitching certain sure *know* they'd headed our way!"

"Maybe the major should have sent up a smoke signal instead of using the wireless," the small Texan suggested, without taking his attention from the rim.

"It'd've been quicker 'n' a danged sight more certain!" Branch asserted, returning his gaze to the top of the slope after having scooped up and donned his damaged Stetson. He went on as they started to walk forward, "They allus work mighty good, 'cepting when it's too windy for the smoke to rise, too wet to light a fire, or too dark to see 'em."

"Or you can't find any wood, have forgotten to fetch along any matches, or don't have a blanket to spread over the fire to send them up," Alvin supplemented, guessing why his partner was speaking in such a fashion and taking no offense over the reason. "I tell you-all, Jubal, those smoke signals surely come up short on a whole heap of counts when you get to looking at them."

"That blasted 'wirey-less' contraption ain't a whole heap better," Branch objected, indicating the hole in the crown of his headdress. "If it had been, *this* wouldn't've happened to my hat."

Reaching the rim without the conversation—which both knew was intended to stop Alvin brooding over the possibility of, for the first time in his career as a peace officer, having helped to kill, or seriously injure, another human being—having caused them to relax their vigilance, the sergeants went cautiously toward Scargill's sprawled-out body. They did not need to make a close examination to assure them that he was beyond doing them any harm.

Watching his partner covertly, Branch saw little sign of change come to the tanned young face, which he knew was being studiously retained in an impassive mold. For his part, the small Texan was telling himself that the body at their feet was that of a criminal who had been trying to kill them and had probably murdered other people with just as little qualm. The thought served to overcome the revulsion that he had started to experience as he first studied the consequences of his accurate shooting.

"Where's that fool dog got to?" Alvin inquired, forcing himself to keep his voice steady and going to pick up the B.A.R.

"Lightning, speak up, blast you!" Branch bellowed. Hearing the steady "chop" notes of the bluetick baying after the fashion of having "treed" its quarry, he deduced it had brought down and was guarding, rather than still either pursuing or fighting with the man who had fled, and he went on in a softer voice, "Could be he's nailed the other son-of-a-bitch."

"Good for him," Alvin replied. "This fool thing jammed on the first shot, which's lucky for us, seeing it's set on automatic." Then his attention was diverted from the weapon's breech and he continued, "This wasn't done just now when he dropped it. I wonder when and how it happened."

"What?" Branch inquired, satisfied that—although he was not thinking of the matter in the exact words—the young man was successfully coping with one of the most traumatic experiences that ever befell a peace officer.

"This groove along the butt," Alvin explained, exhibiting the weapon.

"Lemme take a look!" Branch demanded, stepping forward. Surprised by the vehemence of the reaction from one who was generally so taciturn, the small Texan obeyed without question. Staring at the groove on the butt in a disbelieving fashion for a moment, he next looked at the serial number on the frame. "Well, I'll be damned!"

"*I've* never doubted *that*," Alvin stated. "But how come you've suddenly found it out?"

"This's the same old B.A.R. I toted when your daddy 'n' me was fighting the Germans in France," the elderly sergeant explained, still sounding as if he could not believe the evidence of his eyes. "It was always right lucky for me."

"I'll tell you something, amigo," Alvin drawled, reaching out to tap the empty case that was jamming the breech. "Was I asked, I'd say it still *is.*"

Case Three

THE DEADLY GHOST

"Now, me, not being one of you all-fired smart young cusses, I don't see why us peace officers should go bothering good taxpaying citizens so long's all they're doing is cooking up a swatch of white lightning on their own land," Sergeant Jubal Branch declared, sitting in his shirt-sleeves, bareheaded and with his right foot raised so the Kelly "Petmaker" spur on its Justin boot threatened to add to the scratches left on the top of the table in the past by similar devices. "Moonshiners ain't such all-fired bad hombres, took as a whole. Fact being, I can only mind ever running across one out-and-out mean one. That was Ole Charlie Winthrop, so called to make sure folks'd know you-all was wanting him and not his son, Young Charlie Winthrop."

"Well, yes, admitting to being one of us all-fired smart young cusses, I reckon such would be a reasonable sort of way to name him," Sergeant Alvin Dustine Fog admitted judicially, being attired in much the same informal fashion as his elderly partner, but lounging with his legs astride a chair and its back turned toward the table. "Though his momma and poppa must have been more knowing than the average moonshiners to figure before he was christened that he'd have a Young Charlie one day who could confuse folks who wanted to see him."

"Folks might not've had the book-l'arning you young jasper's been given," Branch conceded, with the air of one who was conferring a favor. "But they surely knowed a thing or four. Anyways, coming from Rio Hondo County like you do, I'd reckon as how you'd've heard tell of Ole Charlie Winthrop."

"I can't come right out truthful and say I have," the small Texan confessed, despite the name seeming to strike a responsive chord without his memory being able to supply any information as to why this should be so. "Or about Young Charlie Winthrop either, comes to that."

The comments were taking place in the bunkhouse of the small ranch, situated some fifteen miles south along the Colorado River below the city of Austin, which had been acquired as the secret headquarters of the Texas Rangers' newly formed Company "Z." Along with some of the other members, Alvin and Branch were relaxing after having completed a day's work on fitting up some of the equipment that had been supplied to help in their unconventional duties. The small Texan's remark about the possibility of them being given the task of locating and halting the operations of illicit liquor stills as their first assignment had provoked his partner's response.

The way in which the two sergeants had worked together during the breaking up of the "Machine Gun Gang" had cemented their friendship and partnership. It had satisfied Branch that Alvin was not only steady under fire, but could shoot another human being when the need arose. This was especially important to the elderly sergeant's way of thinking, far exceeding the excellent exhibitions of gun handling he had witnessed on the National Guard's Walk and Shoot range and along the little-used road near Austin. He had seen one and heard of other young peace officers who—despite their theoretical training in matters pertaining to law enforcement—had lost their own lives, and in one instance caused a partner to forfeit his, through hesitation over firing at another person. So he was pleased to have discovered that the young man he would be working with did not suffer from such qualms. Branch was not a bloodthirsty paranoiac hid-

ing behind a badge, but he had long since accepted there were
times when having to kill in the line of duty was unavoidable,
and as in the case of Cranston Scargill, was even beneficial to
mankind.

For his part, although the matter had not been mentioned by
either of them, Alvin appreciated that the "Machine Gun Gang"
affair had enabled him to take a major step toward gaining complete acceptance by his partner. It had shown in many ways, but
most obviously through the increased banter—which was allowing Branch to pass on the knowledge of peace officer's work
he had acquired and state his sentiments on various matters
while doing it—that passed between them. The repeated refer-
ences to the disparity in their ages and Branch's continual decry-
ing of everything "modern," particularly the educated younger
generation, strengthened rather than weakened their relationship
as the small Texan knew he would only do it with a person he
liked. They were, in fact, rapidly welding into a smoothly functioning team. One in which each would be able to depend upon
the other no matter what kind of peril they were facing, or how
unexpectedly a dangerous situation confronted them.[1]

Although Major Benson Tragg and Branch had expressed
their approval over the way in which the small Texan had behaved on the woodland road outside San Antonio, he knew that
he had still not quelled the reservations of the other members of
Company "Z." They conceded that he had held up his end in
that affair and had done well to bring about the conviction of the
three young men at Austin, but each had been a piece of routine
law enforcement. So all were wondering whether he had the
experience needed to cope with the more specialized and unconventional work that lay ahead. However, he did not resent their
attitude. Instead, he was willing to accept that time and his own
efforts could cause it to change for the better.

"Well, I'll have to admit moonshiners don't go to putting their

1. An example of the way in which Sergeants Alvin Fog and Jubal Branch
could act in complete accord and without needing discussion is given in
Part Ten, Alvin Dustine (Cap) Fog, "A Chore for Company 'Z'," of *J.T.'s
Hundredth.* J.T.E.

names, addresses 'n' 'advertical-ments' saying 'We-all make right good white lightning' in newspapers any too frequent," Branch drawled, throwing a look to where his big bluetick coonhound lay sleeping by the unlit potbellied stove, as if the ranch had been its home for years instead of just over a week. "And, top of that, both of them'd likely be dead 'n' gone afore you-all was borned. Ole Charlie for sure was, seeing's how it's going back to not long after Sheriff Billy-Bob Brackett first took me on as his deputy."

"Land's sakes!" Alvin injected. "That would make it before my *daddy* was born."

"Anyways, Ole Charlie Winthrop had him a still on Whitetail Crick, maybe a mile from Jack County's east line," Branch continued, giving no indication of having heard his partner's comment or the chuckles it raised among the other Rangers who were lounging at ease around the room. "Used to get tolerable riled should folks go wandering about in its 'veecinity.' Which most folks'd got the good sense 'n' 'perlite-icalness' to stay well clear of it. Trouble was, this new bomber boy,[2] he'd be about *your* age, all fresh, green 'n' eager comes down from the North and he didn't have no good sense nor 'perlite-icalness.' Which could maybe account for why we found him all shot to doll rags along that way one morning."

"Had he committed suicide?" Alvin suggested dryly, and watching the exchange of glances passing among the other men, decided they too had heard of a similar verdict having been reached on *very* flimsy evidence at a coroner's inquest for a bomber boy—who had been found dead as a result of a bullet wound—held in Diggers Wells, seat of Jack County and an area well known for the number of illicit liquor that contributed to its economy.[3]

"Well now, being fair-minded duly elected peace officers and

2. "Bomber boy," also known as a "revenuer": an investigator in the Enforcement Branch of the Inland Revenue Service's Alcohol & Tobacco Tax Division. J.T.E.
3. Further information regarding the proclivity of Jack County's citizens for operating illicit liquor stills is given in *The Law of the Gun* and Part Three, "The Trouble with Wearing Boots" of *The Floating Outfit*. (Transworld Publishers' edition) J.T.E.

mindful that voting time was close to hand, that's just what we wondered if it could be," Branch replied, speaking as soberly as the way in which the question had been put to him. "Trouble was, we somehow couldn't figure out how he'd managed to do it by sending *three* point forty-four *rifle* bullets into his back from maybe fifty yards off, 'specially as he only had a belt-gun with him."

"That'd be quite a feat," Sergeant Colin Breda declared, with a matching solemnity. "So what did you-all do?"

"Now, me, I'd allus reckoned's how bomber boys was varmints's could be shot all year round," Branch answered. "But Sheriff Billy-Bob allowed as they was like game critters and had an open 'n' closed season on 'em. Which, being as how it was the closed season on revenuers right then, we was mortal duty bound to do something about it."

"Well, yes," Alvin said didactically. "I can see how there's some who might say you should do, seeing's how the law had been broken a mite."

"And that's just how Sheriff Billy-Bob saw it, in spite of 'lection time coming around real soon," Branch confirmed. "So, on account of where we'd found the body, we trailed along to good Ole Charlie Winthrop's cabin and out he comes, a Winchester 'Ole Yellerboy'[4] in his two hands 'n' looking a whole heap meaner'n a razorback hawg stood stropping its tushes again' the trunk of a post oak, ready to go to fighting over some lil ole gal hawg.

" 'Howdy, you-all, Ole Charlie,' Sheriff Billy-Bob says all per-lite-like, Ole Charlie Winthrop being a right good taxpaying 'n' voting citizen of Jack County. 'We done found us a tolerable dead bomber boy down along the crick a ways. Do you-all know anything about him?'

" 'Well now,' Ole Charlie Winthrop ree-plies, only nowhere near so perlite-like. 'I just reckon I might do at that, seeing as how it was me that killed him!'

4. For the benefit of new readers: "Ole Yellowboy" was the colloquial name for the Winchester Model 1866 rifle, derived from the color of its brass frame. J.T.E.

"And, as soon's he'd done saying it, I'll be 'ternally damned to perdition if he don't up with that blasted Ole Yellerboy and start whanging away at us with it like he was getting the bullets free from the Winchester gun-making company." Pausing for a moment so as to look about him and see the effect of his words upon his audience, he went on, "I tell you-all, amigos, *that* was when we started to get just a mite suspicious of good Ole Charlie Winthrop."

"Why, I reckon any of us just might have done the same in your place, *hermano*," Sergeant Carlos Franco asserted, without so much as a change of expression. Of something over medium height, almost as broad as he was tall and bulky, he wore the attire of a working vaquero and had such a villainous cast of features that his own mother might have found difficulty in loving him. His English was good, but with a suggestion of Hispanic birthright.

"I know I for sure would," seconded Sergeant Hans Soehnen, being big, burly, blond haired and obviously of Teutonic origins. "What did you and Sheriff Billy-Bob do, Jubal?"

"There just didn't seem like there was but one thing we could do under the 'see-cum-stanticals,'" Branch said, shaking his head in a manner redolent of sorrow. "So we just shot good Ole Charlie Winthrop's cabin plumb full of holes 'n' good Ole Charlie Winthrop along of it. Surely miseried Sheriff Billy-Bob 'n' me to've had to do it, though. Young Charlie Winthrop might've got to be Ole Charlie Winthrop, which pleasured him some, seeing's how he'd got him a Young Charlie Winthrop of his own by that time, but he couldn't never whomp up a swatch of White Lightning nowheres near so good as his dear 'deep-harted' pappy. Say one thing about him, though. He wasn't so all-fired ornery as his pappy had been about folks straying around the family still. Fact being, he'd let 'em come as close as maybe three-quarters of a mile off from it afore he started in to tossing lead their way, and he allus made sure as how he didn't *never* wound nobody too bad."

"Now, that's what I've always admired," declared Sergeant Aloysius Bratton, who dressed like the carnival roustabout he had once been and spoke with a broad Irish brogue. "A right neighborly and considerate sort of a man."

"And me," agreed Sergeant Alexandre "Frenchie" Giradot, who was tall, slim, wiry, swarthily handsome and always contrived to appear dapperly dressed. He boasted that his ancestors had been Parisian *apache*[5] and his accent had a Gallic timbre. "But, *mon ami,* knowing something of how the good taxpaying citizens in Jack County feel about the making—and *selling*—of white lightning, I would not expect them to take too kindly to what you and Sheriff Billy-Bob had done."

"You're not just whistling 'Dixie'; they didn't take kindly to it, 'mon hammy,' " Branch confessed. "Why, afore a week was out, Sheriff Billy-Bob 'n' me found our names'd become a by-word and a hissing all through Jack County. There was even some talk of having Judge Burtram Rothero heave us both out of office for 'extry-ceeding' our legally appointed official duties. I tell you one and all, I was worried to a muck-sweat. Was I to've lost my badge, I'd've had to start *working* for a living."

"Which's a thing we're all scared of happening," Bratton commented. "But, seeing's how you're sat here among us still wearing a badge, and I've *never* heard of you doing nothing else but being a peace officer, I reckon it didn't come to *that.*"

"It didn't," Branch admitted, exuding an air of relief. "But, by cracky, I'll tell you it was close."

"How'd you avoid it?" Alvin inquired.

"*I* didn't," Branch confessed. "What I heard was your grandpappy and Miz Freddie dropped by one night to 'sociabelize' with Judge Rothero.[6] Over dinner, 'long of other

5. *"Apache"* used in this context does not mean the Indian nation of that name. Pronounced "a-pash," it is the name given by Parisians to a class of small-time criminals who once infested the city's streets. They are best known for the "apache dance," which it is claimed they originated. In this, the man throws his female partner around the room and drags her across the floor by the hair. J.T.E.
6. Details of a very much earlier and less sociable meeting between Dusty Fog and Burtram Rothero—long before the latter became a judge—are given in Part Five, The Civil War Series, "A Time for Improvisation, Mr. Blaze" of *J.T.'s Hundredth.* J.T.E.

things, they got to talking 'accidental-like' about our fuss. Seem's how Colonel Dusty took to saying as how he'd never heard tell of Sheriff Billy-Bob going out hunting for moonshiners, only after genuine law-busters and as how having a revenuer gunned down that-aways was reckoned as being genuine law-busting in some quarters. Top of which, letting such happen without doing nothing to bring the 'miss-cree-ant' in was like to 'antagic-onalize' all the rest of the bomber boys so bad, they'd come a-swarming into Jack County thicker'n fleas on a back-country mountain-cur[7] 'n' they'd go to a-chasing and a-prying every which way until life wouldn't be fit for living, 'cause nobody'd be able to whomp up a cooking of white lightning in peace, nor move any of it that was already made."

"Trust Colonel Dusty to think up something as slick as *that*," Sergeant David Swift-Eagle remarked. Tall, powerfully built, in his late thirties, despite having his black hair cut short and wearing the attire of a working cowhand, his coppery-brown aquiline features attested to his nationality. He was, in fact, a pure-blood Kiowa Indian. "I bet the judge paid mind to what he said."

"Sort of," Branch affirmed, but nothing in his demeanor showed whether the result had been favorable or not. "He said as how he reckoned the good taxpaying citizens of Jack County couldn't't've looked at it that way, so it was his right and bounden 'ee-lected' duty to warn 'em. Which he did."

"I just figured he *might*," Alvin stated sardonically, being aware that the Rothero family had long derived the majority of their income from the moonshining activities of the Jack County residents. He had also noticed with pleasure the general concurrence with Swift-Eagle's praise of his paternal grandfather.

"Now, me, I took it right kindly of him to stand by us that way," Branch declared. " 'Cause, after he'd done it, afore you-all could say, 'Pass me the jug of white lightning, Aunt Selina-Mildred,' everybody in Jack County—including Young Charlie Winthrop, who was now Ole Charlie Winthrop on account of us

7. "Mountain cur": a mongrel with a mixture of coonhound blood, generally used for hunting small game, such as raccoon, which take to the trees when pursued. J.T.E.

—was all neighborly to Sheriff Billy-Bob and me 'n' saying as how we hadn't had no choice but to do what we'd done, way things stood when we done it."

"I reckon we're all right relieved to hear that justice and reason prevailed," the small Texan drawled, glancing across the room as a vehicle of some kind came to a halt at the front of the bunkhouse. "And I reckon the story must have a moral some place."

"It for sure has," Branch confirmed. "Goes to show as how folks'll support their friendly neighborhood peace officers, happen they get shown how doing it'll benefit the 'communally.' Top of which, it taught the fellers running the stills not to go acting too 'impeterous' when folks strayed in the 'vee-cinity' of their stills." Footsteps had crossed the porch while he was speaking, and discovering he was in error by assuming they heralded the arrival of the other two members of the company when the door opened, he continued in what sounded like an ingratiating tone as he hurriedly brought down the elevated foot. "Why, howdy you-all, Major. We didn't know as how it was *you* just drove up."

"That figures," Major Benson Tragg replied sardonically, glancing to where the big bluetick raised its head slightly and gave its tail a single, briefly lethargic wag. "Happen you had, you'd all have been dashing around like that fool hound dog, pretending to be doing some work instead of just sitting here and letting me catch you loafing this way."

"I was just saying this very minute as how it was time we started to do something," the oldest of the sergeants prevaricated, but giving off an aura of speaking the truth. "Now, wasn't I, partner?"

"Like good old General Georgie Washington said when he was asked if he'd chopped down his momma's cherry tree, I cannot tell a lie," the small Texan responded, exuding an equally spurious veracity. "So I'll have to up all honest and truthful to say 'yes' to that."

"Times like this, I find myself wishing that blasted 'lucky' B.A.R. hadn't jammed!" the commanding officer of Company "Z" snorted, crossing the room to toss his briefcase onto the table and sitting next to the two speakers. "Something tells me

I'm going to regret asking this, but do you-all believe in evil spirits, Jubal?"

"Why, sure, Major, I believe in 'em good enough to take the odd snort, or six, on 'occasional,' " Branch replied, then an expression of innocence pervaded his leathery features and he continued in what might have been tones of conscious virtue. "Afore them goddamned Yankee pussyfooters[8] up to Washington, D.C., brought in their blasted 'Prohibitical' law, that is. But not since, being a duly sworn 'n' duty-bound peace officer who—"

"I feel as if I'm going to fetch up!" Tragg interrupted grimly, making a wry face. Swinging his gaze to the youngest of the sergeants, he went on, "And, was I to be loco enough to ask, what kind of fool answer are *you* going to come up with?"

"*Me,* sir?" Alvin answered in a mock unctuous fashion and went on, provoking a sotto voce yet clearly audible mutter of "apple polisher" from his partner, "Why, *I'm* not the kind to go wasting your invaluable time that way. For shame! I conclude you're talking about the kind of 'evil spirits' who go roaming around after dark, all white and spooky, wailing and clanking chains fit to scare a body to death. Not those other sort, which're all *some* old-timers who should know better think about, and go to guzzling given half a chance, law or no law."

"I couldn't have put it better myself," the major asserted, paying just as little apparent attention to Branch's equally distinct exclamation of "He's a blasted *young* snitch as well!" and noticing it brought grins from the other sergeants at the table. He was aware that such seemingly inconsequential persiflage was a sign the partners had developed a firm respect and liking for each other and adopted it as a means of strengthening the bond between himself and the men under his command, knowing the time could come when he would have to send them on assignments that would not only put their lives in jeopardy, but might be construed as breaking certain constitutional laws. "That's just the kind I meant."

"Well now, blast it!" Branch objected, his demeanor register-

---

8. "Pussyfooter": a sanctimonious person who advocated temperance enforced by law. J.T.E.

ing asperity. "Why didn't you-all say straight out 'n' clear what you was after, Major, so's *I* wouldn't've got to wasting your '*un*-valuable' time neither. What you're wanting to know about ain't evil spirits, it's 'ha'nts.' "

"And *I* thought a razor-sharp old-timer like you-all would for sure know *that* without needing to have it run through the branding chute slow and easy," Tragg answered, opening his briefcase. "So I didn't bother to spell out word for word that it wasn't hard liquor I was meaning."

" 'Scuse me for billing in, Major," Sergeant Swift-Eagle said, sharing his superior's and Alvin's knowledge that a "ha'nt" was the colloquial name for a ghost. "Would there be any particular 'evil spirit' you're thinking about?"

"There would, Dave," Tragg confirmed soberly. "So particular, in fact, that it could have caused somebody to be killed."

"Whooee!" the small Texan exclaimed. "And Grandmomma Freddie always reckoned that over here in what she used to call the 'Colonies'[9] we don't have any for-real, out-and-out, doing-meanness—or bringing-misfortune-to-anybody-who-sees-it ghost like the one of the Dowager Duchess of Brockley in England, who she used to tell scary stories about to us Hardin, Fog, and Blaze kids around Halloween."[10]

"I tell you," Branch complained quietly, directing the words to the other sergeants rather than his partner or superior. "It's a mortal sin 'n' shame Miz Freddie didn't fright' some respect for his elders into *one* particular Hardin, Fog, 'n' Blaze kid."

"I wouldn't want to be gainsaying Miz Freddie's word, see-ing's what she did for Uncle Waxahachie Smith,"[11] Tragg drawled, once again paying no discernible attention to the el-

9. Like many English people of that period, Mrs. Winifred Fog, frequently expressed the opinion, perhaps a little tongue in the cheek in her case, that the world was divided into two parts, Great Britain—as it was then—and its Colonies. See dedication in *Kill Dusty Fog!,* also "Brit"'s' comments in *Rio Guns.* J.T.E.
10. For further comments respecting to the Dowager Duchess of Brockley, see *The Remittance Kid* and *The Whip and the War Lance.* J.T.E.
11. The service that Mrs. Winifred Fog rendered for Waxahachie Smith is described in *No Finger on the Trigger.* Other details of his career are given

derly sergeant's comment. "Only I reckon, happen I'm right in my thinking about what I've heard, this particular 'ha'nt'—as Jubal will have it called—maybe hasn't got around to being one of those for-real, out-and-out, doing-meanness-or-bringing-misfortune-to-anybody-who-sees-it kind like they have back in England, but I figure he'll do for us 'Colonials' until one comes along that is." His gaze turned to the Kiowa sergeant as he went on, "It's the Ghost of Brixton's Canyon I'm talking about, Dave."

"Him, huh?" Swift-Eagle replied, and although there was little observable change to his tone and demeanor, all his companions could see he was very interested. "Sounds like he's gone some further than just scaring folks down Grouperville way?"

"He could've gone a whole heap further this time," Tragg commented, then swung his gaze to the youngest sergeant. "Have you-all heard of him, Alvin?"

"I can't say I have, sir," the small Texan replied. "Has he been around for long?"

"Not too long, as ghosts go," the major admitted. "Ebenezer Brixton was a Yankee geologist who drifted down to Grouperville early in the summer of '19. Seems he was taken with the notion that there was a vein of gold in the walls of a canyon out on the badlands, as folks thereabouts call a patch of pretty rough and rugged country that starts maybe five miles south of the town. He was so sure, he bought up a fair piece of land around it, brought in a bunch of Chinese coolies and special mining gear from out of state to do the digging."

"Something tells me he didn't have a whole heap of luck with it," Alvin commented, feeling sure that such an event as a gold strike could not have been kept secret if it was made, and unable to recollect having heard any reference to it.

"He didn't, from all accounts," Tragg answered and Swift-Eagle nodded in concurrence. "He wouldn't allow anybody but the coolies into the canyon even, much less to look around the diggings. Not only did he have the land posted all around it, he

in *Slip Gun,* and he makes a guest appearance in *The South Will Rise Again.* J.T.E.

had some pretty tough hombres he'd brought in along with the coolies and gear to make sure folks stayed off. None of the coolies ever went into Grouperville, and when the guards did, they pretty soon made it known they didn't aim to answer any questions, nor favor any being asked. Anyways, one day early in '20, he paid off all the guards and coolies and sent the equipment back where it came from, allowing he'd been wrong about the gold. A few days later, a cowhand hunting for strays by the edge of the badlands heard one hell of an explosion, and having heard Brixton was finished digging, went over to see what was doing. When he got there, he found the entrance of the workings had been blown up, and going by the look of things, Brixton along with it."

"Is that what had happened?" Alvin inquired, as the major stopped speaking and looked at him with the air of expecting some comment or question.

"Everything pointed to it being that way," Tragg admitted. "When Sheriff Fat—*Big*—Jim Healey was told about it, he went out there and found a note saying Brixton was so sorrowed at having wasted his friends' money and having been proved wrong, he couldn't face up to living anymore."

"So he'd committed suicide," Alvin guessed.

"That's how it looked to the sheriff and the way the Grouperville coroner's inquest saw it," Tragg agreed. "Seems Fat—*Big*—Jim had been out to see Brixton the day before the explosion and everything that had been there then, including his car, was still there. Which, seeing as how he didn't own a horse or anything else he could have ridden off on and there was no place, other than Grouperville, near enough for him to have walked to, he could hardly have left."

"Didn't the sheriff get any notion that he was intending to kill himself when they met the day before?" the small Texan inquired, once more deducing he was expected to raise some point and noticing the others were not offering to anticipate him, but appeared to be waiting to hear what he had to say.

"*Fat* Jim Healey wouldn't hardly have a notion whether it was day or night," Branch asserted, and, as Swift-Eagle gave a grunt of agreement, elaborated, "He wouldn't be the smartest jasper you'd come across, even if he was on his lonesome when you met him."

"I'll bow to your superior wisdom, sir," Alvin declared. "But didn't *anybody* think it might be a reasonable precaution was they to try to dig out the workings and make sure Brixton wasn't just buried alive?"

"Even Fat Jim Healey wouldn't overlook *that*," Tragg stated, without bothering to correct the sheriff's sobriquet—and continued, after a quiet but audible, "Not so long as somebody else thought of it for him," from Branch and another brief signification of concurrence by the Kiowa sergeant—"Only, according to what he told the coroner's inquest, there was no way they could have dug out the workings with what they had on hand. All the special equipment had been sent away and nobody in town knew where it had gone. There's never been any other mining around Grouperville, so there wasn't anything else in that line to be had thereabouts. Then his deputy, who allowed to have done considerable hard-rock mining, said there was no chance at all of anybody living through such a bad cave-in, at least not long enough for equipment to be found and brought in. So, when it was mentioned that the town could wind up by having to pay for the hiring of the gear, the verdict came out that Brixton was dead by misadventure and there was no mention of suicide."

"Even if any kin he might have weren't too happy about there having been no attempt to make sure he really was dead, the verdict could help them claim should he be insured," Alvin remarked, being aware that coroner's juries occasionally produced findings of convenience. "But how did you hear about the suicide note?"

"Fat Jim told Cap'n Gaskin about it when he asked for one of us Rangers to go out and look the canyon over," Swift-Eagle explained, referring to the commanding officer of the company from which he had been transferred. "I was sent, and what I saw, I was inclined to agree with what the deputy said about nobody being able to live through such a cave-in, especially was he minded to kill himself."

"But that wasn't the end of it?" the small Texan drawled, more as a statement than a question.

"It wasn't," Tragg confirmed. "Brixton might not have found gold, but he'd blown into an underground water course and made himself a fair-sized drinking hole in the canyon. So a couple of Chicano goat-herders decided to set up camp there, goats being just about the only kind of critters that can find enough grazing to live on out in the badlands. They only stayed there one night, though. Went rushing into Grouperville next morning, scared close to white-haired and telling how they'd seen a ghost in the canyon. They allowed it was all white, glowing, and came floating through the air wailing and moaning. When their dogs went for it, something knocked them off their feet before they got even close and they lit out yelping like their butts was burning. So one of the herders cut loose at it with a scattergun, and although it jerked like it was hit, it just kept coming across the water at them and they took to running."

"It went *through* the water?" Alvin asked.

"Nope," Tragg corrected. "Way they told it, it floated just above the surface without so much as raising a ripple."

"Could whatever it was have *jumped* over?" Alvin wanted to know.

"Depends whereabouts it was when it crossed," replied Swift-Eagle, to whom the question had been directed. "Way I recall it, the water come from a crack at the bottom of one wall, widens into a pool in the middle of the canyon, then narrows as it runs out under the other wall."

"And they reckoned it came over in the middle," the major supplemented.

"What did the sheriff do about it, sir?"

"Told them the canyon was private property and he'd throw them in the poky if they went trespassing there again."

"Didn't he go to see if there was anything in their story?" Alvin inquired.

"You-all don't know Fat Jim Healey," Branch sniffed. "Does he, Dave?"

"Not if he reckons he'd do any more work than he has to," Swift-Eagle declared. "Which he'd figure riding out across the badlands on what could be a wild-goose chase wasn't worth the effort."

"He did," Tragg confirmed. "Seems he just allowed they'd been swilling tequila so much they'd been seeing things, and let it go at that."

"Only it still didn't end there," Alvin guessed, wondering what the conversation was leading up to; but convinced that, whatever it might be, he was to be involved.

"Not by a long country mile," Tragg agreed. "A couple of young cowhands went out to the canyon a few nights later, figuring to prove white folks wouldn't let themselves be scared off like the Chicanos. They concluded that, if they saw whatever it might be, they'd ride up and rope it, then fetch it back to show around town. Well, it showed all right. But, before they could get close enough to throw a loop, their horses were spooked so bad they were thrown, and when they tried to go after it on foot, something they couldn't see knocked them both off their feet."

"Something?" Alvin queried.

"They didn't know what it was and didn't stick around long enough to try to find out," Tragg replied. "All they could say once they hit town again was that the thing had still been a fair ways off from them when it happened. From then on, folks took the notion that the thing must've been Ebenezer Brixton's ghost haunting the canyon. Fact being, 'most every time anybody's been out there after dark, it's showed up and those who tried to get a closer look have been knocked down like the cowhands and the goat-herders' dogs were."

"Does the same thing happen if anybody goes there in the daytime?" Alvin asked.

"Nope," the major answered. "Only after dark."

"Now me, I'm only a half-smart old-timer," Branch remarked. "But I never heard tell of a 'ha'nt' coming out to be seen in the daytime."

"Or me," Alvin confessed, giving off an aura of martyrdom. "Only, seeing I'm a mite skeptical about whether there are such things, excepting for the ghost of the Dowager Duchess of Brockley, who must be true because *Grandmomma Freddie* said she is, I'm wondering if maybe somebody doesn't want folks around the canyon after dark?" He paused and glared defiantly at his partner as if anticipating an argument, and when none was forthcoming, went on. "What's more, I'm sort of surprised nobody's gone in there, figuring the same way I do, to try to find out if maybe there *is* gold there in spite of what Brixton said before he went and killed himself after making sure nobody could walk in and check up on him too easily."

"Nobody can," Tragg explained. "The day after the coroner's jury had brought in its verdict, who should show up but Brixton's out-of-town lawyer? Seems like he'd made a will leaving the property to his only living kin, a cousin he'd lost touch with, but was convinced was still alive. He was so certain sure of that, he'd arranged for there to be enough money available, should anything happen to him, it would pay the taxes and keep the place safe until the said cousin could be found to claim it, which hasn't happened yet."

"So that means the canyon's still private property and nobody can work it without the owner's go-ahead," Alvin remarked, seeing the ramifications of such an arrangement had not escaped the other men in the room. "But that was one hell of a coincidence, him having made such a will, and having committed suicide, the lawyer showing up when it was most needed. It puts me in mind of when old Elmo Thackery met his end."

"Likely," Tragg said, being conversant with the events that occurred as a result of the stipulations in a will made by the extremely wealthy rancher whose name the small Texan had mentioned.[12] And, anyways, Reece Mervyn's got a habit of showing up when he's needed."

"*Reece Mervyn!*" Alvin repeated. "But he's—!"

"Hogan Turtle's tophand shyster," Branch finished for his partner, referring to the current head of a family that had been prominent in the criminal activities of Texas even before independence was won from Mexico in 1836.[13]

---

12. For further details, see *The Fortune Hunters.* J.T.E.
13. Information respecting two earlier heads of the family, Coleman and his son, Rameses (Ram) Turtle, is given in *Ole Devil and the Caplocks*—which, along with the other volumes of the Ole Devil Hardin series, covers some aspects of the Texans' struggle for independence from Mexican domination —*Beguinage, Beguinage Is Dead!* and by inference, *The Quest For Bowie's Blade.* J.T.E.

"I didn't know he went in for that kind of legal work," Alvin protested, having no doubt the major and the rest of the sergeants shared his and Branch's knowledge about the status of the man in question.

"He'd do *any* kind of law wrangling, was he paid enough," Branch asserted. "Most 'specially when it could be something's he'd likely not need to raise too much sweat over for his pay and might get them mucky-mucks in the state attorney general's office thinking as how we may be way off the trail when we allow he's crookeder'n the bends in the Twisting River, wherever in hell's name *that* might be."

"Something's starting to give me a li'l hint there could be a whole heap more to it than just *that*," Alvin declared. Then, although he had lost the mock unctuous tone he had employed on his superior's arrival as soon as he deduced the conversation was about a matter of some importance, he went on, "In fact, I'll go so far as to say I'm getting a sneaking suspicion you-all reckon so, too, sir."

"There could be," Tragg conceded, taking several documents from his briefcase. "I'd be tempted to go even further and say I'm just about sure there is."

"*I've* been saying so ever since I first heard about Brixton's 'ha'nt' scaring folks out of the canyon," Branch inserted, exuding an air of conscious virtue. "Only nobody *ever* listens to *me*."

"There's some who'd say they were wise not to," Alvin countered. "Wasn't you saying something about it maybe having killed somebody instead of just scaring them off this time, sir? Way you've been talking, it's not done that before."

"There's nothing to *prove* it has this time, comes to that," Tragg warned, picking up the top sheet of paper. "Fact being, most everything seems to suggest it *hasn't*."

"But not *everything*?" Alvin suggested.

"Not *everything*," the major confirmed, laying just as much emphasis on the second word. "Seems that a bunch of young cowhands had been drinking in Soskice's Hotel a few days back and one took to boasting he could go out and fetch back Brixton's ghost should it show itself. There were bets laid and he took off on his lonesome, as was called for, to do it. When he hadn't come back by noon the next day, a search party went looking for him. They found his body about a mile clear of the canyon, with nothing to suggest he'd been any closer."

"Which there likely wouldn't be, what I know of the badlands back of Grouperville," Branch put in, looking to and receiving a nod of confirmation from Swift-Eagle. "The ground there's harder'n a Yankee banker's heart."

"Like you say, likely there wouldn't be," Tragg conceded. "Anyways, according to Sheriff Healey's findings, the cowhand had either fallen or been thrown from his horse where they found him. As he was going down, the Peacemaker he'd been toting—stuck in his waistband—slipped out, fired when it hit the ground, and sent the bullet through his chest to kill him."

"Such could've happened, was he loco enough to be cocked and with six bullets in the cylinder," Branch stated in a judicial fashion and with a defiant glance at his partner. "Which most young cusses don't have enough good sense not to."

"It *couldn't* have happened had he been toting an automatic, they only go off when they're meant to," Alvin affirmed, despite knowing his declaration to be incorrect, the relative merits of the two firing systems being a topic upon which he and the elderly sergeant frequently found themselves in opposition. Then, having concluded that none of the other Rangers had a high regard for Sheriff Healey's intelligence or ability as a peace officer, he went on, "Had the Peacemaker been fired, sir?"

"Yes," Tragg replied, indicating the sheet of paper on top of the small pile he was holding. "But whether it happened the way the sheriff reckons isn't all that certain. At least, according to this, there wasn't even a trace of burning on the body from the muzzle flash. Which there *should* have been, seeing as the Peacemaker was firing black powder shells and he must have been hit from pretty close if it had happened the way it was supposed to."

"Which same looks to an uneddicated ole country boy like me's if good ole Sheriff *Fat* Jim Healey, who we all loves and respects so dearly, could've *maybe* made him just a li'l mite of a 'mistook,' " Branch drawled and once again turned a challenging gaze to the small Texan as if expecting an argument. "How-all do you smart young jaspers see it?"

"They do say such can happen to the best of us, which I'm starting to get a right sneaky sort of feeling Sheriff Fat—*Big* Jim Healey doesn't rate as being," Alvin answered. Then, having observed that the information to which his superior was referring had been handwritten on what appeared to be a page torn from a school exercise book, he deduced it had not originated via an official source and inquired, "Who's sent us the word about the killing, sir?"

"The letter isn't signed," Tragg replied, perceiving that the young sergeant's powers of observation and astute judgment had not gone unnoticed by the other men. "But taken with the suspicions I've been getting ever since I heard the stories about Brixton's ghost haunting the canyon, I still reckon it's worth acting on. So that's what we're going to do."

"Should Sheriff Healey right kindly ask us to sit in, of course," Alvin grinned, being aware that the Texas Rangers had no legal right to participate in a local investigation unless their assistance was requested by the county or municipal law-enforcement agency in whose jurisdiction the incident had taken place.

"Of course, *if* he should have a mind to do it," Tragg answered blandly. "On the other hand, should it happen to slip his mind and he *doesn't* invite us, which's more likely, Company 'Z's' going in regardless. That's what you loafers out here on the spread are being paid to do, and way I see it, the time's come for you-all to start earning your money."

The assembled sergeants exchanged glances and the same thoughts were running through every mind. The events in the badlands near Grouperville could be the result of some form of illegal activity. So this was to be the first of the official "unofficial" assignments which Company "Z" had been formed to handle. Their future in such an unconventional capacity, perhaps even as Texas Rangers, depended upon whether their activities met with success—or failure.

"Howdy you-all, *Mister* Hollingshead," greeted the only customer in the barroom of Soskice's Hotel, having looked around on hearing footsteps entering. His formerly pleasant Texas drawl became increasingly less amiable as he continued, "I haven't seen you-all since—"

About six foot in height, tall yet conveying an impression of possessing wiry strength, with rusty-red hair and a handsome, Indian-dark face, the speaker appeared to be in his late twenties. His attire was that of a working cowhand and had seen considerable hard use. Watching from behind the counter, Abel Softly concluded he disliked the person who had just come in and would bear watching on that account. Although he had behaved in a friendly fashion since his arrival shortly after the bar opened and had had only one schooner of beer, there was an air about him that suggested to experienced eyes that he might not be slow to turn a feeling of animosity into open aggression against whoever had aroused it.

"You're mistaken. My name *isn't* 'Hollingshead'!" the newcomer interrupted, speaking irritably and with the accent of a well-educated Southron. Not very tall, he was blond haired and sturdily built, appearing to be slightly younger than the cowhand. In spite of the horn-rimmed spectacles he had on, his face was tanned as if he spent much of his time out of doors. Nothing in his attire, not even the white Stetson with a "Montana peak" crown,[14] implied that he might have any connection with the cattle business. Nor did the rest of his garments offer any clue as to how he might earn his living, being comprised of a brown corduroy Norfolk jacket with matching trousers tucked into the calf-high legs of untanned boots more suitable for walking than riding, an open-necked gray flannel shirt and a multihued silk cravat. Having made the statement in a manner that showed he considered the matter was closed, he went on in an only slightly less irascible tone, "Who do I see about taking a room for a few days, bartender?"

"There's a bell on the desk in the lobby," Softly answered, with just a trace of asperity in his voice. However, although he disliked the way in which he had been addressed, he refrained

14. "Montana peak": a hat with a crown similar to those worn by the Royal Canadian Mounted Police, and prior to being changed for berets, Boy Scouts. J.T.E.

from offering to correct the small man's misapprehension with regards to his exact status in the hotel. "Happen you go and give it a bang, the clerk'll come and tend to you."

Big, burly, with scanty brown hair plastered down by a liberal application of bay rum, the man behind the counter had florid features that generally appeared jovial. He was wearing a collarless blue-and-white striped shirt, a pair of trousers in a loud checkered pattern, and well-polished black town boots, but there was nothing about his appearance to suggest he was other than he seemed to be. However, while he had not attempted to revise the newcomer's assumption that he was no more than an employee, the nominal owner—among others—knew this was anything but the case. It was he and not Oliver Soskice who gave the orders, or made the decisions, about the way in which the hotel should be run on behalf of the actual proprietor. He also had various other responsibilities in Grouperville and the surrounding district that went far beyond the continued operation of the establishment. In fact, although he generally tried to avoid letting it become discovered by strangers until he knew more about them, he was a person of much greater influence and authority than would have been the case if he had been merely a bartender.

"Like hell I was mistaken!" the cowhand growled indignantly, after the newcomer had turned and strode from the room in a swaggering fashion redolent of arrogant self-assurance. "That son-of-a-bitch is Otis J. Hollingshead, or my name's not Dick Blood!"

"He's for sure got a mighty high opinion of himself," Softly commented, having watched the departure with the gaze of one well versed in the study of human nature. He decided the small man's bearing was caused by a belief that he was a person of considerable importance. If this was the case, it might prove worthwhile to learn more about him, and from what had been said, the means to do so could be close at hand. "And, happen he *is* who you reckon, he's mighty shy of letting it be known."

"He's who I said," the cowhand asserted, having returned his gaze to the man behind the bar. "Only could be there's what *he* reckons's a right good reason for stopping it being known."

"You don't mean he's an owlhoot on the run from the law, do

you?" Softly asked, despite his instincts suggesting this was not the case.

"Naw!" Blood answered in a bitter tone. "At least, not unless helping some goddamned rich oilman to sneak away honest folks' land without telling 'em what's waiting to be got out from under it's been made again' the law. Which I don't reckon, the pull them rich Texas tea-raising son-of-bitches have in Austin, they'll've let that happen."

"I don't follow you-all, friend," Softly stated, sounding far less interested than he was feeling.

"He allows to be a 'gee-hello-pissed,' " Blood explained, still bristling with what appeared to be indignation. "Or some such similar thing."

"A *what*?"

"A 'gee-hello-pissed.' He goes sneaking around on folks' ranges, looking at rocks and stuff he digs up 'n' allows he can tell from 'em whether there's oil, gold, or whatever buried under it."

"Do you mean a 'geologist'?"

"Yep," Blood confirmed. "That's the son-of-a-bitching brand he laid on hisself. After he's through sneaking around secretlike and doing it, he passes the word to whoever's hiring him so's they can buy out the folks's owns the land without saying why, or paying a fair price for it."

"Is that what he did to *your* folks?" Softly suggested, employing a show of sympathy that he felt sure would elicit any further information the cowhand possessed.

"Like hell he did!" Blood snorted, with what sounded like a mixture of annoyance and disappointment. "I wouldn't be hungry-bellied and looking for a riding chore if he *had*. The son-of-a-bitch allowed there wasn't nothing under *our* land. So it was them goddamned Hickey bunch down the trail a-ways as got *their* land bought by the Counters and not *us*."

"That sure was hard luck on you-all," Softly drawled, with well-simulated commiseration. He now considered that, as the Counter family had been involved,[15] his customer's antipathy

15. After his marriage to Dawn Sutherland—whom he had first met during the events recorded in *Goodnight's Dream* and *From Hide and Horn*, Mark

where the newcomer was concerned had arisen more from the result of the negative report than out of any genuine and justified objections to the land-grabbing propensities of men engaged in the oil-producing industry, which had supplanted cattle raising as the major factor of the economy in some parts of Texas. However, sounding no more than marginally concerned, he went on, "So he's a geologist, is he?"

"He is!" Blood affirmed.

"Well," Softly sniffed, still appearing far from interested or impressed. "I don't reckon he's come to do any of his 'geologisting' around these parts. It was proved by that loco mining man, Brixton, there's nothing valuable in the ground hereabouts."

"*He* was after *gold,* what I heard," the cowhand pointed out. "Could be somebody's got took with the notion there might be *oil* in this neck of the woods. Which being the case, either the Counters or some of them other land-grabbing oil bunch could've sent him to nose around secretlike and see if there is. Happen they have, he for sure wouldn't want folks hereabouts to find out who and what he was."

"It wouldn't help him to do his work if they did," Softly conceded, then continued after a shrug that apparently registered disappointment. "But good luck to him—and whoever's hiring him—should it be so. Only I don't reckon it is, more's the pity seeing how something like that could bring in plenty of business for us at the hotel. I tell you, friend, things have been so blasted quiet around here, what with Prohibition and all, the boss was saying he can't hardly afford to keep *me* on much longer. Can I get you-all something else?"

"Nope, *gracias,*" Blood answered, pushing his glass across the counter, from which he had been drinking beer sold in open

---

Counter had bought a ranch that proved to be the center of an extensive deposit of oil. While the family's fortune was mainly based upon this industry from then onward and they continued to increase their holdings, there is no evidence to support the suggestion that they were other than scrupulously honest where their considerable acquisitions of land were concerned and they were noted for their fair dealing. J.T.E.

defiance of the Volstead Act.[16] "I reckon I'd best be on my way and see if I can find me a riding chore at one of the spreads hereabouts. I'll likely be seeing you-all again, should I be lucky."

Watching the cowhand strolling leisurely toward the street door, a frown came to Softly's face. Despite his comment about the paucity of trade, his reaction was not caused by the thought that Blood's departure would leave him with no further customers requiring his services and wares. Because of his true status, he was far from as indifferent to the arrival of a man who might be a geologist than he had pretended while speaking with the cowhand. Nor did his curiosity stem from the possibility of an increase in the hotel's business and revenue should the newcomer's investigations prove fruitful. Rather the opposite, in fact. The last thing he wanted was for there to be an influx of people around the town, even if they possessed money to spend in the barroom.

The buzzing of a telephone's bell from close at hand diverted Softly's speculations from the possible reason for the visit by a geologist, particularly one who clearly had a desire to remain incognito. Although there was a switchboard at the reception desk, he was aware that the sound had neither originated from nor had been routed through it. A "candlestick" pedestal telephone stood on a shelf beneath the bar, where it was out of the customers' sight. It was an extension from the telephone in his private quarters, and the hotel's staff had strict orders that he alone must answer it. Walking to the end of the counter, he picked up the instrument by its pedestal and lifted the earphone.

"It's Mr. Plant calling from Austin, Mr. Softly," announced the female operator at the exchange in the town's post office, without waiting for the man behind the bar to announce his

16. "Volstead Act": the Eighteenth Amendment (Prohibition) to the Constitution of the United States of America, defining intoxicating liquors as those containing more than one half of one percent alcohol and forbidding the manufacture, transportation and sale of such liquors for beverage purposes. Introduced by Representative Andrew J. Volstead of Minnesota, the Act was ratified—over the President's veto—on October 18th, 1919, and repealed in 1933. J.T.E.

identity. She had been informed of the instructions regarding the use of that particular telephone.

"*Gracias,* Miz Berkley," Softly answered and, knowing that the caller was the confidential assistant to his genuine employer's legal adviser, continued, "This may take some time. So, happen you-all've any shopping or chores to do, this'd be a good chance for you to do them."

"Well, now," the woman replied, in a calculating tone and showing no surprise at the suggestion in spite of knowing her departure would leave the switchboard unattended by its official operator. "I was thinking I'd like to go along to the general store. They've the most darling hat there I'd just love to have, only I don't reckon they'd hold it for me until I get my next paycheck. So there's no real point in me going, is there?"

"There's no reason why you shouldn't go," Softly declared, being aware of what was expected of him. "Get the hat, happen you're so minded, and tell them to charge it to the hotel."

"Why, that's right neighborly of you-all," the woman cooed, trying without any great success to sound as if she had not anticipated the offer would be made. "Just so long as it's only a *loan,* mind. I'll pay you back comes the end of the month."

"I know I can trust you to do just that," Softly declared, exuding such sincerity that he might have believed the repayment would be made. "You go and get that hat, Miz Berkley; it won't take me more than five minutes and I'll be through by the time you come back."

"Very well," the woman said. "I'll put you-all through and go."

"All right," Softly announced, having watched through the window of the barroom, which commanded a view of the post office across the street, until the tall, angular, middle-aged exchange operator had emerged and walked off in the direction of the general store. As the telephone was only used for calls of a highly confidential nature, he was grateful to have found her so willing to desert her duties when he had broached the subject on his arrival in Grouperville. So, as on previous occasions, he had had no hesitation over authorizing her to charge a purchase to the hotel even though he knew the money would never be refunded. He considered it was a small price to pay for ensuring privacy during the conversation which was about to take place. "Go ahead. She's left."

"I've just been informed that Joel Meeker's taking an interest in the story about there being gold in Brixton's Canyon," Wilfred Plant obliged, in his nasal midwestern accent and without any preliminary greeting. "What is more, he claims to have located the cousin who is the beneficiary of the will."

"He can't have!" Softly protested, knowing the man who had been named was one of the most unscrupulous financiers and speculators in Texas, but equally aware that there was no such person as Ebenezer Brixton's long-lost cousin.

"I'm perfectly aware of *that*!" Plant declared, with some impatience. "But for obvious reasons, we can hardly come right out and say why it isn't possible."

"I never thought *your boss* could!" Softly answered, annoyed as on other occasions when they had conversed by the other's attitude of condescension. "Thing being, what's *he* figuring on doing about it?"

"Mr. Mervyn was on vacation in New York when the news reached me, but he's already canceled it and is coming back," Plant replied stiffly, being equally disenchanted by the reminders that he was only the lawyer's assistant; particularly as they were made by a man he considered to be a social and mental inferior. "The moment he arrives in Austin, he will apply for an injunction preventing any occupation of, or working on, the property until, as is stipulated in Brixton's will, the identity of the claimant has been verified to his satisfaction."

"Which there's no way it can be," Softly stated complacently.

"Don't be too sure of *that*," Plant warned, his tone brightening a little despite the context of the words. "If the need arose, *we* could supply somebody with sufficient documentary evidence to convince a court he was who he claimed to be, and Meeker has legal advisers who are *almost* as capable. So he's sure to have done something along those lines."

"If his shysters are only *almost* as capable, why worry about them bringing out their proof?" Softly challenged. "Seeing as how *you're* so much slicker, you should right easy be able to show it's a fake."

"I don't doubt *we* can and *will,* if necessary!" Plant asserted, his tone losing the pleasure it had acquired while he had considered he was proving the other man in error. "But Meeker appears to have anticipated the injunction will be imposed and has made arrangements for a clandestine preliminary investigation to be carried out before it takes effect. Possibly he wants to know whether it will be worthwhile before investing money in fighting a court action, should one become necessary, to prove his man's identity. Whatever the reason, he's hired and is sending a geologist to find out."

"Would that be Otis J. Hollingshead?"

"Yes! But how did *you* know?"

"He's just now arrived and taken a room here," Softly explained, silently thanking providence for the cowhand having been present to make the identification.

"You let *him* take a room at the hotel?" Plant almost yelped.

"I did!" Softly declared with defiant finality, resenting the questioning of his actions by one whom he regarded as no more than a passer-on of messages.

"Are you *sure* it is Hollingshead?" Plant demanded.

"He tried to make out he wasn't," Softly answered, his voice expressing resentment at the continued doubting of his word. "But there was a cowhand in the bar who remembered him from when he was working for the Counter family—"

"And *you* still let him—?" Plant interrupted, wanting to fix the blame.

"I didn't find out who he was until *after* he'd gone to register, and I hadn't heard from you then, either," Softly put in. "But even if I'd known, I'd still've let him. That way makes it easier for us to keep an eye on him."

"I suppose you acted for the best," Plant conceded grudgingly, having no doubt that his employer would consider this to be the case. "Anyway, now he's there, you'll have to make sure he doesn't start nosing around the canyon."

"Yeah. I'd sort of figured I'd have to. I'll tell Healey to warn him the canyon's private and posted land, so he's to stay off."

"That won't do. Even if Meeker hasn't given him a letter of authority from the 'cousin,' or some other document to offer what passes as a legal right to go there, having the sheriff warn him will make them sure there's gold to be had there."

"Which being the case, I'll just have to see he's stopped some other way."

"There mustn't be another killing!" Plant warned hurriedly. "Hollingshead's got important connections. He's not just a no-account cowhand."

"I'd some notions on that score myself," Softly said dryly. "And I aim to have it fixed so it looks like it's got nothing to do with what he's come here for."

"I'm not sure I understand!" Plant protested.

"There's no reason why *you* should," Softly countered. Having been thinking fast, he had decided what would offer a satisfactory solution. "But what I'll do is make sure he'll not be in any condition to go out there for at least a week. Only it'll happen in a way that'll look like an accident, not because somebody wants him stopped doing his work."

"How will you do it?" Plant inquired.

"*You* leave that to *me*!" Softly commanded. "If he's down for a week, can your boss get that injunction slapped on before he's back on his feet?"

"It will be in effect by the end of the week at the latest," Plant promised. "Are you going to close down at the canyon, just in case you can't stop him?"

"I can't do that!" Softly declared, finding the questioning of what was his responsibility growing increasingly distasteful. "There's a collection being made tonight, so it'll have to go through. Anyway, I'll have a pillow put under his head by sundown."

"You're sure?"

"I'm sure! Miz Berkley's coming back. Is there anything else?"

"There's nothing more at *this* end," Plant admitted. "But, whatever you do, make certain that—"

"*You* make certain your boss gets that injunction and leave me to see Hollingshead can't move before it's on," Softly ordered,

nd despite realizing there were other points that should have
een discussed, he hung up before the caller could reply.

Remembering comments that had suggested that other mem-
ers at his level in Hogan Turtle's organization found Plant's
omposity as irritating as he did, Softly returned the telephone
o its place of concealment and went to the street door. In spite
f the reason he had given for terminating the conversation, Mrs.
Berkley was only just leaving the general store when he stepped
nto the sidewalk. He had not been able to see her at the time he
vas making the excuse. Although he had made a mental note to
ell the desk clerk to keep him informed of any telephone calls
nade or received by Hollingshead and intended to make a simi-
ar request to Mrs. Berkley, which would cover the situation
hould contact be established off the premises, had he not left the
arroom to look for her. Instead, he was searching for the means
y which he hoped to bring his scheme to fruition.

Apart from a dust-coated 1922 Duesenberg Model A two-
eater sedan, which Softly had never seen before, standing unoc-
upied opposite the entrance to the lobby, no vehicles were
arked in the vicinity of the hotel. Deciding the sedan must
elong to Hollingshead, he gazed around. A grunt of annoyance
roke from him as he discovered that Blood was already driving
rom the town in an open-topped old car. As the cowhand had
nly arrived in Grouperville that morning, Softly had hoped to
tilize his animosity toward the geologist to bring about the dis-
blement in a manner that would lessen the chances of the real
eason being suspected. Accepting that this would not be possi-
le and he must make use of somebody with closer connections,
Softly returned the wave given by Mrs. Berkley and walked back
nto the barroom.

"Hey, Miguel!" Softly called on reaching the counter, and
vhen a voice from the kitchen behind it answered, went on, "Go
nd tell the sheriff to drop by and see me—!"

"When do you want him to come, *señor*?" the man in the
kitchen put in.

"Straightaway," Softly stated in a manner that suggested he
xpected an immediate response to the summons. "When you've
een him, go find the Skinner boys and Fred Mulley. Tell them to

get their butts around here, pronto. I've got something for them
to do."

Watching Sergeant Jubal Branch climbing out of the battered
looking Ford Model T four-seater sedan and, followed by Lightning, cross the sidewalk toward the street door of Soskice's Hotel's barroom shortly before half past one, Alvin Fog felt a tingle
of anticipation mingled with just a trace of apprehension. With
his partner's arrival in Grouperville, the time was at hand to
continue with the plan outlined by Major Benson Tragg during
the meeting at the ranch. So he turned from the window of the
room he had been allocated on signing the register with a different name to that which Abel Softly had been given by the "out of
work cowhand." Nor had the latter been any more truthful, or
accurate, when identifying himself as "Dick Blood." In reality
he was Sergeant Mark Loncey Scrapton of the Texas Rangers
and another member of Company "Z."

Having been summoned by the state attorney general—one of
the few people who knew of Company "Z's" existence and purpose—and shown the anonymous letter describing the mysterious aspects surrounding the death of the cowhand in the
badlands, the major had stated his belief that—because of its
connection with the other stories about Brixton's Canyon being
haunted—there had been foul play and not an accident. Accepting there was no legal way by which the truth could be
ascertained, they had concluded the circumstances warranted
the kind of independent and clandestine investigation for which
the company had been formed. It was, in fact, to serve as a
proving ground to test their ability to perform the specialized
duties that were envisaged.

Appreciating how the future of Company "Z" depended upon
the outcome of their first official "unofficial" operation, Tragg
had set about preparing for it with a determination to do everything possible to ensure its success. He was helped in his planning by having some knowledge of conditions in Grouper
County, especially with regard to the ownership of Soskice's Hotel. Prior to taking up his new appointment, he had been working in conjunction with the attorney general's department to try

to bring about Hogan Turtle's downfall. Their efforts had been without avail so far, but a reasonable quantity of data about the master criminal's organization was in their possession. Making use of this, the major had seen a way in which the investigation could be carried out. Displaying the aptitude that explained why he had been selected to command the unconventional law-enforcement team, he had wasted no time in starting to collect the extra information and the means by which to send them into action.

A visit to the current head of the Counter family, an old and trusted friend, had produced the name of the most suitable specialist in the profession that formed a part of Tragg's plans, and also secured a promise of any further cooperation that might be required. While one of Company "Z's" sergeants possessed the requisite physical attributes to pose successfully as the man in question—apart from his hair being the wrong color and that could be changed without difficulty—unless meeting close acquaintances, which was considered unlikely, he was the youngest and least experienced of them. However, having faith in Alvin Fog's ability, the major had not considered this would be detrimental to the conducting of the investigation. He was aware that pretending to be a geologist sent to make a secret examination of Brixton's Canyon could put the small Texan in danger if his suspicions should prove correct, but he believed this could be reduced to an acceptable level. What was more, he considered the selection might prove beneficial. The successful conclusion of the assignment would remove any doubts or misgivings the other members of the company were feeling over the newcomer's inclusion in their number.

So effectively had Tragg carried out the groundwork in Austin that, by the time he reached Company "Z's" secret headquarters, he was ready to lay a plan of campaign before his men. Furthermore, he had brought along everything they would require in order to put it into operation.

Noticing how much of the conversation about the events in and around Brixton's canyon was being directed at him, Alvin had deduced that he was to play a leading role in whatever was forthcoming. So he was not surprised to learn this was the case,

although he was impressed by the discovery of how much would
be expected of him. The major had pointed out the dangers involved, but he could not fault the precautions that were being
taken to help him circumvent them. Nor had he had any doubts
that he was being put to the most serious test he had yet faced.
Not only would his conduct have a decisive effect upon the outcome, but his complete acceptance by the other sergeants hung
in the balance, and a successful conclusion would take him far
toward attaining it.

Not only had the small Texan been given documents that
would establish his pretended identity, unless they should be
subjected to a far more extensive examination than would be
likely under the circumstances, but he was supplied with suitable
attire. A car had been hired in Otis J. Hollingshead's name and
the equipment a geologist would require to perform the kind of
research that had, supposedly, taken Alvin to Grouperville was
procured from the Counter family. It was sufficiently used to
prevent the suspicion that might have fallen upon it if it had all
been brand-new. The suitcase in which he was transporting the
tools of his temporary trade had a well-concealed false bottom
wherein reposed his armament. In addition to the two Colt Government Model automatic pistols, the shoulder holster, spare
magazines and ammunition, he had a Very pistol and half a
dozen cartridges.[17] The automatics, the rig in which he could
carry one of them and the boxes of bullets would not offer any
clue as to his real identity if the suitcase should be searched and
its secret discovered. Neither would the Very pistol, which was
just as untraceable, be regarded as out of the ordinary, as Rance
M. Counter had said such a device was frequently owned by
geologists as a means of signaling for help in case of emergency.
However, as a precaution against such a contingency as a search
of his room, the small Texan had his Texas Ranger's identification card and badge hidden in the hollowed-out heels of the

17. "Very pistol": a discharger for firing brightly colored flares; "Very
lights" as a means of signaling or providing hurried illumination of an area
at night. Invented by the United States' ordnance expert, E. W. Very (1847
–1910) and still in use. J.T.E.

untanned boots he was wearing, a similar installation having been made to the footwear of every member of Company "Z."

Apart from having Sergeant "Frenchie" Giradot's wife dye Alvin's hair blond, the major had decided nothing further beyond wearing appropriate clothing and horn-rimmed spectacles was needed to disguise him. As Grouperville was neither a mining town, nor in a region that produced or might have deposits of oil awaiting discovery, it was unlikely that anybody had had such a close acquaintance with Hollingshead to know the small Texan was an impostor. Should Softly seek verification after the disclosure of his "identity" by "Dick Blood," it could only be acquired quickly via the telephone or an exchange of telegraph messages. Whichever means might be employed, the genuine and bogus geologists were sufficiently alike in size, build, and with the changing of Alvin's hair color to blond, general appearance for him to match what would of necessity be a far from extensive description. What was more, as any attempt to locate Hollingshead would probably be based upon comments regarding a former employer made by the "out of work and resentful cowhand," it was doomed to failure. One of the reasons for selecting him had been that he was currently engaged upon a highly confidential mission for the Counter family, with his whereabouts known only to its leading member and his absence would lend strength to the deception.

There had been another aspect that Tragg had regarded as likely to reduce the danger of the subterfuge being detected. He had seen its advantages as soon as he learned of Reece Mervyn's vacation. If the lawyer had been present in Austin when the rumor of Joel Meeker's interest in Brixton's Canyon instigated by the major reached his office, he might have ascertained it was unfounded. As it was, Tragg had felt sure Wilfred Plant would be disinclined to assume such a responsibility, and on contacting his employer by telephone for instructions, would be told to call Softly to pass on a warning that the "geologist" would arrive to carry out a secret investigation and must be delayed until after legal action was taken to prevent it. Having heard of the antipathy with which many of Turtle's "middle management" men regarded Plant and suspecting Softly—having known him else-

where—could be included in their number, the major had deduced that a mutual hostility might prevent them from engaging
in any too fruitful and informative a discussion on the matter. If
that proved to be the case, it was unlikely they would draw any
conclusions that could put the furtherance of the scheme at jeopardy.

Tragg had warned Alvin that his arrival in the town as Otis J.
Hollingshead and his pretense of having a desire to remain incognito was likely to produce some indication to support their
supposition of illegal activities taking place in and around
Brixton's Canyon. Whatever form these took, they could not be
happening without the knowledge and approval of Hogan Turtle's senior man on the spot. Nor, as he almost certainly exercised control over the local law-enforcement officers, would
Softly hesitate before taking action if he considered the newcomer might pose a threat to his employer's interests. On the
other hand, the major believed it was unlikely he would go to the
extremes with which the cowhand had been dealt. Not only
would the intended victim be thought to have the backing of an
unscrupulous but wealthy and influential financier, there was to
be a Texas Ranger who was aware of his "identity" in the vicinity.

So, having set his superior's plan in motion with Scrapton's
assistance, and remaining in the hotel room until his partner
arrived to help continue it, all that remained for Alvin to do was
carry on as he had been instructed and see if there were any
developments.

Glancing around and taking mental note of where each item
was positioned, so he would be able to tell at a glance whether
his property had been disturbed and possibly searched in his
absence, the small Texan left the room and locked the door.
Then, having made sure there was nobody in the vicinity to see
what he was doing, he set about employing a ruse that his paternal grandfather had learned from Belle Boyd, the legendary Rebel Spy,[18] and put to good use, to ensure he would know if there

18. For the benefit of new readers: some details of the career of Belle "the
Rebel Spy" Boyd are given in: *The Colt and the Sabre; The Rebel Spy; The*

had been an unauthorized entry while he was away.[19] Taking a piece of black thread from the right-hand pocket of his Norfolk jacket, he fastened one end to the top of the frame and the other to the upper edge of the door. Satisfied that he had done all in his power to preserve the secret of his identity, he strolled toward the stairs. As he was descending to the ground floor and crossing the lobby, he wondered when—if at all—something would happen to confirm Major Tragg's suspicions.

"Y-You want a m-meal, sir?" asked the plump and pompous-looking desk clerk, when Alvin inquired about the possibility of obtaining lunch in the hotel. Throwing a glance redolent of apprehension at the door inscribed MANAGER'S OFFICE, PRIVATE and which stood slightly ajar, he continued with a noticeable hesitancy. "Y-You *can* have one here if you wish, but the dining room is closed and you will have to eat it in the bar."

"Gracias," the small Texan replied, darting an equally surreptitious gaze in the direction to which the other had looked, without managing to see if they were being watched or overheard. "I'll do just that."

"Y-Yes, sir," the clerk gulped, once more throwing a hurried peep over his shoulder. "I-If you go in and sit down, a waiter will attend you."

Despite the casual way in which he had given his acceptance, Alvin was far from relaxed as he walked toward the door offering access to the barroom. It was obvious to him that the desk clerk had been ill at ease and believed they might be under observation from the manager's office while supplying him with the information. Drawing conclusions from the nervous attitude, he decided that the precautions that had been taken for his protection might soon be put to the test.

Bloody Border; Renegade; The Hooded Riders; The Bad Bunch; Set A-Foot; Part 8, Belle Boyd, in "An Affair Of Honor," *J.T.'s Hundredth; To Arms! To Arms! in Dixie; The South Will Rise Again; The Remittance Kid; The Whip and the War Lance* and Part 5, Belle Boyd, in "The Butcher's Fiery End," *J.T.'s Ladies.* J.T.E.

19. What the results were on two occasions when Captain Dustine Edward Marsden (Dusty) Fog felt the need to employ the precaution are described in *Viridian's Trail* and *Beguinage Is Dead!* J.T.E.

The first thing to strike the small Texan as he entered the barroom was that business had improved since his earlier visit. While it was still far from packed, there were now several customers present. They were either standing by the bar, or as in Branch's case, sitting at the tables. Seeing them caused Alvin to feel a sense of relief. Although the elderly sergeant's official status might not be known, with so many potential witnesses around, whatever might have been arranged for his discomfiture was unlikely to be too serious. He doubted whether it would entail gunplay and was confident that he could protect himself for a sufficient length of time in the event of a bare-handed attack, to allow his partner to intervene and save him from injury. On the other hand, should he be in error with regard to the use of firearms, Branch would be just as able to defend him on the pretext of wanting to safeguard the other customers rather than himself specifically.

The small Texan was left in no doubt over where he was expected to position himself. While some of the other tables were unoccupied, only one was covered with a clean white cloth and had a complement of silverware to indicate it was intended for dining rather than merely drinking illicitly sold liquor. So, catching his partner's eye, he gave a brief and negative shake of his head. Branch was supposed to rise and greet Alvin as "Mr. Hollingshead," but he took the hint and remained in the chair he had selected so that his back was to the wall. Nor did the big bluetick stir from where it was lying apparently asleep beneath its master's table.

Studying his surroundings as he was walking forward, Alvin could not detect anybody other than his partner who was displaying an especial interest in him. The lack of curiosity appeared to extend to Softly, who was still carrying out the function of bartender and gave him no more than a quick glance before looking elsewhere. There were four places set at the table, so he selected the one that put his back to Branch as this allowed him to keep the rest of the room under observation.

On sitting down, the small Texan saw Softly look at the Mexican waiter who was standing near the kitchen door and nod in his direction. Although the recipient of the signal was not doing anything else, Alvin thought he seemed reluctant to carry out what had clearly been an order. In fact, it was not until Softly started to walk toward him that he moved forward. As he approached in a reluctant manner, the small Texan thought he was exhibiting a similar nervous fashion to the desk clerk, and apparently shared the knowledge that had created the latter's apprehension.

"How's the chili con carne?" Alvin inquired after a brief perusal of the menu he had been given, having a liking for that particular fiery delicacy. He gave no sign of noticing the waiter's thinly disguised agitation.

"I-Is not ready yet, *señor*," the waiter replied in somewhat stilted English, darting a look pregnant with concern toward the counter.

"Then I'll wait until it is," Alvin stated, in a tone that suggested he would not welcome an extended conversation.

"B-But that won't be—!" the waiter commenced, sending another worried glance to where Softly was engaged in serving a customer. His voice was pitched to little more than a whisper, which nevertheless still throbbed with urgent anxiety.

"Goddamn it!" the small Texan growled, not only contriving to feign annoyance without speaking sufficiently loud for his words to reach the man behind the bar, but managing to be equally unobtrusive where the other customers were concerned. He realized that by doing so he was preventing his partner, being some feet to his rear, from gaining information about the situation and he accepted this rather than chance putting the Mexican's life in danger. Going on, he continued to adopt a similar low tone, "Do you-all want me to tell the manager you're so blasted work-shy that you're trying to turn me from eating here and won't need to serve me?"

"N-No, *señor*!" the waiter gasped, making no attempt to conceal his alarm at the suggestion. Yet, despite his feelings, he continued, "I just thought—"

"Don't *think*, just do as you're told," Alvin advised, sitting back on his chair with the air of one who considered the last word had been uttered on the subject. He did not like behaving in such a fashion, but knew it must be done. As the Mexican seemed on the verge of saying something more, he noticed that Softly was looking in their direction and went on in a more audible tone that had lost its assumed timbre of irritation, "I'll have a bowl of chili and some refried beans on the side."

"*Sí, señor,*" the waiter assented, after pausing for a moment as if contemplating some further remark. He did not give a shrug of resignation, but the gesture was implied in his demeanor. Then, becoming aware that his employer was watching, he went on quickly, "Can I fetch you anything to drink while you're waiting?"

"Nothing," the small Texan refused. "I'll have some coffee with the meal, though."

Watching the Mexican turn and make for the kitchen, walking with a stiff-backed posture that expressed righteous indignation over having taken a not inconsiderable risk while attempting to do a favor and having had his efforts spurned by their intended recipient, the small Texan was grateful for the warning he had been given. Silently promising to make amends for his apparently inconsiderate behavior at a propitious moment, he decided to subject the other occupants of the barroom to a further surreptitious and more extensive examination, while waiting for the meal to be delivered. By doing so, he might learn what was intended and who would be involved.

As he was commencing, Alvin thought wryly how much easier his task would be if he possessed Leon Gonzales's encyclopedic knowledge of, and faith in, the science of physiognomy. After dinner one evening, during a brief visit to Polveroso City the previous year, the famous Spanish criminologist—who, with his associates, George Manfred and Raymond Poiccart,[20] had been touring the United States giving lectures to law-enforcement agencies, and while in Austin, made suggestions that led to the

20. George Manfred, Leon Gonzales, and Raymond Poiccart were the surviving members of the "Four Just Men" organization. Although the following volumes do not cover the tour of the United States, or meeting with Jackson Fog, see *The Four Just Men; The Council of Justice; The Law of the Four Just Men; Again the Three* and *The Three Just Men* by Edgar Wallace. J.T.E.

formation of Company "Z"—had spoken at length of employing a study of the shape of the human skull, features and expressions, as a guide to detecting a criminal nature or intentions. Although neither he nor his father—who had met and become friends with the trio while in Britain with the American Expeditionary Force prior to going on active service in France—had considered the methods were as infallible as their guest implied, the small Texan felt his present situation would have offered an expert physiognomist an ideal opportunity to give a demonstration.

Lacking such specialized ability, Alvin was compelled to rely upon his own judgment and had to admit it did not help him to draw any conclusions. The customers appeared to be the usual cross-section of the population found in any small town throughout the Texas range country. With the exception of three cowhands who were standing at the bar, their attire suggested they were either the owners or employees of Grouperville's various businesses. None of them looked in any way sinister, suspicious, or as though they were paying any more discernible attention to his presence than they had on his arrival. Certainly he could see nothing to lead him to select the man, or men, who might pose the threat that he was expecting, to his continued well-being. Nor could he detect the slightest indication of what, if anything, was being contemplated.

Wondering if he might have read something more sinister than actually existed into the behavior of the desk clerk and the waiter, perhaps even allowing his imagination to run riot as Major Tragg and Branch had warned might happen while engaged upon such a deception as he was carrying out, the small Texan brought his gaze to rest on the three cowhands. Unlike some peace officers he had known, he had no antipathy where their kind were concerned and therefore was not automatically led to assume they were the men he was seeking. For all that, as they were the exceptions in the room as far as appearances went, he considered it advisable to devote a longer scrutiny to them than he had given any of the other customers.

Tall and well built, none of the trio exceeded Alvin's age, and they were wearing what was clearly their working clothing. As

they were standing with their backs to him, he was only able to
see their faces reflected in the far-from-spotlessly clean mirror
behind the counter. This prevented him from acquiring much
information, other than his guess at their ages, but he decided
the tallest and shortest, although there was only a couple inches
difference, were sufficiently alike to be brothers. They were blond
haired and their companion was darker in complexion. While
their features were pleasant rather than surly, none appeared to
be in a cheerful mood. Taken with the way in which they were
merely sipping at their schooners of beer and kept glancing from
the clock on the wall to the street door, the fact that each had
retained his batwing chaps[21] suggested they were waiting for
somebody rather than being in town on an extended visit. Just
about the only thing that could be considered even remotely out
of the ordinary was that a pair of rubber galoshes were standing
on the floor between the tallest and shortest of them.

Despite Alvin's assumption that he was in danger, or soon
could be, he was unable to change a lifetime's habit of pondering
over anything that he found to be unusual. Nor did he attempt to
stop himself in the prevailing circumstances. Having failed to
locate any evidence to support the supposition that he might be
in jeopardy, he was willing to let his thoughts be diverted from
the main issue for a while. He had found adopting a similar
course on other occasions was beneficial to concentration, particularly when—as at that moment—the subject responsible for the
change seemed sufficiently trivial to avoid causing any marked
relaxation of his general vigilance. By allowing his attention to
turn elsewhere, his mind might link apparently unconnected

21. "Batwing chaps" are made of heavy bullhide with wide, flapping wings
that snap on, as opposed to the "shotgun" variety—so called because they
are said to look like the twin barrels of a shotgun with a choke at the
muzzle—having the outside seams sewed together all the way down the leg.
Both kinds are intended to protect the wearer's trousers and legs while
working. However, cowhands in the Southwestern cattle-raising states prefer the former kind, as they are cooler and there is no need to remove the
spurs from one's boots when taking them off. Being weighty and cumbersome, they are generally removed if the wearer anticipates spending some
time on foot. J.T.E.

pieces of information it had instinctively absorbed, and produce a solution to his dilemma.

Sitting with every appearance of being completely at ease, the small Texan gave his consideration to whether there might be a special significance to the presence of the galoshes. While they were not old, they had been subjected to sufficient wear to rule out the possibility that they were freshly purchased in the town, which might have offered a reason for them being in the bar-room. Thinking of the deductions he had formed with regard to the trio's imminent departure, he wondered if the galoshes could have been brought so as to be available for use in whatever task was awaiting them when they left the hotel.

Suddenly another possibility, spawned out of the latter consideration, sprang to Alvin's mind!

It was one that created the gravest implications!

Although sometimes bought by men whose work frequently entailed standing or wading in water, galoshes were far from a generally accepted style of footwear in the range country of Texas. As Alvin knew, many cowhands tended to consider their use implied an effete and less-than-manly attitude, no matter how wet the task concerned might be. In fact, the average member of that hard-working fraternity was inclined to treat those who wore them with something close to contempt.

The small Texan had never earned his living as a cowhand, apart from when he had supplemented his spending money during school vacations, but he had grown up among them. So he was aware that, although they no longer wore handguns openly except when working on the range, and increasingly used motor vehicles for purposes that had formerly been performed on horseback, the cowhands of the present were little different in temperament from their predecessors who had ridden with his paternal grandfather and the other members of the OD Connected ranch's legendary floating outfit.[22] In general, they were

22. For the benefit of new readers: a "floating outfit" was a group of cowhands employed by a large ranch to work its more distant ranges. Taking food in a chuck wagon, or "greasy sack" on the back of a mule, they would be away from the ranch house for several days at a time. As is told in the

still as fun loving as ever and inclined to play with a zest similar
to that with which they carried out their frequently long and
often grueling hours of work. A visit to town could produce
antics just as wild and irresponsible (backed by an equal generos-
ity when paying compensation for any damage or inconvenience
that ensued) as would have a trail crew celebrating the end of a
cattle drive from Texas to the shipping point on the railroad in
Kansas during the mid-1800s.

Having witnessed many examples of the ebullient nature of
cowhands, the small Texan appreciated how nothing was considered to make a resounding success of a spree in town than having
a good fight. So, if it had not been for the way they were dressed
and were behaving, he might have believed they had brought the
galoshes in the hope of provoking a derogatory comment to
which offense could be taken as an excuse to start a brawl. Only,
in this instance, there could be a more sinister motive.

When what appeared to be a chance fracas started, Alvin
could be injured even though not ostensibly involved. In that
way, he could be rendered incapable of performing the supposed
investigation in Brixton's Canyon for long enough to allow an
injunction preventing it legally to be brought into effect. He remembered how an illustrious ancestor, "Ole Devil" Hardin, had
employed similar tactics to deal with a group of potential dissi-
dents during the final stages of Texas's struggle to free itself from
Mexican domination in 1836.[23]

Even as the small Texan was arriving at that unpalatable point
in his train of thought, he saw the tallest of the cowhands glance
into the mirror behind the bar and address a brief sotto-voce
remark to the others. Although he was unable to hear what was
said, they all began to turn around.

Tensing slightly, so as to be ready to rise and defend himself at
the first suggestion of trouble, Alvin realized he was not the
object of the trio's attention. They were staring not at but past

author's Floating Outfit series, because of General Jackson Baines (Ole
Devil) Hardin's prominence in the affairs of Texas, the men employed in
that capacity by his OD Connected ranch were frequently sent to assist his
friends who found themselves in difficulties or endangered. J.T.E.
23. Told in *Ole Devil at San Jacinto*. J.T.E.

him to where a thickset, white-haired and cheerful-featured man entered from the street.

Studying the newcomer's attire, as the tallest cowhand raised a hand to wave a greeting, the small Texan concluded that—in spite of the way he was dressed—he could be the person for whom the trio were waiting. Bareheaded, he had on a collarless gray flannel shirt and faded blue bib overalls, the legs of which were tucked into a pair of earth-encrusted, calf-high, low-heeled boots. If he worked on the same ranch, however, it seemed unlikely to be in a capacity that entailed much riding. He walked stiffly, in a manner that suggested he had at some time sustained a sufficiently serious injury to have brought his days as a horseman to an end.

"Howdy, Tombstone," the tallest cowhand drawled, speaking louder than when he had addressed his companions, his tone and bearing implying that the elderly man was a person for whom he had considerable liking and respect. Reaching down, he lifted the footwear that had aroused Alvin's interest and went on, "We heard from poor ole Ewen's momma this morning and she allowed as how we should give all his working gear away. So, seeing as you-all took such a shine to these galoshes of his, you may as well have them."

"Why, that's right neighborly of you boys," the newcomer declared, as the other two nodded concurrence. His Texas accent had a timbre that supplemented the jovial lines of his leathery, tanned face. Accepting the gift he was being offered, he continued, "Digging graves after there's been rain's sure painful for my tired old feet. They don't take kind to getting wet no more."

"Poor ole Ewen's momma was always worrying about him getting his feet wet, seeing's how that was what took his daddy off just after he was born," the shortest of the trio commented in a bitter tone. "Which's why she sent those damned things to him. And as she'd come over to visit with him 'n' he'd just seen her headed back to home was how come he'd got 'em on when he come in here that night. If he *hadn't* been—"

"Don't start going into *that* again, amigo," the third cowhand requested soothingly. "Ain't *nobody*, 'specially his momma, blames *you-all*. He was mighty set on going out to the canyon, hunting for ole Brixton's ghost afore you—and the rest of us—started in to hoorawing him for having to wear 'em.''

"Why, sure," seconded the tallest of the three and glanced at the clock on the wall. "Anyway, we'd best finish our beer and get going. The boss'll be through at the store by now and he said for us not to keep him waiting."

"See you-all around, Tombstone," the third cowhand promised, when they had carried out his companion's instructions.

"Allus pleased to see you young'n's, just so long as it's not in my official capacity," the elderly man replied, placing the galoshes on the floor by his feet and reaching for the schooner of beer Softly had filled without needing to be told. After the cowhands had set off toward the street, he swung his gaze to rest briefly on the table at which the small Texan was sitting and went on, "I didn't know you'd took to serving food in here, Abel."

"It's only while they're giving the dining-room floor a good scrubbing," the man behind the counter answered, throwing a glance toward the lobby.

Allowing himself to relax as the trio walked by without paying the slightest attention to him, Alvin looked in the same direction as Softly. He saw nothing beyond the entrance to the barroom and once more wondered whether he was imagining the danger. In spite of his apprehension, the cowhands had only been waiting to present the galoshes to Tombstone. From the conversation he had overheard, he deduced these had belonged to the young man who was found dead in the badlands and had been worn on the night that the incident had taken place.

Much as the small Texan would have liked to discuss the situation with his partner, he realized that deviating from the original plan would make this difficult. As they had not shown any sign of recognizing each other when he arrived, it might arouse Softly's suspicions if they should do so now. Being uncertain of how to act, he decided the best course was to do nothing until a suitable moment came for them to establish contact. Seeing the waiter coming from the kitchen with his meal on a tray, he concluded that he might as well eat while awaiting an opportunity.

Then a disturbing thought struck Alvin.

Suppose the food had been tampered with in some way?

Being so highly spiced and fiery to the palate, chili con carne would be ideal for masking the taste of any kind of noxious potion.

"Take a hold of yourself!" the small Texan ordered silently. "There's no way they could know what I'd order, or even if I'd be eating here."

For all that, Alvin drew only slight consolation from the thought. It was, he realized, far from as comforting as it had appeared at first. The odds favored him eating at the hotel. Finding a table prepared in the bar, with the dining room fortuitously closed, lent strength to that supposition. What was more, he recollected how the waiter had tried to dissuade him when he ordered the chili. However, the remembrance aroused further speculation. If the food had been tampered with, why had it been considered necessary to have him eat in the bar?

It was not, if the remarks Alvin had overheard passed between Softly and the elderly man were any guide, because this was the usual day on which the dining room's floor was scrubbed. The fact that that explanation had been required suggested it was not closed for such a purpose on other occasions.

Before the small Texan could give any further thought to the matter, or come up with a satisfactory reason for testing his theory regarding the possibility of tampering with the food, the waiter reached the table and set down the tray.

"Hey, this looks good," Alvin enthused as the bowl of steaming red chili was placed in front of him, but he was watching the Mexican's face and not the food.

"*Sí, señor,*" the waiter responded. "The coffee isn't ready yet—"

"Fetch it as soon as it is," Alvin replied, unable to detect any suggestion as to whether his latest suspicions were justified or that the excuse about the coffee was genuine.

"*Sí, señ—!*" the waiter began, but the words broke off as he stared at the entrance from the lobby. Giving a gulp of alarm, he went on hurriedly as he started to back away, "I'll fetch it for you!"

While the Mexican was turning to walk rapidly away Alvin swung his gaze across the room and studied the three men who were entering. All wore cowhand-style clothing that he suspected was grubby and untidy by choice rather than through being worn for work, but they were a far different proposition from the trio who had presented Tombstone with the galoshes. The one in the lead was the oldest, being in his forties, of medium height, thickset, and had a brutish, scowling face. Taller by two and three inches respectively, his companions were lean, with surly features in need of being shaved, and were clearly brothers. There was something arrogant and truculent about all three of them. It could have been accounted for by their slightly lurching gait, which implied they had been drinking elsewhere before arriving in the hotel.

Alerted by the waiter's reaction at the sight of the trio, the small Texan sensed that the situation he had envisaged might be commencing. He noticed the calculating way they were looking at him as they approached, still in the loose arrowhead formation, and he guessed their purpose was similar to that which he had suspected of the cowhands. Running his trained gaze over each in turn, he spotted a significant bulge at waist level under the left flap of the leader's open jacket. However, he could not detect anything to suggest either of the other pair was armed.

While conducting the survey, Alvin picked up the tablespoon with his left hand and lifted the bowl of chili on his right palm as if about to start eating. Instead, he sat still and without allowing any trace of his awareness regarding their possible purpose to show. Then all doubts about their motives ended as the stocky man came to a halt at the opposite side of the table, but his companions continued to walk until they were level on the small Texan's right and left.

"Hey, four-eyes," the leader said, teetering truculently on his heels. His name, Alvin learned later, was Fred Mulley. "You're sitting at *our* table."

"I didn't see any reserved sign when I took it," the small Texan replied in the silence that fell following the stocky man's words. He sensed that every eye in the room was turned to the table. Without laying down either the spoon or the bowl, he moved his chair back slightly as if meaning to rise and went on equally mildly, "But that being so, I'd best let you have—"

"Don't pull that gun!" Mulley bellowed, lunging forward, confident that David Skinner—to the intended victim's left—and his younger brother, Dennis—on the right—would lessen the chances of the room's other occupants seeing that such an action was not taking place.

Ready for the first act of hostility, Alvin swung his right arm. Exhibiting an accuracy equal to when firing his Colt Government Model automatic pistol, he flung the bowl so its contents gushed out to meet the oncoming man. Caught in the face with the stewlike liquid, which was hot from cooking as well as by virtue of the spices it contained, Mulley might have thought himself fortunate that his eyes had closed instinctively an instant before it reached him. Despite this, he let out a howl reminiscent of a cat that was being scalded, and his aggressive advance became an anguished retreat. Rising swiftly, their original purpose forgotten, his hands began to paw at and wipe the thick red chili from where it was burning his face. As he went, displaying a rapidity that matched the throwing of the bowl, his would-be victim's spoon-filled left fist hooked beneath the edge of the table and pitched it over after him.

Such was the alacrity with which the small Texan responded to what they had believed would be an unanticipated assault, the Skinner brothers stood and stared instead of attacking the moment things began to go wrong. In exculpation, neither had expected there would be any need for them to participate in such a manner. On hearing how small the potential victim would be, it had been decided to let Mulley carry out the disablement. The brothers' presence should have been to support his assertion that the man who had aroused Softly's animosity provoked the fight by trying to draw a gun, and also to act as a reminder of the danger of reprisals if anybody offered to disprove the excuse.

Seeing the table overturned and Mulley blundering backward, Dennis recovered from his state of surprise somewhat more quickly than his elder brother. Taking a couple of paces closer, he thrust out his hands. The right caught hold of the Norfolk jacket's offside lapel and the left grabbed Alvin's right arm. As he began to pull his captive from the chair, he became conscious of just how bulky and hard a bicep he was grasping. Realizing that the small Texan was far from being as puny as he had imagined, he was not sorry to see his sibling start to move forward with clenched fists.

Bending the motion smoothly with the strain being exerted to lift him from his seat, Alvin rose faster than he was being pulled. As the chair went flying behind him, he brought his straight left arm around and up in a wide arc to rake the head of the spoon he was still holding across his attacker's face. Although the tip only just grazed Dennis's nose he could not prevent himself from jerking back his head and relaxing his grip slightly. The small Texan's arm, having gone by, bent, and its elbow rammed into the man's chest with sufficient force to effect his release.

Nor was Alvin a moment too soon in attaining his freedom. A glance over his shoulder as he delivered the elbow blow warned him that the elder brother was closing on him. Setting his full weight on his slightly flexed left leg, he raised and folded the right beneath him. By inclining his torso forward, he avoided the left fist that was driving in his direction. Stabbing to the rear with the elevated boot, he caught his would-be assailant hard and where such an attack would produce the best result. Even as agony ripped from David's groin and he was brought to a halt, his discomfiture was not at an end. Descending immediately after delivering the kick, the small Texan's foot served as a pivot upon which he swiveled. Given added impetus by the turn, his open left hand was sent in a slap to the side of the head, which knocked its recipient in a twirling sprawl to crash on the floor. Already in considerable pain, the impact jolted all the breath and any semblance of cohesive thought from David.

Granted a brief respite by the brothers' intervention, Mulley contrived to partially clear his vision. Having done so, he could hardly believe the sight that met his eyes. Discovering that his companions had met with even less success than he had when coping with their proposed victim, he darted forward with the intention of resuming his attack. Alert to the possibility, Alvin turned and dealt with it in much the same way he had when rendering Hubert Blitzer hors de combat in the cabin of the hotel at Austin.

Finding his left wrist caught by two powerful hands, which gave a mighty heave to propel him across the barroom, the leader of the would-be attackers could neither halt his headlong progress nor retain his equilibrium. He had a vague idea that he was rushing in the direction of a tall, lean, leathery-faced figure that was rising from a chair against the wall. Clad in ancient range clothes, the man in question was reaching beneath his jacket with his right hand. However, at that moment Mulley was too concerned by his own predicament to devote any thought to what the other was doing, or anything else for that matter. So he failed to notice that the man toward whom he was approaching, while without any human companions, was not alone.

Although Mulley had never done any more work than was necessary, he had of necessity acquired a horseman's skill in breaking a fall. Feeling himself going down, he instinctively ducked his left shoulder and contrived to alight rolling until coming to a halt a few feet from Sergeant Branch's table. He was shaken, but not so severely injured that he was unable to force himself into a sitting position facing his intended victim. Then, snarling with rage, he sent his right hand toward the revolver that was to have been planted on the geologist to excuse the attack.

Driven backward for a few steps by the impact of the elbow upon his chest, Dennis Skinner saw what he considered to be his chance. However, he had noticed how the small man had served his brother and was handling Mulley. Having a strong streak of cowardice under his viciously bullying nature, he was disinclined to tackle such an obviously competent antagonist with his bare fists. So, instead of advancing immediately as his stocky companion was flung toward the wall, he dipped his right hand into the pocket of his Levi's pants. Not until his fingers were entering the holes of the brass knuckle-duster that reposed therein did he offer to move forward.

Just as Mulley's fingers were enfolding the butt of the revolver, he heard a deep and menacing growl rumbling from close behind him. Looking over his shoulder, he found himself confronted by the snarl-rippling and powerfully toothed mouth of a big bluetick coonhound, which was standing beneath the table. Its eyes were fixed upon him and its sleek, well-muscled body seemed to be quivering with a desire to spring forward.

"I'd leave it be, was I you-all," remarked a dryly sardonic drawling voice. "Ole Lightning there don't take kind to having guns waved about near him."

Without waiting to discover what the third of his attackers meant to take from the pocket, Alvin darted in. Bending at the waist, he wrapped his arms around Dennis's legs just above the knees. Clamping them together, he straightened up and lifted, then threw his captive from him. The tall man landed on his feet, but that did not prove to be any advantage. He staggered a couple of steps to the rear, the hand emerging to join its mate in a flailing attempt to keep his balance.

Following Dennis on the run, the small Texan leapt to deliver a thrusting kick with the left foot. Struck in the center of the chest and feeling as if it was being caved in, the attack ruined whatever chance he might have had of remaining erect. Sent spinning toward the entrance to the lobby, his spine collided with the frame of the door and the back of his head met the wall, hard. Rebounding, he went through to collapse unconscious at the feet of the man who was approaching from the now wide-open door of the manager's office.

As he twisted his head around, the first thing to meet Mulley's gaze appeared to be a contradiction of the warning that had been uttered. His still smarting and running eyes took in the sight of a Colt Frontier revolver, its hammer drawn to the fully cocked position, dangling in a deeply bronzed hand that looked as strong and hard as granite. Nor did he miss the point that, while the weapon was in plain sight, the bluetick paid no attention to it despite what had been said on the subject. So, raising his gaze to the hard and unsmiling features of the speaker, he left the revolver thrust in his waistband and exposed the empty hand. The dog stopped growling, but it remained on its feet and continued to display an alert readiness he felt sure would change into an attack if he made the slightest hostile gesture. With that disconcerting thought in mind, except for looking from the speaker to the entrance to the lobby, he sat as if turned to stone.

Alighting from delivering his version of the *yoko tobi geri*—side jumping kick—of karate, still without his exertions having dislodged the horn-rimmed spectacles, Alvin decided its recipient would not require any further attention. So he swung around to find out whether he would need to continue defending himself against the other two. By the time he had completed the turn, halting in a defensive posture that was strange to Occidental eyes, he was equally confident that there was nothing more to fear from either. Although the stocky man might have been physically capable of resuming the attack, Branch and Lightning were clearly acting as effective deterrents, and the second of the brothers sprawled limply where he had fallen.

Satisfied that the fighting was over, the small Texan allowed his hands to drop and turned his gaze to the other occupants of the room. Not for the first time, he felt grateful for the process of hereditary reproduction that had given him such an unobtrusively powerful physique. As in the case of his maternal grandfather, he found his outward appearance was a tremendous asset when backed by the thorough training he had received in the unarmed combat techniques of the Japanese martial arts. These qualities combined to offer an initial edge when he was in contention against larger men who were unaware of their existence.

Even without possessing Leon Gonzales's knowledge of physiognomy as an aid to reading facial expressions, Alvin could tell that the customers and the waiter were most impressed by what they had witnessed. Furthermore, if the smiles and nods of approval—those of Tombstone and the Mexican being particularly noticeable—were any indication, not a few of the onlookers were far from displeased by the treatment he had inflicted upon the trio. In fact, he concluded that the general consensus of opinion considered his actions to have been not only correct, but praiseworthy.

However, pleasing as he found the obvious approbation of the majority of the men on his side of the bar, it was to Softly that the small Texan devoted most of his attention. There was an expression of amazement mingled with baffled anger on the usu-

ally professionally jovial features of the burly man as he glared
from each of the supposed assailants in turn and to their intended victim. Try as he might, he could not prevent his
clenched fists from banging on the top of the counter. Then his
gaze snapped toward the door that gave access to the lobby.

Following the direction in which Softly was glaring, Alvin
found no difficulty in identifying the man who lumbered across
the threshold. The tarnished badge of office, displayed on the
food-stained vest of an expensive if rumpled and badly creased
three-piece suit, provided all the confirmation that was necessary.

Big and built on massive lines, although he had long since run
to seed in a manner that suggested why his nickname had been
changed from "Big Jim" to "Fat Jim," Sheriff James E. Healey
had bristling black hair tinged with gray. The perspiration on his
greasily pallid porcine features indicated he was out of condition;
and they were embellished by bushy brows from beneath which
peered buttonlike, shifty eyes. Apart from something slender and
less bulky than a gun causing his jacket's right hand pocket to
sag and bulge, there was no sign of him being armed. However,
the brown derby hat perched on the back of his head, the grubby
white silk shirt, a large diamond stickpin in his red, white, and
blue striped necktie and a thick gold watch-chain stretched
across his bulging stomach offered suggestions that he had some
source of income beyond his salary from Grouper County's tax-
payers.

Despite having watched Dennis Skinner entering and crashing
unconscious upon the floor of the lobby, Healey had formed no
conceptions of what might be awaiting him when he reached the
barroom.

Skidding to a halt as he crossed the threshold, an exclamation
of profane astonishment burst from the sheriff. Knowing the
brothers and their companion, he could scarcely believe what he
was seeing as his gaze went from David to Mulley and then was
directed at the small young man they were supposed to have
beaten up. After studying Alvin for a moment, he looked at
Softly in search of guidance. Realizing that he could hardly expect verbal instructions under the circumstances, he gave

thought to how he might retrieve the situation. Remembering what the man behind the counter had said about the geologist's arrogant nature, he decided there was a way in which he could bring about the desired result.

"All right, hombre!" Healey rumbled, resuming his interrupted advance without so much as a glance at the other occupants of the room and confident that none of them would dare raise any objections to the way he intended to act. Reaching into his pocket as he went on speaking, his right hand grasped the leather lead-loaded sap that reposed therein. He was ready to take it out and use it as soon as the geologist made any kind of provocative response. "Why did you jump these gents?"

"Reckon you-all've gotten your reins just a li'l mite twisted there, *Big* Jim," Branch called, before Alvin could reply, having made an accurate guess at what the local peace officer had in mind. He returned the Colt to its holster as he strolled forward with leisurely appearing speed. However, as Lightning remained under the table instead of accompanying him, Mulley showed no inclination of trying to take advantage of his departure. "It wasn't Mr. Hollingshead there as started the fuss."

"Who asked—? Oh, it's *you*!" Healey spluttered, changing the wrathful question as he realized with whom he was dealing. He had failed to notice the elderly sergeant standing by Mulley on arriving in the barroom, due to his consternation over the situation awaiting him there. Then the full implication of the other's comment struck him and he continued, trying to sound amiable, but retaining his hold on the sap in the hope that he would be granted an opportunity to use it as he had planned, "Do you know this jasper?"

"We've run across one another here 'n' thereabouts," Branch confessed, shoving the lapel of his jacket aside to hook his left thumb in the armhole of his vest. By doing so, he exposed the silver star-in-a-circle badge of office that was attached to the latter garment. "Don't you-all know him?"

"No!" Healey asserted, only just preventing himself from answering in the affirmative, and concluding something more should be added, went on, "So *you* saw what happened, then?"

"From start to end," Branch replied, speaking somewhat

louder than was necessary to ensure his words carried all around the room. "Which I don't know how anybody else figures it, but in my 'considered hoe-pinner-on' as a sergeant in the Texas Rangers, it sure looked like what a legal-minded shyster'd call a clearcut case of tried-for 'haysalt and batterizing's' went wrong."

"You mean's it was *them* who picked on *him*?" the sheriff demanded, trying without any great conviction to sound as if he considered the possibility unbelievable and hoping the geologist would enter the conversation, or do something to justify him taking out and using the sap.

"It for sure wasn't the other way around," Branch confirmed, and he did not need to look to know his partner shared his suspicions with regard to the local peace officer's intentions, so was avoiding presenting the opportunity.

"Why'd *they* do it?" Healey challenged.

"Looked to me like they'd been taking drinking liquor, which's again' the 'Prohibitical Law' for shame, until it'd set 'em on the prod and looking for a fuss," the sergeant offered blandly, ignoring the fact that he had been transgressing in a similar fashion, if with less aggressive results. "Could be they figured as how Mr. Hollingshead, being a stranger 'n' what they took for a dude, would make easy pickings. Trouble being, doing the kind of work he does, he's had to learn to take care of hisself better'n somewhat should he get picked on that ways."

"Well, I don't know about that—*them* causing fuss, I mean," Healey objected, directing a menacing scowl around the room. It was intended to serve as a reminder that anybody who expressed disagreement with his sentiments would face painful repercussions after the sergeant had gone. "Those boys aren't usually trouble-causers, even happen they've taken a snort or two."

"I'm not the man to gainsay it, seeing as how you-all know 'em and I don't," Branch declared, apparently accepting the attempted exculpation. "Maybe they've got a 'miss-like' for Mr. Hollingshead—or what he does—from some other place?"

"Would they have?" Healey demanded, glaring at Alvin and oblivious of Softly's attempts to will him to raise the matter of the geologist's employment, as he had disclaimed being acquainted.

"I've never seen any of them before they came in here," the small Texan stated, standing perfectly still and holding his voice to such a neutral tone that it precluded any emotion that could allow an attack to be made upon him.

"Are you—?" the sheriff began, hoping an expression of doubt over the geologist's veracity would produce the required response.

"Hey, though," Branch put in, exuding a helpful air. "Maybe they was worried that you'd come to do some of that fancy 'gee-hog-olising,' or whichever you call it, of your'n hereabouts."

"They're wrong if that's what they think!" Alvin claimed, sounding as he had when denying his "identity" earlier that morning. "I'm only here on vacation."

"Huh!" Branch grunted. "Do you *always* tote a gun when you're on vacation?"

"Gun!" Alvin snorted, with well-simulated indignation, but still refraining from making any gesture that the sheriff might choose to construe as threatening. "What gun?"

"The one that feller concluded you was reaching for and tried to stop you pulling," Branch elaborated, indicating Mulley with a snapping motion of his right thumb and forefinger, yet never taking his eyes from the local peace officer.

"Goddamn it, man, I *never* carry a gun!" Alvin snapped, raising his arms slowly until they were outstretched at shoulder height. "Go ahead and search me if you think I do."

"Might be best was *you* to do it, sheriff," Branch drawled, showing none of the delight he was feeling at the way his young partner had anticipated his wishes.

"Huh?" Healey grunted, knowing that the suggestion of the geologist being armed had only been uttered by Mulley as an excuse for starting the attack, and seeing no point in performing what he knew would be an unproductive task.

"Do what you want," the elderly sergeant drawled, confident that between them, he and Alvin could prevent the local peace officer from turning the search into a reason for using the sap. "Only, happen you don't, there's some as might think as how you-all was scared to do your legal and 'eelectrical' duty on account of who he is—or could be working for."

"Blast it all, man!" Alvin interrupted, deciding a denial would be expected by Softly if nobody else, but continuing to stand as if turned to stone. "I've told you that I'm not working for *anybody* right now."

"That's what you told us," Branch admitted, but his voice registered what appeared to be thinly disguised doubt. "And, which being the case, you don't have no 'objections' to the sheriff here searching you?"

"Of course I don't object!" Alvin replied. "That's why I'm standing like this. Go ahead and search me, sheriff."

Even as Healey was congratulating himself upon how the geologist was playing into his hands, he began to appreciate that this was not the case. After such evidence of compliance, he could not exploit the opportunity without the possibility of serious repercussions at a later date. If there had been only witnesses who lived in the town present, he could have carried out his intentions secure in the knowledge that whatever reason he gave for felling his victim would pass without question.

Sergeant Branch of the Texas Rangers was an entirely different proposition!

That the elderly peace officer should have intervened struck the sheriff as being significant. From remarks he had made, he was clearly aware of the exact nature of Hollingshead's work and the kind of men who made use of the geologist's talents. Which offered a suggestion to the sheriff as to why he had felt the need to intrude. The thought that Branch might have been motivated by nothing more than a desire to see justice done never occurred to Healey, such altruism being foreign to his own nature. Instead, the only reason he could envisage was that there must be some form of financial benefit involved.

Perhaps Branch had been hired to accompany and watch over Hollingshead!

However, after considering the possibility for a moment, Healey discarded it. While there had been an occasional corrupt Texas Ranger, he had never heard the slightest suggestion of Branch belonging to that category. Rather the opposite, in fact. Of course, finding himself a chance onlooker, he might have decided it could prove advantageous to his career if he performed a service that might gain him the approbation of whoever was currently hiring the geologist. His comments had made it obvious that he discounted the claim of being on vacation and that he had the influential status of the employer in mind when giving his advice to the sheriff. In which case, he would not countenance an unjustified attack upon Hollingshead, whose behavior indicated no resistance was contemplated.

There was yet another objection to making the intended assault, the sheriff suddenly realized as he glanced about him in search of inspiration and noticed in passing two victims of the earlier attempt. That the small geologist had successfully fought off three larger, heavier assailants implied an exceptional skill at bare-handed combat. In fact, Branch had not appeared to be surprised that he should have been able to cope with the trio's attack.

The conclusions Healey reached warned him that Hollingshead was a person, small size notwithstanding, against whom it would be dangerous to attempt hostile actions. Although the sheriff had at one time acquired a well-deserved reputation for competence as a roughhouse brawler, those days were long behind him. Too much liquor, good food, and easy living had reduced his former powers to such an extent that, particularly as there were residents of his jurisdiction present to see what happened, he felt disinclined to chance receiving similar treatment to whatever had felled the geologist's previous attackers.

Yielding to the inevitable, Healey glanced at Softly as he was bringing his empty right hand from his pocket. Barely able to restrain a shrug of resignation as he met the scowling gaze that was being directed at him, he went toward the motionless geologist. Feeling sure that there would be no concealed weapon for him to find, he set about doing as Branch had suggested and Hollingshead authorized. It was obvious to anybody with experience in such matters that his heart was not in the task.

"He's not carrying a gun," the sheriff announced, making no attempt to conceal his disappointment—although it was not, as some of the onlookers assumed, caused by the failure to discover a weapon—after having completed what the two Texas Rangers considered to have been a far more perfunctory search than either of them would have made.

"Seems like you-all was 'miss-tooken' then, mister," Branch called, looking around as Healey stepped away and Alvin lowered his arms. "So, happen you're up to it, maybe you'd best go and see how bad your amigos are hurt."

"Call off that goddamned dog of your'n first!" requested Mulley, to whom the comment and suggestion had been directed.

"Who, ole Lightning?" the sergeant asked, sounding puzzled. "Why shucks, he's too all-fired lazy to bother you none."

Looking behind him for the first time since Branch had walked away, Mulley found that the big bluetick—having obeyed the finger-snapping signal—was lying down and appeared to be asleep. Nor did it offer to move as he rose cautiously and walked to where, still behaving in a dazed fashion, David Skinner was sitting up.

"Do you-all want to have 'em arrested for jumping you, Mr. Hollingshead?" Branch asked, as Mulley was helping Skinner to stand up. Before Alvin could reply, however, he turned to the local peace officer and went on apologetically, " 'Scuse me, *Big* Jim, I'm a mite out of line. T'ain't for *me* to be asking *that*. This here's *your* bailiwick 'n' I'm just passing through, unofficial-like."

"Shucks, sergeant," Healey replied, only just managing to conceal the alarm he felt over the prospect of having to arrest the three local men—particularly as the possibility had never entered his head—if their intended victim was to prefer charges against them. "You're only trying to help."

"Why, sure," Branch declared, with such an appearance of sincerity he might have been speaking the truth. "How about it, Mr. Hollingshead?"

"Excuse me, sheriff!" the desk clerk said, coming from the lobby and providing a most welcome interruption as far as the local peace officer was concerned. "But I think somebody should send for the doctor. I've been looking at the man lying in the lobby and believe he needs medical attention."

"Is he hurt bad?" Healey demanded, although it was noticeable that David Skinner—who had been helped to the bar by

Mulley and was holding a drink that Softly had given him—did not display any interest or concern over his brother's condition.

"I'm *not* a qualified medical practitioner," the desk clerk replied, making little attempt to conceal his antipathy for the sheriff. "But I served with the Red Cross during the war and it's my opinion that the doctor should see him as soon as possible."

"So he's hurt *real* bad, is he?" Healey said with greater satisfaction than regret, as a flash of inspiration struck him. Then, instead of offering to act upon what most people would have considered to be sound advice and should have been his first priority, he swung toward the small Texan, continuing, "It seems to *me* that it'll not be Fred Mulley and the Skinner boys I'll be arresting."

There was a timbre of vindictive satisfaction in the sheriff's voice as he was making the pronouncement. Despite no opportunity presenting itself so far, he was confident that he could solve Softly's problem. Provided Branch did not stay in town, once he had the geologist in the seclusion of the jail and with only his solitary deputy as a witness, the pretense of an attempted escape would allow the two of them to inflict sufficiently serious injuries to achieve the results that were required and had so far been thwarted.

"Howdy, Abe," Healey greeted, with an obvious lack of enthusiasm, on entering the supposed bartender's living quarters at Sostice's Hotel some two and a half hours after the abortive attempt to render the geologist incapable of carrying out an examination of Brixton's Canyon. In view of what had happened, he had hoped to postpone the interview for which he had been summoned. "Miguel said you wanted to see me."

"You must have took some finding!" Softly complained and went on in equally bitter tones, "Goddamn it! What a no-good waste of time and money all around. That son-of-a-bitch Hollingshead's still on his feet and able to do what he's been sent here for."

"Well, you can't blame *me* for that!" the sheriff asserted as vehemently as he dared, being uncomfortably aware of just how much he was dependent upon the man he was addressing for

retaining his lucrative official position in Grouper Count
"Who'd've thought a short-grown runt like him could take o
the Skinner boys and Fred Mulley?" When there was no r
sponse to the question he had posed as evidence that he was n
trying to place the blame for the failure upon his host, he adde
what he hoped would be considered as exculpation where I
personally was concerned. "And Branch billing in like he d
stopped the little bastard saying or doing something I could ha
used as an excuse to bust his head open with my sap."

"So I saw," Softly admitted, showing no sign of being moll
fied by anything he had just heard and seeking a scapegoat fe
the recriminations he was sure would be forthcoming over th
lack of success in carrying out the promise he had made to Wi
fred Plant. "And he's *still* walking around as free as a go
damned bird."

"There wasn't no way I could've held him if I'd took him in
Healey answered hurriedly, being equally disinclined to have th
onus for the fiasco placed upon him. "The kind of lawyer he'd'
sent for wouldn't just have stopped at having any case I brougl
again' him thrown out of court, he'd likely've hauled *me* in fro
of the judge for false arrest and—"

"Goddamn it!" Softly interrupted. "Even *if* you'd've let hi
send for a lawyer, you could've fixed his wagon afore the son-o
a-bitching shyster got here."

"That's what I was figuring on doing," the sheriff pointed ou
"But he told Branch as how he wanted him to stick around
make sure he got his legal rights should he be took in. An
Branch allowed, with the kind of backing he'd got, there wasn
nothing he could do but do it. Then he warned me what'd ha
pen was I to take Hollingshead in. And knowing why he's here,
figure it made good sense not to."

"You told a goddamned *Texas Ranger* we know about Meek
sending Hollingshead here?" Softly demanded, almost in
shout, having contrived to follow most of the somewhat mu
dled explanation.

"No!" Healey asserted, and although he refrained from add
ing, "of course not," the words were implied in his tone. "B
going by what Branch told me down to the jailhouse, Ho

ngshead's figuring on marrying into the Counter family and
ou know what that bunch are like for standing by their own.
hey'd've set up more fuss and hollering than I reckoned you, or
Ir. Turtle, would want should he have been hauled to the poky
or hurting one of *three* fellers who jumped him, then got worked
ver 'cause he was supposed to be trying to escape."

"We've rode out fuss and hollering afore now," Softly
rowled, despite silently conceding the point. Having had his
opes raised by deducing what was intended to follow the geolo-
ist's arrival at the jailhouse, then seen them dashed again, he
ould not resist the temptation to make the sheriff squirm. Be-
ore he could say anything more, there was a knock on the door
nd he bellowed, "Come in!"

"I've fixed it, boss," announced the man who entered, and
omething in his attitude suggested to the sheriff that, whatever
he task had been, it was not connected with his normal duties as
ssistant bartender.

"He didn't see you, did he?" Softly demanded, giving added
upport to Healey's summation.

"He kept quiet about it if he did," the man replied, grinning
roadly. "Which I don't reckon he would have if he'd seen me."

"I don't reckon he would at that," Softly confirmed, showing
leasure for the first time since the sheriff had arrived. "Go and
nake sure Joplin knows what to say."

"Sure, boss," the man assented, and left, closing the door.

"Where are Mulley and the Skinners?" Softly asked, as soon
s he and the sheriff were alone.

"Down to Minnie Morgan's chicken ranch,"[24] Healey replied,
vondering what instructions were to be given to the owner of the
own's only service station.

"How bad's Dennis hurt?" Softly inquired, before the sheriff
ould attempt to satisfy his curiosity.

"The doctor allowed he might have a concus—something-or-
ther."

"Can he be moved?"

"The doctor reckoned the best place for him'd be at home and

4. "Chicken ranch" : a colloquial name for a brothel. J.T.E.

in bed," Healey replied, deciding that the news brought by the assistant bartender had put Softly in a more amiable frame of mind. "But Mulley 'n' David was threatening to come after Hollingshead with guns—"

"The stupid bastards!" the manager of the hotel snarled.

"I figured you wouldn't want it," Healey stated, relieved to hear that his handling of the situation had been correct. "So I told them you said they was to stay put and leave him be until you gave the word."

"Thank God you've done *something* right!" Softly said, almost jovially. "Now you can go and tell them I said for them to get the hell back to their place and stay there until I pass word they can come into town again. Only, happen you get asked, say you sent them there straight after the doctor'd seen Dennis."

"I'll see to it," Healey promised, and taking advantage of the other's improved humor, continued, "Who's likely to come asking about them?"

"Don't make no never mind who it is," Softly answered, "just so long as you tell him what I said."

"I will!" the sheriff affirmed. "But what about Hollingshead?"

"You can leave him to *me*," Softly ordered, and watching the alarm that came to Healey's face, went on impatiently, "Don't worry. I'm not wanting *you* to do anything about him. I've just made sure he can't get out to the canyon tonight, and I'll have things rigged so he'll not be feeling up to going any place except his bed for a spell, the next time he has a meal here."

"You're not going to have him poisoned?" the sheriff said nervously. "Hell, that'd bring Branch back on the run."

"Why would he come back?" Softly challenged, being unaware until that moment of the elderly sergeant's departure. "*You* won't be sending for him."

"He might come, just the same, should he hear," Healey warned. "I took the notion from what he said, him being close to having to retire through old age, he'd jump at the chance to do something likely put him in good with the Counter family."

"He would, would he?" Softly growled, then was struck by a thought. "Hey, though, if that's what made the old bastard bite in, we could be worrying for nothing."

"How do you mean?"

"I was thinking Meeker could've had him sent along to make sure nothing happened to Hollingshead."

"I don't reckon so," Healey objected, and having told of the deductions he had formed with regard to the sergeant's nonintervention during the attack, went on, "Besides, from what Branch told me, he's in Major Tragg's Company. He's one son-of-a-bitch who's *never* been in *anybody's* pocket and he wouldn't be doing no favors for a longhorn like Meeker."

"So you don't reckon he was sent to wet-nurse Hollingshead?" Softly inquired.

"I—I—!" Healey faltered, his instincts rebelling against making a definite statement on such an issue in case he should be proved wrong.

"Why was he here then?" Softly demanded.

"He allowed he was just passing through on the way to San Antone to identify a feller who's been picked up by the sheriff, and only stopped by for a beer," Healey replied. "But to make sure he doesn't just go along the trail a ways then come sneaking in again, I've told Callaghan to follow him until it's certain he's left the county and isn't coming back."

"*Bueno,*" Softly praised, although somewhat sardonically, as he was surprised to learn the sheriff had shown such forethought in having the precaution taken. "And don't look so worried. No matter whether Branch wants to foot-lick to the Counters or not, what I've got in mind for Hollingshead won't look like anything he'll figure needs for him to come back and poke his nose in, should he hear about it."

"Just what are you going to do?" the sheriff wanted to know.

"There's no time to tell you all about it now, and if you don't know, you'll look surprised when you hear," Softly answered, drawing amusement from keeping the clearly perturbed peace officer in suspense, particularly as he now considered his affairs were at last progressing in a satisfactory manner and the danger of further intervention by the elderly sergeant was removed. "You'd best go and send those three useless knuckleheads out of town. And should you be asked, don't forget that they left at least a couple of hours back."

"I'll remember," Healey promised sullenly, accepting that an
further attempt to elicit information would be futile.

Leaving the room, the sheriff drew what small consolation h
could from the thought that he had done his best. He could no
only await developments and hope that, whatever they might be
they would not lead to the return of Branch. However, lik
Softly, he was satisfied that he had done all that was necessary t
prevent this happening unexpectedly in the immediate future.

Neither of the conspirators would have been so complacen
about having ensured that the elderly sergeant could not remai
in the vicinity of Grouperville without their knowledge if the
had been able to witness what was taking place at that momen
some fifteen miles along the road to San Antonio.

Driving a dirty black 1918 Dodge Brothers' Four coupé at a pac
suitable to his needs, Deputy Sheriff Waldo Callaghan was pay
ing little attention to his surroundings. Although the vehicle wa
the property of the Grouper County sheriff's office, its neglecte
and dilapidated condition was discreditable to the two peace of
ficers who should have been responsible for its upkeep and main
tenance. For all that, it seemed to be a match for its solitar
occupant's appearance. A big, flabby, shambling man in his earl
fifties, he had thinning white hair and unprepossessing features
Dressed in a mixture of range and town clothes, all of whicl
were in need of cleaning, he clearly neither washed nor shave
too regularly.

Despite being even more lazy and incompetent than the sher
iff, Callaghan was performing his current duty at least accept
ably, if resentfully. Not that it made any greater demands upo
his limited intellect than was necessary to drive at a sufficien
distance to prevent the man in front, in the aged-looking Forc
Model T sedan, from becoming aware that he was being followe
along the narrow dirt road. Callaghan was helped by the rollin
terrain they were traversing and was satisfied that he was achiev
ing his purpose.

A loud popping sound, followed by the hiss of escaping ai
jolted the deputy out of his complacency. Although the coup
swerved, he was not traveling at such a high speed that what h

knew must have been a blowout posed any threat to his safety. Putting aside his speculations on how he might avoid completing the drive to the county line, particularly as the man he was following was showing no sign of returning or even of halting with the intention of returning later in the day, he had no difficulty in bringing the vehicle to a halt. Hauling himself laboriously from the driver's seat to the ground, he lumbered around the hood. Halting, he glared at a deflated tire, which long use had left entirely bereft of its tread.

"Goddamn it!" the deputy snarled, bestowing a kick to the wheel and walking to the rear of the coupé without examining the damage. His only thought on the matter was that the tire, in common with the others on the vehicle, was in such poor condition he was surprised a blowout had not happened sooner. Glowering at the spare wheel attached to the trunk compartment for a moment, he turned his gaze in each direction along the road and found that, apart from the Ford—which was disappearing over a rim about three-quarters of a mile away—there was no sign of life. "Just my son-of-a-bitching luck. There's nobody around I can make change 'em for me."

A more observant person than Callaghan would have noticed that, instead of having pierced the bearing surface of the tire, as might have been expected, whatever caused the damage had passed through the walls, leaving round holes just over a quarter of an inch in diameter, the one on the outside being slightly higher. Being idle by nature, he was too annoyed by the prospect of having to change the wheel himself to pay any attention to what otherwise might have suggested something unusual had taken place to produce the puncture. Instead of giving thought to the cause, he did nothing more constructive than mutter a string of profanity as he raised the lid of the trunk compartment and lifted out the tools with which to effect the transfer.

While seeking assistance, the deputy had not troubled to extend his search as far as the ridge to his right, which formed a bush-covered skyline something over a quarter of a mile away. Nor, even if he had looked there in the course of his scrutiny, would he have detected anything to have aroused his suspicions. To be fair, even while the blowout was being produced, a much more alert and keen-sighted person than Callaghan might have been excused for overlooking the means by which it was caused.

Despite the need for extreme accuracy, there had been little more than an inch of the barrel protruding beyond the bushes in which the weapon's user was hiding as he was taking aim and dispatching the bullet that pierced the coupé's tire. Nor had there been an audible notification of what was happening. The somewhat bulbous nature of the muzzle, compared with the size of the aperture at its center, indicated it was equipped with a device capable of reducing the sound of the cartridge's powder charge being detonated to no more than a sharp hiss, which could not be heard on the road. Furthermore, although the clacking of the bolt being operated to eject the spent case and thrust a live round from the magazine into the chamber could not be silenced, it was drowned by the noise from the coupé's engine and the blowout, so went unnoticed by the deputy. As a final precaution against discovery, there was no sign of the weapon to be seen by the time its victim was leaving his vehicle.

Having played his part in helping to establish Alvin Fog's "identity," Sergeant Mark Scrapton had had a good reason for his hasty departure from Grouperville. Despite being aware that the deception might put the small Texan in jeopardy, he had had to make preparations for another duty and knew Jubal Branch would be available to provide any protection that might prove necessary.

The second, potentially as important, task that the young sergeant had been given was a further example of the foresight employed in devising Company "Z" 's plan of campaign. Having surmised that the presence of a known Texas Ranger claiming an acquaintance with, and interest in, the welfare of the geologist would arouse suspicion, probably to the extent of causing Branch to be followed when he left the town to ensure he did not slip back instead of going straight to San Antonio as he had announced was his intention, Major Tragg had thought up a way to counter the eventuality. The idea was based on Sergeant Swift-Eagle's estimation of which local peace officer would be sent to keep Branch under observation and his assertion that, if he was correct, the man in question would prove too stupid to realize something other than an accident had caused the blowout. He had also suggested what action Callaghan might take after making the coupé fit to travel.

However, the success of the plan hinged upon whether a tire could be punctured!

Although Scrapton had only acquired the Holland & Holland .375 Magnum rifle shortly before joining Company "Z," he had attained sufficient knowledge of its handling traits and proficiency in its use to be considered the best man for the vitally important duty. Nor, in his opinion, could he have employed a more suitable firearm to carry it out. Not only was it fitted with the latest type of telescopic sight, which permitted the greatest utilization of the powerful cartridge's potential for accuracy at long ranges, but it also had a Moran silencer[25] attached to the muzzle, and there was no superior device of that nature available.

Possessing hereditary instincts that supplemented the thorough training in such specialized work he had been given during his formative years and that, in part, had gained him selection for Company "Z," Scrapton had known what precautions he must take against being detected. He had chosen his firing position with care, making sure that he would be able to shoot from its concealment. As soon as he was satisfied he would not need to fire again, he had withdrawn the Holland & Holland from the forked stick upon which it had rested as an aid to aiming until it too was completely hidden by the foliage. Now, watching what was happening on the road, he was convinced that his actions had not betrayed his position. His fear that the damage to the tire might arouse the deputy's suspicions had not yet material-

25. "Moran silencer": designed by banker-financier Leo Moran, see *The Clue of the Silver Key* by Edgar Wallace. Although Mr. Moran never had his invention manufactured commercially, as is indicated in *"Cap" Fog, Texas Ranger, Meet Mr. J. G. Reeder,* he allowed several to be produced for men he considered were making significant contributions to British law enforcement. Some of those that were allocated to the Three Just Men were presented to various prominent peace officers they met during their tour of the United States, Major Benson Tragg and Sheriff Jackson Marsden Fog being two of the fortunate recipients. J.T.E.

ized, but he had been told he might be fortunate in that respect and could only hope for the best.

"Looks like Dave's called it right about him so far," the young sergeant mused, as Callaghan removed and shoved aside the punctured tire, still without submitting it to any examination. Glancing affectionately at the weapon he was holding, he continued, "Dutchy-boy, you're one hell of a straight-shooting gun. Happen he'd been alive to see you-all, I reckon Grandpappy Lon[26] would have wanted to trade me that old 'One of a Thousand' of his for you."[27]

Having duplicated a sentiment that had frequently occurred to him when using the Holland & Holland rifle—a present from his parents and godfather, Sheriff Jackson Fog, to celebrate his promotion to sergeant—in less demanding conditions, Scrapton settled down to maintain his surveillance. While he was ready to employ the patience he had learned was required for the kind of work he was doing, he hoped that he would not be compelled to puncture another of the coupé's tires. Even if the deputy was as incompetent as Swift-Eagle had suggested and events appeared

26. As the author's regular readers may have deduced, Mark Loncey Scrapton was the grandson of Loncey Dalton Ysabel—better known as the Ysabel Kid—who was, along with Dusty Fog and Mark Counter, a leading member of the OD Connected ranch's floating outfit and a noted marksman with a rifle. Sergeant Scrapton had adopted the sobriquet "Blood" on Company "Z"'s first assignment, as it had been a favorite alias of his illustrious forebear; see *Hell in the Palo Duro; Go Back to Hell* and Part Three, The Ysabel Kid in "Comanche Blood," *The Hard Riders*. J.T.E.
27. When manufacturing the extremely popular Winchester Model 1873, the makers selected those having barrels found to shoot with exceptional accuracy to be fitted with set-triggers and given a special, fine finish. Originally, these were inscribed "1 of 1,000," but this was later changed to script, "One of a Thousand." The title was a considerable understatement, as only one hundred and thirty-six out of a total production of 720,610 rifles qualified for the distinction. Those of a grade lower in quality were given the name "One of a Hundred," but only seven were so designated. The practice commenced in 1875 and was discontinued in '78, allegedly because the management decided it was not good policy to suggest the company produced different grades of gun. The rifle to which Sergeant Scrapton referred was won by his maternal grandfather, the Ysabel Kid, at the first Cochise County Fair; see *Gun Wizard*. J.T.E.

to be bearing out, he would be unlikely to overlook the cause of a second blowout. In fact, he was almost certain to become suspicious if another one should occur. However, if the need arose, the young sergeant was confident that he could fire with equal accuracy and produce the desired effect.

What was more, although they were not yet as close as their respective maternal and paternal grandfathers had been, Scrapton and Alvin Fog had become good friends since their enrollment in Company "Z." So, knowing that the small Texan's life might depend upon preventing Callaghan discovering that Branch was rejoining the other members of the company instead of going to San Antonio, Scrapton was willing to employ even more severe measures to keep the meeting a secret.

"Where the hell are those three goddamned drunken sons-of-bitches who tried to jump me at the hotel?"

Listening to the wrathful words and staring at the speaker, as he brought his feet down from resting on his desk, Sheriff Healey realized that the inquiry he had been warned would be forthcoming was taking place. He also concluded that the way could be opening for him to do as he had intended, during the open phases of the conversation that had followed the abortive assault in the hotel's barroom. Having burst into his office at the jailhouse without even knocking on the door, the geologist had delivered the demand for information in a manner to which he might be justified in taking exception. Nor, as his deputy's continued absence suggested that Jubal Branch had spoken the truth about going to San Antonio, was it likely anybody would inquire too closely into his reason for attacking Hollingshead in the immediate future, and provided he took precautions, the news might not even reach the elderly sergeant at all.

Even though much of it was assumed and in no way blinded him to the risk he was taking, there was an understandable reason for the small Texan's angry behavior.

After his partner had dissuaded the sheriff from arresting him and they had taken their departure, Alvin had requested that he was brought another meal. Having set the overturned table upright while the conversation was taking place, the Mexican

waiter had obeyed with an alacrity that was a marked contrast to
his previous reluctance. The eagerness with which he had responded prevented Softly, who had belatedly thought of how the
geologist could be rendered temporarily incapable of visiting
Brixton's Canyon without the need to resort to physical violence,
from adding what was known in some circles as a Mickey Finn
to the highly spiced food.[28] Although the small Texan had been
unaware that such measures were being contemplated, he had
eaten without his previous fear of the chili con carne receiving
noxious additives. After the waiter's reaction to his treatment of
the three hard cases, Alvin Fog was convinced that the waiter
would have warned him if this had been done.

Having eaten without suffering any ill effects, or further interruption, Alvin had returned to his room. He had found the
thread attached to the door unbroken, so felt sure his property
had not been searched. Going in, he had kept watch from the
window that overlooked the main street. Seeing Branch driving
out of the town, followed a short while later by the dilapidated
black Dodge Brothers' Four coupé, which he had noticed parked
in the alley alongside the jailhouse when he had arrived, he had
concluded that Major Tragg had once more guessed accurately
about the opposition's reactions. He hoped Mark Scrapton
would be able to do as instructed.

Although he did not anticipate that there would be any further attempts to attack him in the hotel, Alvin had decided it
would be advisable for him to remain in his room for the rest of
the afternoon. As a precaution in case he was wrong in his assumption, he had taken off his Norfolk jacket and opened the
special suitcase. Removing the shoulder holster and one of the

28. Mickey Finn, also known as "little Michael," or a "shoo fly": a strong
purgative such as is given to constipated horses, or a barbiturate, in the
form of a pill or a potion, administered by bartenders to recalcitrant customers. According to Alvin Dustine (Cap) Fog's records, it was the former
variety Abel Softly intended to use, as the effects could be mistaken for a
severe attack of dysentery. The late Lou Clayton, partner and business manager of the comedian Jimmy Durante, was noted for his ability at "slipping
a mickey" when the occasion demanded; see Chapter Six, "The Soft-Shoe
Dancer," *Schnozzola, The Story of Jimmy Durante,* by Gene Fowler. J.T.E.

Colt Government Model automatic pistols from their place of concealment, he had donned the former. Slipping a fully loaded magazine into the butt of the weapon, he had cocked the action, and applying the manual safety without the need for conscious thought, placed it in the rig's retention springs. Putting on the jacket to prevent anybody who should happen to pay a visit discovering he was now armed, he had laid on the bed, and knowing he could be in for a strenuous night, he had managed to take a nap.

On waking, a glance at his wristwatch informed the small Texan he had slept for almost three hours. Feeling peckish rather than hungry, but considering he should make sure of having a good meal before commencing the night's activities, he had decided it could be safer to eat somewhere other than the hotel. So, replacing the thread as he left, he descended to the lobby. The desk clerk was nowhere in sight and a glance informed him that the barroom was almost deserted, not that he had any intention of going in. He felt sure that his former assailants would not be there, but he was disinclined to leave himself open to further measures intended to keep him from carrying out the work which it was believed had brought him to Grouperville.

On walking out of the hotel, Alvin discovered that Softly had adopted less aggressive tactics to circumvent him. Not only were the right front and rear tires of the Duesenberg deflated, they and the spare wheel on the offside running board had been torn so badly by some sharp instrument that there was no hope of repairing the damage. Nor, on visiting the town's only service station, had he been able to obtain replacements. Showing signs of nervousness that had reminded him of the desk clerk and waiter before lunch, the proprietor had claimed there was nothing available suitable for use on his vehicle.

Alvin had intended to travel in the Duesenberg to the vicinity of the canyon, but he knew it was no use protesting over what he suspected was a lie. However, before going in search of an alternative means of transport, he felt he should behave as might be expected of Hollingshead after having discovered the damage to the vehicle. Even before noticing the sheriff fingering the sap, he had not expected to be dealing with an honest peace officer.

Having found Softly in the bar had led him to assume that Healey and his assailants were listening from the manager's office while he was speaking with the desk clerk and the former's prompt arrival had confirmed the supposition. So he had known that paying such a visit to the sheriff's office could prove dangerous, but he wanted to find out whether Branch's warnings about his important and influential connections had been heeded. He had also hoped to discover if the deputy had returned, and should this have happened, what information had been delivered.

Studying the indignant face of his visitor, Healey elected to forgo the opportunity with which he was being presented. He told himself that he was acting as Softly would want by remaining passive, but he knew there was another motive guiding him; a strong instinct for self-preservation. Although the omission was excusable under the circumstances, he had not noticed that the geologist was now armed. It would have taken far keener eyes than his to have detected the carefully designed holster carrying the Colt Government Model automatic pistol. His decision was caused by remembering how the small young man confronting him had defeated three hard cases he would have been reluctant to tackle. So, being alone in the building, he did not relish the prospect of attempting to attack such a competent antagonist.

"What'd you be wanting to know for, *Mister* Hollingshead?" the sheriff inquired, as his unwanted caller showed signs of impatience over his delay in answering.

"The tires of my Duesenberg have been ripped wide open," Alvin replied, deducing from the use of his assumed name and the honorific that his identity was not doubted and watching for any indication of how his news was being received.

"They have, huh?" Healey said, contriving to sound surprised in spite of realizing what the assistant bartender had been talking about in Softly's living quarters. "Did you see *them* doing it?"

"No," Alvin admitted.

"Then how'd you know it was them?" Healey challenged.

"I can't think of anybody else who might have a reason," the small Texan countered. "Not who's here in town, anyway. Do folks often have their cars' tires cut around here?"

"Hell, no!" the sheriff answered emphatically. "Nothing like that's ever happened afore. Only, I can't see as how it could've been them boys as did it. They pulled out as soon as the doctor had took a look at the one you hurt so bad—not that I'm blaming you for doing it, way things was, mind."

"That's white of you," Alvin asserted, deciding that Branch's warnings had been taken to heart and feeling sure the deputy had not returned, or if he had it was without bringing news of Company "Z"'s presence in the neighborhood. "But couldn't one of them have done it before they went?"

"I don't reckon so," Healey replied, then decided to improvise a reason. "I went around to make sure they left."

"Maybe one of them sneaked back?"

"I dunno about that."

"Why not go and ask them?"

"Their place's a good ten miles off, and I've no way of getting there just now. This here's a poor county and we've only got one car 'n' my deputy's using it."

"How soon will you get it back?"

"Not afore sundown, at the soonest," Healey guessed. "Was you figuring on going someplace in your car today?"

"It wouldn't matter if I wanted to," Alvin declared in a bitter tone, giving no indication of noticing the satisfaction that the sheriff was clearly experiencing over his predicament. "The tires are ruined and I can't get them replaced until the feller at the service station has some more brought in from San Antonio, or maybe Austin." He paused, then went on as if the thought had just occurred to him, "Where's the livery barn, sheriff?"

"*Livery barn?*" Healey repeated, losing the smug expression as he considered the implications of the question.

"That's what I want," Alvin confirmed, concluding that the possibility of him hiring a horse had not occurred to the local peace officer, and hoping Softly had been equally lacking in perception as he remembered the behavior of the service station's owner. "I suppose there is one in this godforsaken town?"

"Sure there is," Healey admitted. "You ain't figuring on going after them boys, looking for evens, are you?"

"No!" Alvin stated definitely. "But I want to do some hunting while I'm here and figure I'll have better results riding than on foot."

"That's for sure, there's not many wild critters close in," the sheriff conceded, trying to sound as if he accepted the explanation. "The barn's on South Creek, out back of town. Only, I don't know whether there'll be any hosses for hire. Do you want me to come and show you the way?"

"There's no call for that," the small Texan replied. "By the way, is Sergeant Branch still around?"

"He pulled out a while back, headed for San Antone," the sheriff answered. "Was you wanting him?"

"I thought I'd buy him a meal for helping out the way he did," Alvin explained. "And you, too, of course."

"Like I said, he's left," Healey said hurriedly, showing more alarm than pleasure at the invitation. "And I'm right busy just now!"

"I'll have to let you take a rain check on it in that case," Alvin drawled, receiving a warning from the other's reaction that his supicions with regard to the food at the hotel might be justified. "Well, as I've nothing else to do, I think I'll go and see if I can get a horse before I eat. Maybe you'll be able to join me then."

"I don't reckon I'll be through that quick," Healey replied, his lack of enthusiasm even more noticeable.

"We'll make it tomorrow sometime, then," Alvin promised with assumed cheerfulness. "Sorry I bust in on you like I did, Sheriff, but I was riled about my tires. I still think it could have been one of those three who did it, but I reckon I can count on *you* to see justice is done."

Leaving the jailhouse, the small Texan did not do as he had claimed straightaway. Instead, although he crossed the street and entered an alley that would allow him to reach his destination, he only went halfway along it. Turning when satisfied that he could not be seen from the sheriff's office, he walked back and peered cautiously around the corner of the building on the right. He was not kept waiting for long before Healey emerged from the jailhouse, and as he expected, hurried along the opposite sidewalk in the direction of Soskice's Hotel.

"I surely do admire a loyal son-of-a-bitch, even when he's as crooked as a sidewinder's trail," Alvin mused, after having watched the sheriff disappear into the lobby and he was resuming his interrupted journey. "Only, given a smidgin of good Texas luck, you'll be too late to stop me getting something to ride."

"Gee, mister, I'm real sorry," the hostler said, acting in an almost identical fashion to the proprietor of the service station, when the small Texan made the request that had brought him to the livery barn. "All our riding hosses are out grazing on the range and won't none of them be back afore tomorrow."

"What time are you expecting them to be brought in?" Alvin inquired, deducing that—unlike the sheriff—Softly had anticipated and countered his attempt to procure an alternative means of reaching the canyon.

"B-by noon, I reckon," the hostler replied dubiously, having received no instructions with regard to how he should answer such a query.

"That'll be all right with me," Alvin drawled, hiding his disappointment at the unforeseen eventuality although he knew it could prevent him from carrying out his next part in the assignment. "Will you save me one that's gun-steady? I'll be using him for hunting."

"I—I don't know if we've got one—!" the hostler answered.

"I'll come and take a look, anyway," Alvin stated.

Making no attempt to press the matter further, the small Texan strolled from the barn. He glanced around, without seeing anybody, as he set off toward the small grove of cottonwood trees that separated the establishment from the main street. Before he had taken his third step, he heard something from the left and slightly to his rear.

It was similar to the clicking made when a revolver was being cocked!

Instantly, Alvin swung in the appropriate direction. While doing so, he commenced what he hoped would be a sufficiently rapid protective action to keep him from being shot. At the same time, he was thankful that he had taken certain precautionary measures since leaving the sheriff's office.

During the interview with Healey, Alvin had kept his jacket buttoned to lessen the chance of his armament being noticed and perhaps used as an excuse for hostile action. However, he had had nothing more reliable than the sheriff's word that his would-be assailants were no longer in the town, and he knew that if they had remained, they might be seeking revenge. He was equally alert to the possibility that, after Softly had been informed of his intentions, a violent attempt might be made to prevent him from reaching the livery barn. With such contingencies in mind, he had unfastened the jacket as he was entering the alley opposite the jailhouse and had left it that way. So there was nothing to impede the passage of his right hand as it sped across to draw the Colt.

Even as the small Texan completed his rapid turn, with the automatic's barrel pointing in the required direction and his thumb depressing the manual safety catch, he wondered why no shot had been fired at him. Then he discovered that there was no need for concern and a threat to his existence was not intended.

"You done that *real* slick, Mr.—Hollingshead—is it?" remarked the elderly man who had answered to the name "Tombstone" in the barroom. Stepping from behind the end of the building as he was speaking, he dropped the twig that he had bent so that it crackled and conveyed the impression of a revolver being cocked. "Fact being, like when you-all was picking up the toes[29] of those three knobheads at the hotel, way you done it put me in mind of somebody I used to know."

29. "Picking up the toes": a colloquialism for inflicting punishment. It was derived from the cowhands' roping term meaning to make a catch by throwing the lariat's loop so as to trap an animal's forefeet. Generally, the method was employed to punish a horse that persisted in breaking out of the wrangler's rope corral when part of a remuda. While dangerous to carry out, the throw was used on a basis of kill or cure as the other members of the remuda could pick up the habit if the perpetrator was allowed to go unchecked. A description of how such a throw was made and its effect is given in *Trail Boss*. J.T.E.

"Who might that be?" Alvin inquired, knowing "knobhead" was a derogatory term for a mule, or a stupid and uncouth person, as he was applying the safety catch and returning the pistol to its holster.

"Colonel Dusty Fog, no less," Tombstone answered. "You-all wouldn't be kin of his, now would you?"

"What makes you think I am?" Alvin challenged.

"You feature him a whole heap," the elderly man replied.

"Go on," Alvin scoffed, he hoped convincingly. "I've always heard tell that Colonel Fog was real big—"

"Which same's *way* out, *happen* that's what you-all heard," Tombstone declared, looking amiably skeptical. "He was about your height and build, with blondish hair same as your'n when he was younger. Should I need to tell *you*, that is."

"Are you saying I'm lying?" the small Texan growled, simulating indignation and making a mental note to avoid having his hair dyed blond in the future unless it was unavoidable.

"Nope," Tombstone corrected calmly, still exuding friendliness. "Just playing your cards close to the vest. Which I don't blame you-all none for doing, happen I'm guessing right about you."

"And what are you *guessing*?" Alvin wanted to know, although he had a suspicion that he could supply the answer.

"That you're not what, or who, *some* folks reckon you are," the elderly man obliged. "Only, was I asked and happen I'm right, I'd say we'd best go somewheres a mite more private-like afore we get to talking turkey."

"Have we anything to talk about?" Alvin questioned, despite a growing conviction that the other was to be trusted.

"I reckon we've plenty, should I be calling the play right," Tombstone stated, with no suggestion of resenting the interrogation. "Because, should I be, I'm the feller's wrote the letter that got you-all—and Jubal Branch, likely—sent here."

"That being the case, we'd best talk turkey," Alvin affirmed. "And I'll go along with you that we'd better do it somewhere we won't attract attention. How about going into the barn?"

"No," Tombstone refused. "Bernie Hislop, the owner, can be trusted, but I'd sooner not get him into high water. Happen you

can come around to the back door of the post office in half a
hour, we'll be safe enough there."

"I'll be th—!" Alvin commenced.

"Yes, sir, Mr. Hollingshead," Tombstone interrupted, raisin
his voice and pointing to the northeast. "Happen you're lookin
for some good hunting, you should try out on the Forked Bo
range." Then he swung his gaze beyond the small Texan an
raised his right hand in greeting. "Howdy, Marty. I was ju
telling Mr. Hollingshead here there's nothing to hunt in the bad
lands."

All through the conversation, Alvin had noticed that the e
derly man was keeping the cottonwood grove under observation
He had not looked that way since swinging around, or hear
anything, but realized that somebody was coming and suspecte
it was not a person who might be considered friendly. Turning
he gazed at a medium-sized, thickset man clad in a collarles
white shirt, Levi's pants and heavy, low-heeled boots.

"Was you reckoning on going out to the badlands?" the new
comer demanded, rather than asked, his bearing arrogant.

"I hadn't made up my mind," Alvin replied, "not knowing th
country hereabouts."

"Like I said, Mr. Hollingshead," Tombstone remarked
"You'll have better luck anywhere else in the county."

"I'll keep it in mind," Alvin promised. "Only, I won't be go
ing *anywhere* until the horses are brought in tomorrow. Thank
for the advice, anyway."

Strolling toward the grove, the small Texan decided that th
newcomer must be one of Softly's employees, who had been sen
to ensure that the owner of the livery barn carried out the in
structions that had been given. He did not know, however, tha
he had been talking to the man who had torn open the Duesen
berg's tires.

"Nobody's watching you, young man, are they?" Mrs. Berkle
asked worriedly, having opened the door that gave access to th
living quarters at the rear of the post office, in answer to Alvi
Fog's knock.

"No, ma'am," the small Texan affirmed. "I've made sure of it."

"Come in, then," the woman ordered.

"Something tells me you could be a Texas Ranger," hinted Tombstone, who was sitting at the table in the spotlessly clean dining-room, after the visitor had entered and been settled in another chair.

"That something's telling it right," Alvin confirmed.

"But I thought you fellers could only come into a town if you was asked by the marshal, or the sheriff," Mrs. Berkley objected. "Which Healey wouldn't have done."

"We've been given special authority to come here without an official invitation, ma'am," Alvin explained. "But I've no *written* proof and I can only hope you'll take my word for it."

"Whose word are we taking?" the elderly man inquired.

"I'm Sergeant Alvin Dustine Fog," the small Texan introduced, then smiled and added, "But I've been told I'm a heap better looking than Grandpappy Dusty was."

"Would you-all've been buying drinks for whoever told you *afore* they said it?" Tombstone asked, also smiling and extending a work-hardened right hand. "No matter. My name's Gabriel Wisdom Cole—"

"And your daddy was U.S. Marshal Solly Cole,"[30] Alvin supplemented, shaking hands with a man who had followed his father's footsteps and become an equally famous peace officer. "But how come—?"

"How come I'm living here in this one-hoss town and working as a gravedigger?" Tombstone finished the question for the small Texan. "I wanted a quiet life after I turned in my badge is why. Maybe you don't get young hotheads coming after you to see if you're as good with a gun as they've been told, like in Pappy 'n'

30. Some details of the career of U.S. Marshal Solomon Wisdom (Solly) Cole are given in *Calamity Spells Trouble*—although, while producing this title, the author had not learned Marshal Cole's full name—Part Seven, Calamity Jane series, "Deadwood, August 2nd, 1876," *J.T.'s Hundredth* and Part Six, Martha "Calamity Jane" Canary, in "Mrs. Wild Bill," *J.T.'s Ladies.* J.T.E.

Colonel Dusty's day, but when you've picked up the kind of reputation I did for doing your job well, you make enemies, and it's a whole heap more peaceable happen they don't know where you're at. So I'll be obliged if you don't let on we've met 'n' stick to calling me 'Tombstone,' same's everybody else around here."

"You can count on it—Tombstone," Alvin promised. "Now, what's going on in town and out at Brixton's Canyon?"

"Hogan Turtle's took over the town, starting with the hotel," the elderly man replied bitterly. "Now everybody as runs a business here, even my boss, pays off to him through Abe Softly."

"How about the canyon?" Alvin inquired, watching the woman nodding agreement to the retired peace officer's statement.

"There you've got me," Tombstone confessed. "But, whatever it is, you can bet all you've got that Turtle and Softly are up to their ears in it."

"You've no idea what it could be?" the small Texan persisted.

"Nary a notion," Tombstone insisted. "Except it's big enough for them to be ready to kill to stop folks finding out."

"The young cowhand?" Alvin guessed.

"Young Ewen Silvers," the elderly man agreed. "What happened to him got beyond just somebody playing at ghosts to scare folks off. So I figured it was time something was done to find out what the hell's going on out there. Which's why I wrote to—well, I reckon you-all know as much about *that* as I do."

"I wouldn't want to bet on it." Alvin grinned, for he had not been told to whom the letter was delivered any more than he had been informed of its writer's identity. Then he became more serious and continued, "Are you sure he was killed in the canyon?"

"I'd say it's more 'yes' than 'no' to that," Tombstone answered. "Only I don't have even a smidgin of proof on it. All I can say for certain-sure is he wasn't killed the way that lard-gutted son-of-a—sheriff of our'n allowed it'd happened."

"So you said in your letter," the small Texan drawled.

"There's some as would say the answer could be at the canyon," Tombstone commented.

"That's why I'm here pretending to be a geologist," Alvin replied. "Trouble being, I've no way of getting out there. Somebody's slashed open three of my car's tires and the jasper at the service station *says* he doesn't have any to replace them. And when I went to hire a horse from the livery barn, I was told they've all been sent to graze on the range."

"Sid Joplin and Bernie Hislop aren't bad hombres, but they know better than to go again' Abe Softly's orders," Tombstone apologized. " 'Specially as they've both got places as would take fire real easy should they do it."

"They'd have behaved differently if they'd known you was a sergeant in the Texas Rangers," Mrs. Berkley supplemented.

"Likely, ma'am," Alvin conceded. "But I'd sooner that neither they nor anybody else outside this room learn who and what I am. By the way, I hope having me here won't put you-all in any danger."

"Not so long as nobody saw you come in, or sees you going out," the woman declared confidently. "Mr. Softly's got good cause to reckon he can trust me. After all, you could say I'm on his payroll."

"It was *my* idea," Tombstone asserted, exuding protective defiance. "I cottoned on to what could be happening when all of a sudden Ollie Soskice started firing some of the folks as had been working for him since way back and taking on longhorns like Softly. Not long after, Softly got to hinting to Becky about how he sometimes'd be getting telephone calls he'd sooner nobody else was listening to. She wouldn't never've agreed to leave the switchboard untended when such calls come in, even happen she'd've believed they was only from a stockbrocker he deals with like he reckoned, only *I* talked her into doing it. Sure, she took something from him for walking out—"

"I've *never* took *money* from him, mind!" Mrs. Berkley injected, with an air of worried virtue, staring at the small Texan as if searching for his reaction to the admissions. "Only small things, like a new hat or such, from the store."

"We've listed *everything* and put money by to pay back Ollie Soskice should we be able to get Softly and his bunch jailed, or run out of town," Tombstone went on. "It had to be that way, Becky taking those things, I mean. Softly'd likely've got suspicious had she done it free. Anyway, it wasn't often that the switchboard was left completely untended. If I was next door, which I most times was, Becky'd wigwag to me and I'd sneak around the back way while she was going out front for Softly to know she'd left, and I'd go on the Erie hoping to learn something I could use again' 'em. Which I never did, 'cept enough to know that damned 'ghost' wasn't Brixton come back from the dead."

"They never mentioned what was doing at the canyon?" Alvin asked.

"They *could* have," Tombstone admitted ruefully. "Only most all the calls was in some foreign language."

"Most likely either Norwegian or Swedish," Mrs. Berkley offered. "If you speak one, you can get by in the other. I mind it was just after Softly found out my folks were Norwegian and I spoke the language that he started hinting as how he'd take it kind if I'd leave the switchboard untended once in a while."

"And I said she should, when she told me, or they'd likely find some way of getting rid of her 'n' putting in somebody who'd be more obliging," Tombstone continued. "It wasn't until the first call come that we found out Softly and the other jasper was talking a language I don't understand. Fact being, it was only when that shyster's clerk, Plant, called as they spoke English. Which wasn't often. I sort of got took with the notion that him 'n' Softly weren't what you'd call *bueno* amigos."

"I've heard tell Mr. Plant takes some folks that way," Alvin drawled, having been informed by Major Tragg of the animosity the lawyer's assistant aroused amongst those with whom he came in contact.

"Seems like you've heard a whole heap," Tombstone remarked, eyeing the small Texan speculatively and preventing him from asking whether the conversations between Softly and Plant had been informative. "How long did you-all say you've been a Ranger?"

"I didn't say," Alvin pointed out. "But it hasn't been for long."

"Promotion must've come quick," Tombstone commented. "You making sergeant already 'n' all."

"Could have been family influence," Alvin suggested.

"*Could* have," the elderly man agreed unemotionally. "What company did you-all say you was with?"

"I didn't," the small Texan repeated. "But Major Tragg's my commanding officer. You'll not have heard of the company, it's only newly formed."

"It's none of my never-mind, anyways," Tombstone declared, but without any suggestion of suspicion, deducing that the young man must have sound reasons for being reticent. "Anyway, Plant made a call today. Which's how I got to know about you-all being here, Mr. Hollingshead, and what you're reckoned to have come for. The Forked Box boys had passed word they wanted to see me at the hotel, but I'd aimed to drop by and see what Softly had in mind for you. I'd a pretty fair notion what was coming when I saw that table set up for eating and was trying to figure out how to stop it. Only you and old Jubal Branch saved me from needing to bill in." A frosty grin came to his face and he continued, "Like I said out to the livery barn, way you fight puts me in mind of Colonel Dusty."

"He had me taught some of his tricks," Alvin explained briefly.

"That's as maybe!" Mrs. Berkley put in, clearly having no time for what she considered to be masculine digressions. "What I want to know is, how do you aim to go about getting us our town back?"

"I wish I knew, ma'am," Alvin admitted. "Doing it won't be easy."

"Why not?" the woman challenged indignantly. "You've seen and been told about what's happening here."

"I have, ma'am," Alvin replied. "But, trouble is, I've no *proof* that Softly's broken the law."

"That's as right as the off side of a hoss, Becky," Tombstone seconded, before the woman could make the comment she was obviously contemplating. "Even what I heard today wasn't anything that'd pass as acceptable evidence in court. No names were mentioned to connect Softly with Mulley and the Skinners. And knowing him, I don't reckon as he cut open young Fog's tires hisself. Nor that anybody'd admit to seeing whoever it was did."

"How about Sid Joplin and Bernie Hislop?" Mrs. Berkley

asked the small Texan. "They was both told they hadn't to do any business with you-all."

"We might *know* that," Tombstone answered, before Alvin could speak. "But they're not going to stand up and admit it in court."

"Not if was Sheriff Healey's put them there," the woman admitted. "But they would if they knew Softly had been arrested by a Texas Ranger."

"Trouble is, ma'am, even a Texas Ranger has to have *proof* before he can make an arrest," the small Texan explained. "And like Tombstone said, we haven't got anything stronger than suspicion against Softly."

"He's been having me leave the switchboard untended," Mrs. Berkley pointed out.

"And unless Tombstone's heard Plant saying something incriminating to him," Alvin countered, "he'd just stick to his story that he didn't want to chance you hearing confidential information from his stockbroker."

"Gabe heard him telling Plant what he was going to have done to you," Mrs. Berkley declared, looking at the retired peace officer for confirmation.

"I heard him say's how he was going to have Mr. Hollingshead stopped from going out to the canyon, was all," Tombstone corrected. "Sure, Plant said something about there hadn't got to be no more killings 'cause he was more again' their'n such the cowhand, but it'd only be my word again' their'n such was said." Pausing, he slapped his right hand on his thigh and went on, "Well, I'll be 'ternally damned if I hadn't forgot how there was something said about a collection being made tonight."

"Where?" Alvin asked eagerly.

"Out at the canyon, way they talked," Tombstone supplied. "But there wasn't no mention of what it might be, or when it'd be picked up."

"Blast the luck!" Alvin growled. "Seeing that ghosts don't show themselves in the daytime, I was figuring on going out there tonight."

"What's stopping you?" Tombstone inquired.

"It's not that I couldn't walk the ten or so miles to get there,"

Alvin claimed. "But should things go wrong, I'm not what you'd call enthusiastic about the notion of having to run back, or trying to follow whoever collects what on foot."

"Your daddy 'n' Colonel Dusty never took kind to being afoot, so it's likely born in you-all," Tombstone drawled. "And happen that's all that's stopping you, you can start figuring on going. I've got me a hoss that'll get you there and back easy."

"I can't ask you to take the chance of lending it to me," Alvin protested.

"*Lending* it!" Tombstone exclaimed. "Who-all said anything about *lending* it to you? Not *me*. But can I help it, happen I've got him saddled up ready to go out hunting and some sneaky young sidewinder takes off with him?"

"I reckon you can't at that," the small Texan admitted. "Where'll he be, should that sneaky young sidewinder come looking?"

"Yeah! Come on out 'n' show yourself, you goddamned ha'nt. Here's *one* Forked Box hand as ain't scared of you-all!"

Swinging from the saddle of Tombstone's big bay gelding at the conclusion of the challenge he had yelled, Alvin Fog was confident that he would pass as what he was pretending to be. He had altered the crown of his Stetson until it was more suitable to be worn by a Texan, and apart from his footwear—which was unlikely to be noticed in the far from extensive illumination given by a half moon—was dressed as a cowhand. His actions while approaching and dismounting, aided by his tone, suggested he had been drinking.

After acquiring all the information about Brixton's Canyon and its surroundings possessed by the retired peace officer, the small Texan had ensured he was not observed as he left the living quarters of the post office. In addition to the facts he had been given, he had discovered why Tombstone was willing to accept his bona fides in spite of the questions about his length of service. The trust had been fostered by Branch's participation in the affair, which the elderly man had declared was convincing evidence that he was who and what he claimed to be.

Pleased by the tribute to his partner's integrity, Alvin had

made his way to the town's small café. In passing, he had noticed
that the Dodge Brothers' Four coupé belonging to the sheriff's
office was nowhere in sight and concluded the deputy had not
returned. This implied that Sergeant Swift-Eagle's summation of
Callaghan's character was correct in so far as his failing to notice
how the blowout had occurred was concerned, but wrong in
claiming he would use the mishap as an excuse to stop following
Branch. However, the small Texan felt sure his companions had
dealt with the latter contingency and hoped the deputy's continued absence would not arouse the sheriff's suspicions. There had
been nothing to suggest it had when Alvin had met Healey on
reaching the hotel. On the other hand, the sheriff's obvious disappointment and the desk clerk's barely concealed relief as he
had explained why he could not make good the invitation extended at the jailhouse had suggested his fears about the food
being tampered with, if he ate on the premises, could have been
justified.

Telling the clerk that he intended to have an early night and
asking to be called at seven o'clock in the morning, Alvin had
gone upstairs. Finding the thread on the door still in position, he
had decided Softly did not doubt his assumed identity and had
seen no point in having his belongings searched. There was nothing about the appearance of the room to indicate it had been
entered during his absence and the thread replaced on departure
by the one who had paid the visit.

Before making his preparations for setting out later that night,
the small Texan had not restricted himself merely to locking the
door. He had jammed the room's only chair under the handle,
making an unauthorized entry even more difficult. With that
precaution taken, he had discarded the spectacles and changed
his clothing for a dark-blue shirt, a pair of Levi's pants and a
waist-length brown leather jacket that he had brought in his
baggage. In addition to putting four fully loaded magazines in
the latter's pockets, he had tucked the second Colt automatic
pistol in his waistband. Although he had placed a cartridge in
the Very pistol, he had decided against taking more ammunition
for it. With everything he could do at that time completed, he

had turned out the light and laid on the bed to wait for darkness to fall.

Despite being encumbered by carrying the Very pistol suspended on his back with the strap of its holster, as well as his more formal armament, leaving the hotel undetected had presented few difficulties for Alvin. Having made sure there was nobody keeping watch, he had used the rope provided in the room as a means of escape in case of fire and had descended from the second window into the alley. As he had left, he contrived to draw down the window until it was almost closed. When he was on the ground, he had liberated the loop of the rope from the hook on the wall to which it was attached, and pulling it down, he had carried it away with him to lessen the chance of his departure being discovered from outside the building.

Collecting the bay gelding from where Tombstone had left it hitched at the rear of the undertaker's premises, after having ascertained that Healey's deputy still had not returned, the small Texan had ridden from Grouperville without being challenged. The journey to the vicinity of Brixton's Canyon had proved equally uneventful. Although he had waited in concealment for over an hour, his hope that the mysterious collection would take place had not materialized. Nor had he seen or heard anything of the rest of Company "Z," but that had not caused him any anxiety. The plan called for them to approach as near as possible without allowing their presence to be detected, and remain in hiding until he discharged the Very pistol before closing in. If there was no need for the signal to be made, they would withdraw before daylight, and contacting him in the morning, make fresh arrangements. His decision to move forward was not caused by impatience, but through his belief that doing so was the best course to adopt.

After delivering the challenge and resuming his advance on foot, leading the gelding, Alvin glanced at the Very pistol. Finding it bounced uncomfortably while he was riding, he had hung it on the saddle horn and forgot it when leaving his hiding place. For a moment, he thought of returning it to his shoulders, but concluded this might be inadvisable. Although he had seen nothing, his instincts suggested he was being watched. So he considered that if—as was likely—the observer was using an aid to vision, the donning of the signaling device might prevent the "ghost" from being displayed. It could also lead to the unseen watcher shooting instead of merely trying to frighten him away.

Despite the poor light and the sheer walls being in heavy shadow, the small Texan could see along the bottom of the canyon until it curved beyond the stream. Not that there was anything to attract his attention as he walked into the entrance. Then, floating a few feet from the ground and to the accompaniment of an eerie wailing, something white, flapping, and suffused by a pale glow came into view around the bend. Seeming to be moving of its own volition, it drew nearer until hovering above the widest part of the water without making so much as a ripple on the surface.

Despite all he had been told about the way in which the "ghost" behaved, Alvin had to admit he was unable to detect the means by which it moved. Not that he devoted much thought to the subject. Even as he was starting to draw the automatic from his waistband, the erstwhile obedient gelding halted, and letting out a snort of alarm, tossed back its head. The reaction was only brief, but although it did not attempt to bolt, it showed such a reluctance to follow him that he decided against trying to impose his will. Instead, he released the split-ended reins. Like most range horses, the bay had been trained to stand still when they were dangling loose from its bit.

Pausing only long enough to make sure the gelding was responding to its training, Alvin resumed his interrupted advance. It was his intention to try to capture the "ghost" and produce it as evidence that would allow him, in his capacity as the long-lost cousin's agent, to have the area searched in the daylight by the Texas Rangers, who would arrive at Grouperville, ostensibly merely in passing, the following morning.

"Hell!" the small Texan breathed, looking at the shape as it remained fluttering and wailing over the center of the stream and remembered the identification document concealed in his right boot. "I hope those trick heels are waterproof!"

The sentiment came to an end abruptly as thoughts, of such

alarming context that they transcended considerations of the possible damage to his property, began to race through his head.

As was only to be expected, knowing his life might depend upon it, Alvin had learned all he could about the effects produced by the "ghost's" appearance. He had been fortunate in having had an opportunity to acquire a good amount of useful information. Although Tombstone, in the letter that had brought about Company "Z" 's first official "unofficial" assignment had not told all he had discovered, as a precaution against his identity being revealed if it should have fallen into the wrong hands, he had employed the training accrued during his years as a peace officer to gather vital details from the men who were involved in the incidents and he had then passed it on in full during the meeting at the post office.

While the possible significance of it had eluded the small Texan as he was listening to the retired peace officer, one point had emerged. On every occasion the "ghost" had showed itself, it invariably approached the person, or persons, concerned from the other side of the stream and halted over the center at the widest point, where it could only have been reached by wading. Furthermore, in each instance Tombstone had heard it described, the men affected, or their animals, had been knocked from their feet by some unseen force.

Remembering those facts, in conjunction with his words, Alvin's thoughts triggered off another memory.

Only one victim who had been involved with the "ghost" had suffered anything worse than being felled by the mysterious power. Yet, despite having discussed that aspect at length with Tombstone, the potential implications had not struck Alvin until his present train of thought was set into motion by considering the possible results should his boots be immersed in the water.

However, once it came, the realization aroused speculations of an alarming nature!

The cowhand who had been killed, in a manner that could not have occurred as the sheriff claimed at the inquest, had on galoshes instead of the more conventional footwear of the previous participants. Although it was overlooked by most people, the rubber from which such boots were manufactured gave them another quality in addition to being waterproof.

There was a distinct probability, the small Texan became aware, that the previously unconsidered quality had indirectly caused the death of Ewen Silvers.

A sudden blaze of rage burst through Alvin as the possible explanation occurred to him. Apart from the few brief moments when dealing unexpectedly with the fleeing members of the "Machine Gun Gang," this was his first contact with murderers. Nor did the information he had received about the victim lessen the flood of his revulsion. According to Mrs. Berkley and Tombstone, the cowhand had been the sole support of a widowed mother, honest, hard-working, loyal to the ranch upon which he was employed and good natured in all his dealings with others.

That such a person should have had his young life snuffed out to preserve the secret of "Brixton's ghost," which was being employed as a shield for some form of illicit activity, filled the small Texan with the sense of outrage every good peace officer experienced when faced with the ultimate crime of premeditated homicide. It produced a response that, in other circumstances, he would never have contemplated, much less carried out.

"Goddamn you!" Alvin shouted furiously, looking upward, but still retaining sufficient control over his emotions to swerve toward the darkness at the foot of the right side wall instead of continuing into the water. "This's one time your electric shock won't work!"

"He's guessed!" bellowed a voice from the top of the sheer face that the small Texan was approaching. "Get him!"

Fortunately, the words slammed a realization into Alvin of how he had acted. Jerked back to normality, he flung himself onward in a rolling dive that was not commenced an instant too soon. There was the brief red glow of a weapon's muzzle flash and the bark of a rifle from a point close to where the command had been uttered. As he reached the welcome and protective blackness, he heard the eerie *whap!* of lead passing close above him. Next came the rapid clatter of a lever action being operated, and another bullet flew down to kick up a spray of rock splinters not far away.

"Did you get him?" the speaker demanded.

"Damned if I know!" a second and equally harsh voice replied. "He was moving fast when I pulled off at him."

"See he can't get away if you missed!" the first speaker ordered. "I'll go down and have some of the boys make sure he's finished."

Coming to his feet at the end of the rolling plunge, Alvin flattened himself against the wall and gazed upward without discovering any sign of either man's exact location. For all that, while convinced he was shielded from the rifle, what he had heard indicated his position was anything but a sinecure. He did not know what was meant by "go down," but the rest of the sentence warned that the pair above him had companions close by.

Prudence demanded an immediate retreat from the canyon!

Although Alvin was still holding his automatic, there was nothing at which to aim, and anyway, to have started shooting would have betrayed his position. Not that he had intended to open fire. Instead, he started to walk as quietly as he could manage back through the darkness in the direction from which he had come. Before he had taken his fourth step, the rifle above him spat again. This time, he was not the desired target.

Giving a scream as the bullet drove into it, Tombstone's bay gelding went down kicking and rolling in agony for a couple of seconds before becoming motionless.

A bitter curse broke barely audibly from Alvin as he watched the horse go down. All too well he appreciated the implications of the sight. An inborn knowledge of tactics, such as had enabled his paternal grandfather to win promotion to captain in the field before reaching eighteen years of age,[31] backed by the training he had received, gave him a clear understanding of the situation.

Possessed of undoubted courage, but neither impetuous nor reckless, the small Texan conceded that to remain in the canyon was too dangerous to be contemplated. While the sheer wall of the canyon offered a measure of protection, in that it would allow him to see the rifleman silhouetted against the sky should

31. Told in *You're in Command Now, Mr. Fog.* J.T.E.

an attempt be made to locate and shoot at him from the top, he
could not remain in the darkness. However, the loss of the gelding had rendered flight extremely hazardous. Even after he had
sent up the signal to call the other members of Company "Z,"
there was sufficient open country beyond the canyon that would
have to be traversed on foot to make his chances of surviving
until help arrived far from hopeful.

All too conscious of his predicament, Alvin accepted that
there was only one way in which he could respond. Even if he
was inclined to try, he knew surrender would avail him nothing.
His only hope was to reach the sprawled-out carcass of the gelding, retrieve and fire the Very pistol. With that accomplished,
depending upon the circumstances, he could either stay and
make a fight from the protection offered by the body, or try to
escape by beating a retreat covered by gun fire.

Coming level with the carcass, Alvin silently thanked providence for having had the foresight to bring both automatics and
four fully charged spare magazines. No matter which course he
selected, all would be potent factors in the result. However, as he
halted to survey the situation once more, he had no intention of
opening fire immediately. He had carried the pistol from his
waistband concealed behind his right thigh as he was approaching the stream, so there was a chance that the men who had
watched him might not know he was armed. Not only was he
disinclined to let them find out prematurely, he was unable to
locate either man and had nothing at which to aim.

Drawing in a deep breath, the small Texan darted forward as
swiftly as his legs would carry him. Hearing a startled oath from
above, he deduced that the speaker had failed to anticipate how
he would behave and may have assumed he meant to retire
through the blackness until clear of the canyon. Whatever the
reason, there was a delay before a shot came and the bullet
whined away in a ricochet from behind him. Before he plunged
over and dropped to the ground behind the body two more
rounds were expended, but with no greater success, although
each had been progressively nearer to him.

Lying concealed from the rifleman, the small Texan placed his
weapon on the ground. The gelding was on its left side and he

ould not see the Very pistol. Raising his right hand cautiously,
e found that the holster's carrying strap was still around the
addle horn. With a chilling sensation, he realized that the pistol
as beneath the body. His state of mind was not improved when
he tug he gave at the strap failed to liberate it.

Despite realizing he might be deprived of the means by which
o summon aid, Alvin Fog did not panic. Instead, he tried to
obtain sufficient leverage to allow him to drag the pistol from
nder the mass of flesh, bone, and sinew that was pinning it to
he ground. Before he could achieve anything, a rumbling sound
nd spreading glow of light from beyond the stream attracted his
ttention. Barely noticing that the "ghost" had now disappeared,
e watched as an irregular oblong section of the right side wall
egan to pivot outward.

"He's hid behind the hoss!" yelled the rifleman. "I don't know
 he's toting a gun, but I'm covering him!"

Glancing upward, Alvin discovered that the speaker was now
tanding exposed against the lesser darkness of the sky. Scooping
he Colt from the ground with both hands, he wriggled around
ntil he could hold it supported by his forearms on the seat of
he saddle. Already men were peering warily from the opening,
nd as he did not doubt they were armed, he knew there was no
ime to devote to the careful aim that was required to ensure a
it at such a range. So, making the best alignment possible under
he prevailing conditions, he opened fire. Four times in rapid
uccession he squeezed the trigger, and controlling the recoil
vith the assistance of the double-handed grip, turned the barrel
lightly as each bullet left the muzzle. Twice he heard the lead
trike the side of the wall. Then the third shot ricocheted from
he top. A yell of alarm followed the fourth detonation. Tilting
pward as its user jumped backward hurriedly, the rifle dis-
harged harmlessly into the air.

Without waiting to discover whether he had made a lucky hit,
or merely given his would-be attacker a surprise via a close miss,
Alvin rolled until he lay on his stomach at the gelding's rump.
itill using both hands, he emptied the Colt's magazine just as
wiftly in the direction of the illuminated hole. Although once
nore the need for haste had precluded any chance of the accu-

racy of which he was capable in less demanding circumstances
the bullets flew sufficiently near to cause a hurried retreat by the
emerging figures.

"Goddamn it, Eddie!" a furious voice bellowed from ground
level, as the small Texan retired to the concealment of the car
cass. "What the hell are you doing up there?"

"The bastard's got a gun!" the rifleman bawled back, keeping
clear of the skyline, his tone implying that he considered their
intended victim being armed both unsporting and reprehensible

"We *know* he has, you stupid son-of-a-bitch!" the speaker at
the bottom of the wall almost howled, being the man who had
aroused Alvin's curiosity when saying he would "go down" and
obtain assistance. "So kill the bastard, or stop him using it so
we can."

Listening to the conversation, Alvin took advantage of the
respite he was being granted by removing the empty magazine
and replacing it with one of his reserve. For all his success so far
he knew he was still in a very precarious position. If the men
made a concerted effort, and those in whatever lay beyond the
opening emerged while their companion provided covering fire
with the rifle, he would be hard-pressed to deal with the attack

Wondering how soon something would happen, the small
Texan left the second Colt in its shoulder holster. Any shooting
he had to do would at first be over a distance at which he could
attain the best results by aiming and firing double handed
Knowing the danger that existed in that direction would be less
easy to detect than at ground level, he gave most of his attention
to the top of the canyon. It was obvious that the man up there
had learned his lesson. Certainly he was no longer allowing him
self to be silhouetted against the sky.

"Zip!" Eddie yelled, after about half a minute of inactivity, his
voice registering alarm. "There's somebody coming!"

"It'll be our trucks!" the spokesman at ground level replied.

"Like hell it is!" Eddie contradicted. "They're coming from
the wrong direction!"

"Hell, Zip, it must be the bomber boys!" another voice sug
gested, and despite having spoken more quietly than the man he
was addressing, some acoustic quality of his surroundings al

lowed Alvin to hear what he was saying. "Close that goddamned door!"

"That won't be any use!" Zip pointed out, no more loudly, but just as audibly as far as the small Texan was concerned. "That son-of-a-bitch out there knows it's here and we'd be caught inside."

"Then we'll have to take it on the lam!" the new speaker stated, and several other voices rumbled concurrence.

"We can't until that bastard out there's been took care of!" Zip replied, then raised his voice. "Fix his wagon good, Eddie!"

"He's hid behind the hoss I shot," the rifleman answered. "Send up Old Man Thompson to lend me a hand."

On hearing the warning, Alvin had concluded that his companions had been close enough to have heard the shooting and were coming to his rescue. As the conversation went on, however, he realized they must still be some considerable distance away. It was unlikely Eddie would be willing to remain on top of the wall with no other means of escape than his feet, there being nowhere a vehicle—or even a horse—could be hidden in his immediate vicinity, if there was danger close at hand. So he must be convinced there was ample time for him to do as Zip demanded and still make good his departure before the peace officers arrived at the canyon.

Unless the small Texan was mistaken, he considered there was something even more serious behind the latest development. He believed Eddie was intending to employ something more effective than human aid to remove the threat he was posing. The request for Old Man Thompson to be sent up did not refer to one of his associates, but to a weapon possessing very deadly qualities.

Already a number of the special type of gun produced by the Colt's Patent Fire Arms Mfg. Co. for the Auto-Ordnance Corporation of New York had found their way into the hands of criminals. Alvin had a suspicion that he might soon be in contention against one of them. Furthermore, he concluded that the installation behind the opening in the canyon's wall must be of considerable value for a still comparatively rare and expensive Thompson submachine gun to have been provided as part of its defenses. Which explained why Softly and the men who were present did not hesitate to take extreme measures to protect the secret of its existence.

At that moment, however, Alvin was more interested in his own welfare than speculating upon what the installation might be. The presence of the Thompson could render his present position untenable, no matter how effective it had proved so far. If fitted with a fifty-capacity drum magazine, as was likely, the weapon could pour such a volume of .45-caliber bullets his way that he would be driven into the open even should he escape being hit. Once out there, he would be at the mercy of the rest of the men, not that he believed any mercy would be given.

Scanning the top of the wall for the slightest indication of danger, the small Texan saw a sudden glow of light such as might be caused by a door opening. For a moment he was puzzled. Then he realized it must be coming from the entrance by which Zip had gained access to the installation. What was more, he appreciated how it might offer him a chance of salvation.

A glance at the opening informed Alvin that nobody was watching him from there. Rising, he darted swiftly toward the shadows on the left side of the canyon. As there was no outcry or shots sent at him, he felt sure his departure had gone unnoticed by any of his enemies. Turning in the inky blackness, he grasped the Colt in both hands and resumed his scrutiny of the top of the other wall.

Seconds dragged by on leaden feet!

For what seemed a *very* long time to Alvin, apart from the sound of one and then a second vehicle's engines being started inside the installation, nothing happened.

Suddenly, two figures loomed into view at the top of the right-hand wall!

The abrupt manner in which the pair appeared, taken with how quickly they started shooting, suggested they had crept toward the rim in a crouching posture until able to see the body of the gelding without exposing themselves more than marginally. Having aligned their weapons, they straightened up so as to be able to direct their fire more effectively. What was more, the harsh chattering and numerous spurts of muzzle blast emitting

from the slightly shorter man's firearm indicated that the small
Texan had guessed correctly and a Thompson submachine gun
was being used.

Despite the commotion caused by the Thompson and Eddie's
rifle as they poured lead downward, supplemented with the vi-
cious screams of ricochets, Alvin noticed another potential
threat could be forthcoming. Headlights came on in the installation and gears grated as a vehicle was set into motion. If it
should turn his way on emerging, he was almost certain to be
illuminated by the lights. Although he had not meant to shoot
back at the men on the rim, he knew he must revise his decision.

Bringing up the Colt to shoulder height and at arm's length,
the small Texan pointed it at the sky. Doing so allowed him to
look along the cocking slide, although it was almost impossible
to make out the blade of the foresight. Turning his torso until the
barrel merged with the red-spurting bulk of the man using the
Thompson, he began to discharge the contents of the magazine
nearly as swiftly as the other weapon was firing.[32] After either
the fourth or fifth shot, they were leaving the automatic in such
rapid succession that he could not say which it was, he heard a
scream of pain. Dazzled by his own muzzle blast, he did not see
the man jerk, spin around, and throw the submachine gun into
the air. However, the cessation of its fire informed him of what
had happened even before he heard it crash to the ground at the
foot of the wall.

Despite the evidence that he had achieved at least part of his
intentions, Alvin devoted not so much as a second to self-con-
gratulation. Firing at such speed had prevented him from count-
ing how many shots were expended, but he did not need an aid
of that nature to inform him when the weapon was empty. On
the last round being discharged, the front end of the cartridge

32. If the reader considers such a rate of fire from a Colt Government
Model automatic pistol is impossible, the author would like to point out
that on page 61 of *Guns and Ammo,* February 1964, there is a photograph
of Thell Reed, Jr.—one of the finest combat pistol handlers of his day—
shooting, albeit from waist level, so quickly there are *four* empty cartridge
cases in the air at one time. J.T.E.

follower, pushed up by the magazine spring, pressed against and forced the stop attached to the frame into the niche cut in the cocking slide to hold it open as an indication of the situation.

Moving to the left as soon as he received the warning that his Colt was empty, the small Texan set about rectifying the situation. At that moment, the long hours of training and practice he had carried out paid dividends. In spite of the darkness, his left hand found and extracted the third of the spare magazines. Working by instinct rather than visual aid, his right thumb pressed the retainer stud and the one it was to replace slid from the housing in the butt. With the loaded magazine thrust home, he drew down the stop and the slide advanced to make the pistol operative once more. By the time he halted in his new position, he was ready and able to defend himself.

And not a moment too soon!

Coming from the opening, a black 1921 Packard Twin-Six sedan carrying several men began to turn in Alvin's direction. Before its headlights could illuminate him as a target for Eddie, he twisted at the waist. Adopting the double-handed hold again, he sighted and fired twice. A yell of pain rose from the vehicle, and as it continued across the canyon to crash into the left side wall, he presumed he had hit the driver. Although he moved after firing, no shot came his way from the top of the other wall. Nor did the occupants of the car try to regain control of it. Instead, they quit the vehicle and ran, the wounded man clutching his shoulder, back into the installation.

Glancing upward and seeing only the uninterrupted sky line, Alvin decided that Eddie might have retired to take part in the departure. Being aware that there was at least one more vehicle available, he knew another attempt to leave was sure to be made. Considering that a further change of location was demanded, he ran back to and dropped behind the bullet-riddled carcass of the gelding. Even in the poor light, he could see enough of its condition to realize he could not have survived the fusillade if he had remained there.

A couple of seconds after Alvin had taken cover, another Packard came from the opening. So did three men armed with rifles and a Winchester trench gun. Still unaware of how far away his friends might be, he refrained from taking any action. To have disclosed his position would be suicidal. The trio were looking along the canyon as the car turned, holding their respective firearms ready for instant use. What was more, the three men accompanying the driver each grasped a revolver and were displaying an equal state of preparedness.

"Where the hell is he?" yelled the man with the trench gun, as the Packard's headlights illuminated the canyon and it sped, picking up speed, through the shallow water of the stream.

"He must be behind the hoss!" guessed one of the rifle-users. "But I'm damned if I can see him!"

Hugging the ground facedown, Alvin listened to the comments and the Packard approaching. Then, as it was going by, he tilted up and began to fire the automatic. His intention was less to hit anybody than to distract the passengers and lessen their chances of shooting him. Although he caused no casualties as far as he could tell, neither did any bullets come his way while the vehicle was passing. However, with the trio still at the opening, and having a need to reload once more, he was unable to make an attempt to halt its departure despite his supposition that the occupants' intention was to collect reinforcements.

Hearing a rumbling sound, the small Texan raised his head warily. He found that the three men had returned through the opening and its disguised door was closing. Deciding he had guessed correctly about the reason why the quartet had been allowed to leave, he made another change of magazines. Having done so, he rose and returned to the darkness at the foot of the left-side wall.

"Come on, blast it!" Alvin breathed, tucking the third empty magazine into the pocket from which it had come and making a mental note to retrieve the other two at a more opportune moment. "Where the hell are you-all, Company 'Z'?"

As if in answer to the question, lights showed and engines sounded beyond the curve in the canyon. A few seconds later, two vehicles came into view. Alvin identified them as Jubal Branch's Ford Model T sedan and the rugged 1920 Essex Four convertible belonging to Sergeant Swift-Eagle. Each was carrying passengers, the latter having three men clinging to its running boards, but there was no sign of the deceptively dilapidated-looking 1919 Hudson Super-Six Landaulette in which Sergeant Scrapton had visited Grouperville.

"Are you all right, boy?" Branch asked, almost before he had brought the sedan to a halt, looking to where his partner was approaching.

"They tried some," Alvin replied, trying to keep all trace of his relief out of his voice, as he tucked the Colt into his waistband. "But they never so much as nicked me."

"Where are they?" Major Tragg demanded, jumping from the Ford's front passenger seat holding a Winchester trench gun and followed by Sergeant Soehnen, who had shared the back with Lightning.

"They're holed up in a cave, or something, in the right wall," the small Texan answered, watching other members of Company "Z" leaving the Essex and noticing there were two absentees. "They're loaded for bear with rifles and trench guns, maybe even Thompsons. The door looked to be made of thick rock and there's another way out on top."

"Happen any of 'em try to use it, they'll right quick wish they'd not took the notion," Branch declared. " 'Mon Hammy' 'n' young Scrapton's up the other side with their rifles and I reckon's they'll likely be able to do something about it, young as they are."

"*Bueno!*" Alvin enthused, without asking whether the pair had made their ascent on the right or the left. Each was a superlative marksman and armed with a rifle that had a telescopic sight, so they should be competent to prevent an attempt to leave the installation even if it was taking place on the opposite side of the canyon. "Trouble is, sir, one car got by me and it's likely going to Grouperville for help."

"Take out after them, Jubal, Hans, Alvin!" the major commanded, knowing the Ford—decrepit as it might look—was capable of making better speed than Swift-Eagle's Essex, although unable to carry as many men. "The rest of us will keep the others bottled up, even if we can't get in to fetch them out. Likely they'll be ready to holler 'calf rope' soon's they find out no help's coming."

"You-all go in the front, Hans!" Alvin suggested, glancing at the Thompson submachine gun equipped with a drum magazine held by Soehnen. "I'll ride on the running board."

"Why, sure," the burly sergeant assented. "Only you'd best go on the *left* side. I don't reckon Jubal'd take kind to me cutting loose with this old Tommy gun close to his one good ear."

"You can bet your goddamned life I wouldn't," Branch confirmed, having sufficient faith in his partner's ambidextrous gun-handling prowess to go along with the proposal, and ignoring the comment about his ears. "Come on, both of you-all. Time's a-wasting."

"Was I asked, which I don't expect to be," Alvin Fog drawled, holding himself in place on the Ford as he had while attending the firing practice on the day Company "Z" had been ordered to go to San Antonio and help deal with the so-called "Machine Gun Gang," except that he was on the opposite side's running board, "I'd say they're slowing down."

"It looks that way to me," Jubal Branch supported, gazing ahead as he drove the sedan at its best pace and without using its headlights along the far from smooth trail, having covered something over eight miles since leaving Brixton's Canyon.

"He's not stopping, though," Sergeant Soehnen pointed out, as the distant vehicle continued to move. "Fact being, I'd say he's speeding up again. Are you-all thinking what I'm thinking, amigo?"

"I'd reckon that all depends on what *you're* thinking," the oldest of the sergeants replied, then glanced to his left. "Have you-all gotten that fool 'auty-matical' of yours out, boy?"

"I've been trying ever since we left the canyon," the small Texan answered, having duplicated his companions' as yet unuttered suppositions. "But the way you're bouncing this beat-up old Tin Lizzie around, it's all I can do to stay on."

"God blast it iffen you young 'n's don't want *everything* served up on a silk-soft cushion!" Branch snorted, as if more incensed by his partner employing the derogatory—yet, in many cases, respectful and loving even—sobriquet frequently applied to the Ford Model T than he had been at the suggestion of his hearing being defective. "Happen I'll be able to get her running smoother should I put the lights on."

"It *couldn't* run any *worse!*" Alvin snorted, despite realizing why the proposal had been made, and despite being compelled to use his left hand, extracting the Colt from his waistband with none of the difficulty his previous comment implied. "Why don't you give it a whirl and see?"

"Danged if I don't at that!" Branch threatened, apparently with irascibility. "But not just yet a-whiles."

Continuing to drive with no reduction of speed, in case his suppositions should prove invalid and hoping to catch the Packard before it reached Grouperville, the elderly sergeant concentrated on handling the car and left his companions to keep watch. However, as they were approaching the area at which the other vehicle had slowed down, he delivered a warning of his intentions and reached for one of the switches on the dashboard. Throwing it to turn on the headlights, he transferred his hand to the brake and his foot operated the clutch as he prepared to reduce the sedan's pace.

The precaution was justified!

Clumps of bushes flanked the trail at the point the Ford was approaching. Although there was no sign of human beings, the glint of something metallic among the foliage on the left warned Alvin at least one might be present. Bringing up his Colt, he lined it and started squeezing the trigger. As on the previous occasions that night, he did not attempt to take a precise aim. Instead, he directed the bullets so they radiated like the spokes of a wheel. Even as a shriek of agony and the crash of a revolver shot—which was sent into the air instead of at him—rewarded his efforts, he became aware that he was not alone in finding the need to take offensive measures.

Having seen a man armed with a revolver standing among the bushes to the right, Soehnen cut loose with the Thompson he had already been pointing through the window. A rattle of rapid detonations followed the tightening of his trigger finger, the change lever being set for automatic fire. Duplicating the small Texan's methods, he sent a spray of lead that engulfed the would-be attacker in its lethal swathe. Much to his satisfaction, being a realist, he watched the men being thrown backward by the bullets without having a chance to shoot in return.

Once again, an unexpected jolt produced by the far-from-smooth ground beneath the Ford threatened to endanger Alvin. It was, however, more severe and serious than on the previous occasion. In spite of being reduced, the speed at which the car was traveling was greater and the force of the bounce dislodged him. Nor was he able to retain his equilibrium as he alighted on the uneven surface at the edge of the trail. Feeling himself falling, he could not prevent the automatic from flying out of his grasp and he saw another of the men who had left the Packard to halt the pursuit rising from amongst the bushes. Yet, for all the alarm and consternation it was causing him, the mishap was to provide his salvation.

Lining the revolver he was holding, the man fired and missed as his intended target went down so unexpectedly. He was not granted an opportunity to make a second attempt.

Sensing that something out of the ordinary was happening, the big bluetick had been standing on the backseat and was watching what was taking place. Noticing the disturbance amongst the bushes before Alvin's second attacker appeared, it thrust past its master and out of the open window of the Ford. Dashing forward on landing, it attacked just after the shot was fired. Taking off in a bound, it caught the outstretched arm between its powerful jaws. A combination of pain, its weight, and the unexpected arrival caused its victim to drop the revolver as he was sent sprawling.

Contriving to break his fall without injury, although at the cost of some skin scraped from the base of his left hand, Alvin wasted no time before starting to rise. Shaking his throbbing palm as he was getting up, he reached across with his other hand to pull the second automatic from its shoulder holster instead of looking for the one he had lost. A glance around informed him that Branch and Soehnen were already leaving the now-halted sedan. Drawing the Colt from behind his back, the elderly sergeant ran to where his dog was still maintaining its hold on the man's wrist while avoiding attempts to strike or kick it.

"Lie still so's I can call him off!" Branch commanded, halting alongside the bluetick and its captive, then continued without waiting to be obeyed, "Let loose, you fool critter. You can chomp away on him some more, happen he gives you cause."

Jumping clear before the words came to an end, Lightning sat down at a safe distance and watched with what the man, clutching at his lacerated wrist and lying still, considered was an attitude of eager anticipation.

"That's better," Branch stated. "Are you all right this time, amigo?"

"I've grazed my hand is all," Alvin answered, walking toward the man he had shot. Looking down with the aid of a match he struck, there was a trace of relief in his tone as he reported, "This one's hit bad, but still alive."

"We'll tend to him soon as I get a flashlight from the car," Branch promised. "How's your'n, Hans?"

"Dead as a six-day stunk-up skunk," Soehnen replied, having conducted a similar examination of his victim instead of accompanying the elderly sergeant. "How'd you expect, with maybe half a dozen point forty-five bullets in the chest?"

"They do say such ain't 'conducterive' to long life 'n' good health," Branch admitted. "Now, you do any old thing you've a mind while I'm gone, hombre, only that fool Lightning dog of mine'll not take kind to it should you try. Then, soon's we're through 'tending to you 'n' your amigo's hurts, you're likely going to feel 'hoe-bliggerated' enough to do some talking to us."

"Looks like you was mistook," Sheriff Healey said, staring around the corner of the building and along the trail that led to Brixton's Canyon. "There's no car coming."

"It's just not in sight yet," corrected the man who had cut the Duesenberg's tires, moving the shotgun nestling across his bent left forearm slightly and directing a contemptuous glance at the clearly nervous peace officer, as the call of a whippoorwill came from behind them to be answered by another somewhere across the street. "But I'm sure I heard one."

When Zip arrived at Soskice's Hotel and told Abel Softly of what was happening in the canyon, Healey had been summoned for orders. He was to collect his deputy, then accompany Marty and another of the men to the edge of town, where they would wait for and ambush the car that had pursued the Packard if the earlier attempt failed to stop it. With Mulley and the Skinner brothers unavailable, Softly had stated he did not have enough men to go to the rescue of the party at the canyon until the officers who were coming had been taken out of the game. It was, he had claimed, possible that one might be taken alive and induced to tell how large a party was involved, so they would know exactly what they would be up against.

Although the sheriff had not dared to refuse when informed what was expected of him, he was far from enamored of the prospect. Nor, despite having had his salary supplemented by Softly, had he ever envisaged he would have to earn it in such a manner. His uneasiness had increased rather than diminished, after having taken cover with Marty in the alley between the last pair of buildings on the left at the outskirts of the town—with Callaghan and the other man, also armed with sawed-off shotguns in a similar location across the street—as time passed without anything happening. There had been a moment of anxiety when his companion claimed to have heard a car approaching, but neither of the other pair nor Healey had done so. Certainly the sound had not repeated itself, but the waiting and suspense had done nothing to calm, or ease, the sheriff's misgivings.

Across the street, Deputy Sheriff Callaghan was in a no less agitated and despondent frame of mind. Like his superior, he had willingly accepted Softly's money and was now equally disenchanted by the way he was having to repay it. Although he had failed to notice how the tire of the Dodge coupé was punctured, he was not so dull witted that he underestimated the danger of what they were intending to do. If the raiders at the canyon were bomber boys, as he considered likely, they belonged to a federal law-enforcement agency. Killing them would create such a furor that staying in Grouper County would be out of the question. Not that he cared greatly about being compelled to take his departure, except for being aware the authorities would spare no expense nor effort to apprehend those who were responsible. Unimaginative as he might be and not usually given to thinking of the consequences, he could foresee nothing other than a life on the run should the affair end in murder. Yet, again in common with the sheriff, he had lacked the courage to refuse when ordered to participate in the ambush and whatever was to follow.

"Goddamn it!" the man at Callaghan's side grumbled, breaking into his disconsolate thought train after the nocturnal bird's call to his rear answered the one from the other side of the street. "Those son-of-a-bitching 'whips' give me the miseries."

"And me," Callaghan confessed. "Hell though, Ben, Marty must've been wrong about hearing a car."

"Sure," the man agreed. "Happen he had, it'd've been here by now."

Relapsing into silence after the comments, the deputy and his companion looked across the street. They could make out the shapes of the sheriff and Marty, who were speaking to one another, but could not hear what was being said. Nor was anything visible in the alley beyond the pair. Before either Callaghan or Ben could try to satisfy their curiosity on the matter, a double click reached their ears from not too far behind them.

"It's a ten gauge, like its mate, and both lined on you boys!" announced a drawling voice quietly, yet exuding a menace matching the ominous sound each man was sure he had recognized without requiring the identification. "And there's two Texas Rangers behind 'em. Don't stir, or make a sound, else it'll be your last."

Despite the shock each had received, the deputy and Ben had just sufficient self-control to realize resistance would not only be futile, but might prove fatal. So they managed to hold down the exclamations both were on the point of uttering and refrained from turning even to look at the speaker.

"That's the way to live long 'n' stay healthy," the quiet voice praised, after a few seconds had elapsed without either man making a sound or movement. "Now, set down them sawed-off scatters slow and easy!"

Yielding to the inevitable, Callaghan and Ben began to comply with the order.

"Aw, hell, Marty!" Healey protested as, unbeknown to him, the men across the street were laying down their arms. "Zip's boys must've stopped whoever was trailing 'em. The sons-of-bitches would've been here by now if they had—!"

A slight sound such as might be made by a stealthy footstep from the other end of the alley brought the sheriff's words to a halt, causing him and the man by his side to glance hurriedly over their shoulders. Seeing a bulky masculine figure silhouetted in the gap between the buildings, they swung around with alacrity. Any chance that he might be a harmless citizen passing through was shattered by seeing how he threw himself forward and down, raising whatever was in his hands as he went.

"Get him!" Marty bellowed, starting to swing the butt of the shotgun to his right shoulder.

Under the circumstances, the command and movement, which Healey copied, were most ill advised.

After treating the two criminals' wounds and leaving the one attacked by Lightning bound hand and foot with a rope brought from the Ford, the three sergeants had resumed their interrupted journey. Despite having been too afraid of the big bluetick to lie, the man who was bitten could supply no hint of what might be in store for them when they arrived at Grouperville. Discussing the matter once Alvin had retrieved his Colt and the vehicle was moving, they had decided Softly would arrange a hostile reception for them on being told what had taken place at Brixton's Canyon. As nothing had happened on the way, they had planned their strategy and put it into effect.

Forming two groups, although disproportionate in numbers, the party had advanced the remaining distance on foot after having driven as close to the town as they considered could be done without the sedan's engine being heard. While Alvin, Branch, and the bluetick went in one direction, Soehnen had made his way there alone. He had found, as had been decided might be the case, that the men who were waiting to ambush them occupied the first alley on the outskirts. Making the discovery, he had impersonated the call of a whippoorwill. On receiving a similar response to the prearranged signal, informing him that his companions were in position and had duplicated his findings, he started to approach the men he had located. In spite of his stealthy movements, he had been overheard.

Forming an identical conclusion with regard to the ambushers' armament to that made by Jubal Branch, Soehnen responded rapidly on seeing his presence was known. As he dropped to the ground, he thrust the Thompson submachine gun ahead of him. Knowing the pair meant to kill him if they were given the chance, he had no qualms about opening fire without warning of his intentions. For the second time that night, the deadly weapon's stuttering automatic thunder shattered the silence. Fanning away from him at an upward angle, some of the bullets found their billets in human flesh. Both Healey and Marty were hit, the latter suffering a mortal wound. They went down almost simultaneously, and although each discharged his shotgun involuntarily, the buckshot balls winged futilely over the sergeant.

"Straighten up empty-handed and lift 'em high!" Branch commanded, snapping the Winchester Model 1873 rifle—the hammer of which he had drawn back and forward twice while holding the trigger depressed to simulate the cocking of a shotgun—to his shoulder and throwing its lever through the reloading cycle. When the men he was addressing obeyed with alarmed alacrity, he went on somewhat louder, "They get you, Hans?"

"Nary a one," Soehnen replied, rising and walking forward warily but swiftly. "I can't say the same for them, though."

"You got your 'handi-cuffs' about you?" Branch inquired, having identified Callaghan, as he and his partner—who was armed with the Winchester Model 1894 carbine that had been with the rifle in the Ford—reached the two would-be ambushers.

"N-No!" the deputy gulped, ensuring he kept his hands raised. "We was told some owlhoots'd be coming—!"

"*I* believe you, it's the judge you'll be facing you'll have to get to do it," Branch interrupted dryly, taking his left hand from the rifle's foregrip and extracting the pair of handcuffs from his jacket pocket. "Use mine."

"O-On him?" Callaghan asked hopefully, catching the device as it was tossed in his direction.

"Him—and you-all, one wrist apiece," the elderly sergeant

orrected. "And I'd do it quick, was I you; this ole *Lightning* dog of mine gets a mite tetchy this time of the night and's been snowed to chaw on a man for 'most no reason at all."

Hearing its name and drawing the correct conclusion from the intonation that the word was given, the big bluetick let out a low and menacing growl that suggested the rest of the comment about it was correct. Already frightened by the realization of their position, Callaghan showed no hesitation before doing as he was ordered, and Ben did not resist.

"How the hell did you get here, B—Sergeant Branch?" the deputy inquired at the completion of the task, belatedly realizing his captor was the man he had been ordered to watch leave the county. Although he had parked the coupé in concealment after changing wheels, and spent the remainder of the afternoon resting, he had believed he was speaking the truth when telling his superior the departure was made on returning after dark. "You didn't come by—"

"Maybe you was sleeping as I passed," Branch suggested, although this had not happened. "Anyway, we'll talk about that later. Right now, where-at's your boss?"

"Across there," the deputy replied, gesticulating with his un-fettered hand. "Looks like he's—"

"Not Fat Jim," the elderly sergeant corrected. "It's Softly I want."

"Down to the hotel," Callaghan answered, making no attempt to resist as Branch ran an expert hand over him and removed the Colt revolver from his waistband.

"You pair do what you can for Fat Jim and the other jasper," the elderly sergeant ordered, after disarming Ben and throwing both revolvers into the darkness. "You-all set to go, Hans?"

Without needing instructions, Alvin had unloaded the shot-guns while his partner was disarming their captives. Across the street, despite an examination having proven that neither of the men he had shot was in any condition to contemplate further hostilities, Soehnen was completing similar precautions.

"I reckon there's enough shells in my Thompson to see me through," the burly sergeant answered. "Let's get moving."

Leaving the prisoners to fend for themselves, the three men set

off along the street toward the hotel, accompanied by the dog.
They realized that there was no longer any possibility of taking
Softly by surprise as they had hoped would happen if they could
capture the ambushers without noise. However, having heard
the Thompson, the men they were going to confront might be
induced to surrender.

With that thought in mind, the trio watched the building and
its surroundings carefully as they were approaching. Ranging
ahead at a signal from its master, the bluetick lessened the danger of enemies lurking in the alleys and allowed the sergeants to
concentrate their attention on the entrances to the reception
lobby and well-lit barroom.

Reaching their destination unchallenged, the sergeants stalked
silently and warily along the sidewalk. Peering around the door
into the lobby, Alvin found it empty. As he and his companions
resumed their advance, they heard a handgun fired somewhere
on the upper floor. Although curious about the sound, they did
not offer to investigate.

"Well, I'll be damned!" the small Texan exclaimed, after commencing a surreptitious examination through the window of the
barroom. "We didn't need to be so cagey."

Following their young companion as he strode forward with
none of his former caution, the older sergeants saw enough to
share his confidence. Although a few of Softly's men were in the
barroom, they posed no threat as they were covered by shotguns
and other weapons in the hands of the desk clerk, Mexican
waiter, Joplin, Hislop, and three more of the town's male residents.

"Stay out of it, amigo," Branch told the small Texan sotto
voce, knowing it was inadvisable for the geologist's true status to
be exposed. Speaking louder, he went on, "Inside the bar. We're
a couple of Texas Rangers wanting to come in."

"Come ahead!" Joplin ordered, in tones far different from
when he had refused to supply tires for the Duesenberg. "Only
do it slow and careful until we can see for sure who you are."

Approving of the reason for the last part of the invitation, the
two sergeants had the Winchester and the Thompson tucked
under their respective left arms as they walked through the bat-

wing doors. They were wearing their badges in plain view and these, taken with the evidence of their pacific intentions, caused the weapons that had been pointed in their direction to be lowered.

"Howdy, you-all," Branch greeted. "What was that shot just now?"

"Sounded like Tombstone's old Frontier Colt to me," Joplin replied. "Him and Ollie Soskice went upstairs after Softly while we kept these longhorns quiet."

Striding swiftly through the connecting door into the lobby, the elderly sergeant saw the retired peace officer and another man coming down the stairs.

"Howdy, Jubal," Tombstone called. "Figured it was you when I heard the Thompson."

"Looks like you had everything in hand here," Branch answered, having decided against letting it be known he and the gravedigger were acquainted, on his last visit to the hotel. "What happened, Gabe?"

"Got some of my amigos ready should they be needed," Tombstone replied. "We moved in when the gunplay started along the street."

"How about the shot up there?" Branch wanted to know.

"Caught that jasper Softly taking things out of Ollie here's safe," Tombstone explained, indicating his companion, but distending the truth somewhat, as the repository had been brought by the supposed bartender on taking over and was in his living quarters. "Figured he was robbing it and had to throw down on him when he grabbed out a gun. Tell you, though. This's one grave I'll enjoy digging."

"What do you reckon about moonshiners being friendly now, amigo?" Alvin Fog challenged, as he sat with the other members of Company "Z" in the sheriff's office on the morning after his hectic visit to Brixton's Canyon. "Because, I tell you, those bunch last night struck me as being just a teensy-mite unsociable."

"You couldn't call them for real, good ole country-boy moonshiners," Jubal Branch protested. "They was 'perfessery-on-alls.' "

As Major Benson Tragg had suggested, the men at the canyon had surrendered on learning no help could be expected. They had already discovered, via a couple of well-placed rifle bullets when one of their number tried to leave, that there was no escape through the second exit. He was not killed, nor was he meant to be or even injured, but his description of the close call he had had added to his companions' growing appreciation of the danger they were in.

An examination of the area after the surrender had revealed the secrets of Brixton's Canyon and the means by which it had been "haunted."

The Yankee geologist had not been searching for gold, but was enlarging a cave—which originally had only a very small entrance—to be used as an illicit distillery. While doing so, he had tunneled into the other wall around the corner from where Alvin had been in action, blowing it up to provide the excuse for his disappearance and keeping the property unoccupied. He had manufactured the two exits with great care, making the doors so well that each would stand up to a close examination when closed, without revealing their existence. The requisite equipment and an electric generator to supply light and power were installed. As a further precaution, all traces of the occupants and trucks that collected the merchandise, coming across the badlands without going near Grouperville or other human habitation, were removed.

None of the prisoners had been able to say who first discovered the cave, or would admit to Hogan Turtle being involved in any part of the operation.[33] Nor were they any more informative about the decision to employ the "ghost" to scare away un-

---

33. According to Alvin Dustine (Cap) Fog's notes, although Hogan Turtle was never brought to trial for his complicity, subsequent inquiries established he had learned of the cave in his youth from some unspecified source. When the Eighteenth Amendment (Prohibition) was ratified, he had decided to turn it into a secret distillery and made arrangements for the work to be carried out. J.T.E.

wanted visitors, although—whether truthfully or not was never ascertained—there was a mutual agreement that the man with the Thompson who Alvin had killed was responsible for the death of the young Forked Box cowhand.

Discovered where Zip had dropped it on top of the canyon, the "ghost" proved to be nothing more spectral than a flashlight inside a diaphanous white shroud suspended by a length of fishing line from the tip of a long aluminum pole. The eerie wailing originated from halfway up the canyon's wall, via the speaker of a gramophone concealed in a hole. In addition to supplying the installation's other needs, the stream Brixton had discovered and diverted across the canyon served as a conductor for the electric shocks, which had created a stupefying effect upon those would-be investigators who tried to wade out and grab the "ghost."

"There's those as might think you shouldn't've gone nosing around on your lonesome in the first place," Sergeant Bratton remarked.

"I wasn't taken with the notion myself," Alvin admitted, noticing the speculative way in which the other sergeants and Tragg were studying him. "But I didn't know which way whoever was making the collection I'd been told about would come. If they'd run across you-all, there'd likely have been enough fuss to keep the 'ghost' from showing itself. So I reckoned I'd best see if I could bring it out. What I didn't count on was Tombstone's horse getting shot and falling on the Very pistol. It's lucky for me you-all were close enough to hear the shooting."

"*We* didn't hear it, first off," Branch contradicted and pointed to the big bluetick sprawled as usual by his feet. "Ole Lightning here was the one. When he all of a sudden jumped up, looked toward the canyon and started to bawling, we figured we'd best drift over 'n' see why."

"Damned if that fool dog isn't good for *something* on 'occasional,'" Alvin drawled. Deducing from the nods of approval that had followed his explanation that it met with his companions' approbation, he became more sober and continued, "Trouble was that I got so riled thinking how it caused that cowhand to be killed when I figured out what had knocked the other fellers down, I yelled I knew and that's what set off the whole shooting match."

"Day you *stop* getting riled when some innocent and law-abiding feller's murdered by owlhoots is when I'll *start* worrying about you," Tragg declared, and there was a general rumble of concurrence from the rest of the men.

"Gracias, sir," Alvin replied gratefully, but the words were intended as much for his companions as his superior.

"It's almost a pity we'll have to have that place blown up," Tragg remarked, after telling his men the arrangements that were being made to prevent their intervention from receiving too much attention. "Anyway, I've had a call from the attorney general this morning. He says there's a feller the New York police want to talk to, hiding out in Juarez. Jubal, you and Alvin head down that way and see if you can persuade him to come back across the border."[34]

"Straightaway?" the small Texan asked, despite realizing he and his partner were selected to prevent the truth about his visit to Grouperville being made public.

"Why, sure," the major confirmed, smiling. "You've stopped having the easy life of a deputy sheriff now you're a Texas Ranger, Alvin Fog."

Seeing the grins and nods of agreement from the rest of the sergeants that followed their commanding officer's last words, the small Texan knew he had won his acceptance as a Texas Ranger and a member of Company "Z."

---

34. How the assignment was carried out is told in Case One, "Friendly Persuasion," *The Justice of Company "Z."* J.T.E.